Gripping Novels of
Intrigue and Suspense

SIGNET DOUBLE MYSTERIES:

THE BLONDE

and

GIRL IN A SHROUD

More Mysteries from SIGNET

- [ ] **SIGNET DOUBLE MYSTERY—CATCH ME A PHOENIX** by Carter Brown and **NYMPH TO THE SLAUGHTER** by Carter Brown. (#E8825—$1.75)*
- [ ] **THE MINI-MURDERS** by Carter Brown. (#Y7263—$1.25)
- [ ] **SIGNET DOUBLE MYSTERY—SEX CLINIC** by Carter Brown and **W.H.O.R.E.** by Carter Brown. (#E8354—$1.75)*
- [ ] **SIGNET DOUBLE MYSTERY—THE ASEPTIC MURDERS** by Carter Brown and **NIGHT WHEELER** by Carter Brown. (#E8521—$1.75)*
- [ ] **NEGATIVE IN BLUE** by Carter Brown. (#Q6220—95¢)
- [ ] **SADIE WHEN SHE DIED** by Ed McBain. (#E8930—$1.75)
- [ ] **FUZZ** by Ed McBain. (#E8399—$1.75)
- [ ] **HAIL, HAIL, THE GANG'S ALL HERE** by Ed McBain. (#E8855—$1.75)*
- [ ] **THE FOUR OF HEARTS** by Ellery Queen. (#E8894—$1.75)*
- [ ] **HALFWAY HOUSE** by Ellery Queen. (#E8895—$1.75)*
- [ ] **THE CHINESE ORANGE MYSTERY** by Ellery Queen. (#E8759—$1.75)*
- [ ] **THE SPANISH CAPE MYSTERY** by Ellery Queen. (#E8864—$1.75)*

* Price slightly higher in Canada

Buy them at your local bookstore or use this convenient coupon for ordering.

THE NEW AMERICAN LIBRARY, INC.,
P.O. Box 999, Bergenfield, New Jersey 07621

Please send me the SIGNET BOOKS I have checked above. I am enclosing
$_____ (please add 50¢ to this order to cover postage and handling).
Send check or money order—no cash or C.O.D.'s. Prices and numbers are subject to change without notice.

Name _____

Address _____

City_____ State_____ Zip Code_____
Allow 4-6 weeks for delivery.
This offer is subject to withdrawal without notice.

The Blonde

and

Girl in a Shroud

Carter Brown

A SIGNET BOOK
NEW AMERICAN LIBRARY
TIMES MIRROR
in association with Horwitz Publications

The Blonde © 1958, 1979 by Horwitz Publications, a division of Horwitz Group Books Pty Ltd. (Hong Kong Branch), Hong Kong, B.C.C.

Girl in a Shroud © Copyright 1963, 1979 by Horwitz Publications, a division of Horwitz Group Books Pty Ltd. (Hong Kong Branch), Hong Kong, B.C.C.

All rights reserved. Reproduction in part or in whole in any language expressly forbidden in any part of the world without the written consent of Horwitz Publications. For information address Horwitz Cammeray Centre, 506 Miller Street, P.O. Box 306, Cammeray 2062, Australia.

Published by arrangement with Alan G. Yates. Originally appeared in paperback as separate volumes published by The New American Library, Inc.

SIGNET TRADEMARK REG. U.S. PAT. OFF. AND FOREIGN COUNTRIES
REGISTERED TRADEMARK—MARCA REGISTRADA
HECHO EN CHICAGO, U.S.A.

SIGNET, SIGNET CLASSICS, MENTOR, PLUME AND MERIDIAN BOOKS
are published by The New American Library, Inc.,
1301 Avenue of the Americas, New York, New York 10019

FIRST PRINTING (Double Carter Brown Edition), DECEMBER, 1979

1 2 3 4 5 6 7 8 9

PRINTED IN THE UNITED STATES OF AMERICA

The Blonde

Chapter One

"Wheeler Lonely Hearts Club," I said. "Give us a ring and we'll see *you* get one."

"Lieutenant Wheeler!" Sheriff Lavers' voice was surprised. "You sound alive and it's only nine-thirty in the morning. So don't tell me. You got a chick there, something left over from last night. Someone sharing that cozy king-size bed of yours, snuggling up and giving you her undivided attention."

"No, sir," I said. "There's no one in bed here with me."

I waved good-bye to the dusky chick, who didn't look so bedraggled now that she had her clothes on and had fixed herself a bit, as she went out the door. She had a remorseful look on her face but it was her own fault. I had offered to get breakfast but she said she wasn't hungry.

I concentrated on the phone again: "I have a surprise for you, Sheriff," I told him. "You gave me a day off, remember! And this is it."

"I wouldn't let it worry me," he said. "I want to talk to you, it's important. You'd better come down to the office right away." He hung up before I could argue.

I would have ignored him but so long as he kept me detached from Homicide and attached to his office, he was my boss. Like the man says, the second quickest way to get fired is to be rude to your boss. The quickest way is to be rude to his wife.

I put down the phone and put on some clothes, then drove downtown. Twenty minutes later I was inside the County Sheriff's office. There always was one good reason for calling on Lavers. Her name was Annabelle Jackson and she was his secretary. I leaned over her desk and gave a thoughtful scrutiny to the smooth, faintly speckled rise of her magnificent breasts as they swept up from the opening in her shirt.

1

"Hush my mouth, honey chile," I said admiringly. "You get more beautiful every time I see you."

"Haven't you noticed the difference since our last date, Lieutenant?" she said coldly. "I've aged."

"You know how it is," I mumbled. "Homicide."

"I've been thinking about it!" she said. "You were going to call me, as I remember. I've been calling you."

"Busy line?"

"Names," she snarled. "The sheriff said you were to go right on in."

I walked into Lavers' office and he nodded toward a visitor's chair. I sat down without thinking and shot into the air again with a piercing yelp.

"What's the matter with you?" Lavers asked tersely.

"That loose spring," I said. "You should get it fixed. One of these days I'm going to walk out of here with a falsetto voice."

I carefully selected another chair, sat down and lit myself a cigarette.

"You ever watch television?" he grunted.

"Sundays," I said, "my day of rest."

"Ever pick up a show called 'Without Favor'—run by a woman called Paula Reid?"

"Once," I nodded. "It's one of those no-holds-barred interview shows, isn't it? She asked a lot of impersonal questions like, 'How regular is your sex life?' Whichever way you answer she wants to know why."

"Something like that," he said. "She also moves the show around the country, interviews personalities in their own city or home. She arrived here in Pine City this morning and her show goes over on Saturday night from the local station."

"I won't be there," I said.

"You will."

There was a tone of finality in Lavers' voice.

"Who's getting murdered," I asked him, "the rating?"

"She's interviewing Georgia Brown."

"Sweet?" I queried. "I thought she was a song title."

"I don't know why it is," he said wearily, "but I sometimes forget you're a moron! Cast your mind back three years or so, Wheeler."

". . . There was a strawberry blonde," I said nostalgically, "and built like Fort Knox—to stay. She stayed about three weeks as I remember . . ."

Lavers lit his pipe, handling it carefully like a time fuse. "You remember Lee Manning?"

"Came the dawn," I said. "The celluloid Romeo who wrote his own lines for a final exit, I remember. And Georgia Brown was the cause of all the trouble."

"That was the story," Lavers agreed. "But it was never proved. The tabloids made a big play with it and the scandal mags took care of the rest. The old story, liquor, orgies, the works."

"Ah, Hollywood," I said wistfully.

"Georgia Brown was a star in her own right," he went on. "She disappeared right after Manning suicided. Nobody ever heard of her again."

"You mean she worked in radio?"

"I mean she disappeared!" Lavers snarled. "I wish you'd stop being cute, Wheeler. Paula Reid claims to have found her. Claims she's going to interview Georgia Brown on her show Saturday night. She says Georgia was the innocent victim of the Manning scandal but now she'll break three years' silence and tell the truth . . . I quote Miss Reid's own words, of course!"

"The truth about what?"

"About why Manning suicided, the orgies, and so on. The names of the other people involved."

"I might break a habit Saturday night," I said. "This should be worth seeing."

"Miss Reid claims that her life and Miss Brown's have both been threatened. She's been told her show will never make the air Saturday night."

"She wants protection?"

Lavers shook his head. "No, she thinks it's all wonderful publicity. This stuff has been headlines for the last couple of weeks. Don't you read the newspapers, Wheeler?"

"You know how it is," I said. "If I had time to read I'd be an educated man."

"Your stamina must be remarkable!" he said obliquely. "Anyway, whether these threats are real or just a publicity stunt, I don't intend taking any chances while she's in Pine City. That show goes on Saturday night!"

"What's the gimmick?" I asked suspiciously.

"There's no gimmick," he said. "This show is getting nationwide publicity. If anything happens to either of those two women before it takes the air, there'll be headlines coast to coast—"

"Not to mention Walter Cronkite and *Women's Wear Daily*," I said helpfully. "We'd be put on the map, feature in *Time* and *Newsweek*, and skimming some of the tourist cream away from good old Plains, Georgia. Is that how you see it, Sheriff? Or would it be forgotten the very next day?"

"This is serious!" he said in a strangled voice. "That television station is almost plumb center in my area of jurisdiction, and that means I'm responsible. I can see what a story the papers would make of it. 'County Sheriff fails to prevent murder after beautiful woman's desperate appeal!'"

"Sheriff," I said, "you've been reading those paperbacks again. I thought you said Paula Reid liked the publicity?"

"But her secretary doesn't. A girl named Janice Jorgens. She's asked for protection—unofficially, of course. But she's the one to give you concrete details about the threats."

"It seems to be an uncomplicated assignment," I said bitterly.

"Just stay with it," he said harshly. "Remember, I want to see that show go over on Saturday night. That means that both Miss Reid and Miss Brown must still be alive then. I don't give a damn what happens to them from Monday on, when Miss Reid leaves Pine City."

"Yes, sir," I said resignedly.

He puffed his pipe complacently. "That's all there is to it, Wheeler. Let me know how you make out."

"If I find any corpses, Sheriff, I'll send them on to you, collect."

"Don't fall over my secretary on your way out!" he snorted.

"And damage one of those beautiful curves?" I asked in a horrified voice. "You must be out of your mind."

I checked and found that Miss Reid, her secretary, producer, and the rest of her staff had taken over suites at the Starlight Hotel that morning.

I arrived just after eleven-thirty and asked for Miss Jorgens at the desk. I took the elevator to the ninth floor, then walked down the corridor until I reached the right door and knocked.

THE BLONDE 5

The door opened about ten seconds later, and a girl stood there looking at me. She wore a lemon top that swept over the pointed rise of her firm but smallish breasts, and a pair of cream slacks that clung tightly to her hips and thighs and lightly traced the V-shaped bulge of her crotch. Her red hair was clustered in tight curls around her head, her eyes were blue and watchful, her lips full and pouting a little. Her shirt was open almost all the way down to her navel to reveal the inner flanks of her breasts rising from the central cleavage. Her nipples made small indentations against the thin fabric.

"Well," she said finally, "if you're all through, maybe you'd like to tell me what it is you want."

"My name's Wheeler," I told her. "Sheriff Lavers sent me."

"Oh," she said. "Then you'd better come inside."

I followed her into the living room, admiring the way her small buttocks shifted beneath the taut material of her slacks. There was a table in the center of the room, piled high with papers, and a typewriter trying to make itself feel at home on one side. In a two-hundred-dollar-a-day suite it was out of place.

"Are you from the Sheriff's office, Mr. Wheeler?" Miss Jorgens asked.

"Sort of," I said. "I'm also from Homicide when I'm not from the Sheriff's office. I double as a Lieutenant in both parts but they don't pay me any more."

"I can understand that," she said easily. "What do you want to know?"

"Sheriff Lavers tells me you want police protection," I said. "Not for yourself but for Miss Reid and Miss Brown. You also don't want Miss Reid to know anything about it?"

"That's absolutely right," she said. "I could be most embarrassed if Paula ever found out I'd asked for it. She might even fire me!"

"I'll remember that," I told her. "What exactly do you want me to do?"

"These threats worry me," she said, "but Paula won't take them seriously. I'd like you to make sure nothing happens to her—or to Georgia Brown."

"That won't be any trouble," I said. "I'll stay with Paula day and night, and Georgia, too. Are you kidding?"

"For what they must pay you, we could get about one-eighth of a writer," she said thoughtfully. "Even one-eighth of a writer could turn out better dialogue than that."

"Maybe Georgia Brown might feel differently about having official protection." I suggested. "If I could talk her into it, we could keep tabs on her all time up to the show. That would only leave Paula to worry about."

Miss Jorgens bit her lower lip gently with nice white teeth. "I don't know," she said. "If Georgia told Paula about it . . ."

"There must be other jobs you can do in television," I said, "like standing in front of a camera and breathing deeply?"

"One-sixteenth of a writer would do," she said almost absently. "Georgia Brown's address is one of television's best-kept secrets right now. Only two people know it, myself and Paula."

"And Paula won't tell."

She looked at me for a moment: "Lieutenant, if I give you the address, you'll handle it tactfully, won't you?"

"You'd be surprised how tactful I can get," I said. "Ask me back here tonight and I'll give you a demonstration."

"What did they have you doing before they gave you this assignment?" she asked. "Filing correspondence?"

"Give me the address and you can halve your problem."

"All right," she said abruptly.

She walked over to the desk and sat down. She lit herself a cigarette and the nails of her right hand beat a faint tattoo on the desktop for a few moments.

"All right," she repeated slowly. "I have a feeling I'm going to hate myself for this. She's in apartment 4-A at 1105 Lake Street. She's under the name of Jones, Miriam Jones. Say that I sent you or she won't open the door."

"Jorgens sent me," I said. "Do I knock three times and ask for Miriam?"

"You can go screw." She took a deep breath and the opening of her shirt expanded outward over her breasts so that I just caught a brief impression of the rim of one pink areola before the shirt slipped back into place. "Are you sure they couldn't send someone else, Lieutenant? It really had to be you?"

"They sent the best man available," I said modestly. "This is Pine City, not a metropolis."

"Handle her gently," she said, "Georgia Brown is a badly frightened woman."

THE BLONDE 7

"I always handle my women gently," I said. "It's a Wheeler trademark. I'll come right back after I've seen her and tell you all about it. We can have dinner," I looked around the suite appreciatively, "here."

"You can tell me about it in ten minutes," she said. "I'm going to be busy tonight. We've only got seventy-two hours before the show."

The door opened suddenly and a woman came in without knocking. "Janice, about that——" She stopped abruptly when she saw me. "Sorry," she said distantly, "I didn't know you had company."

"That's quite all right, Paula," Miss Jorgens said nervously. "This is Mr. Wheeler, he's a . . . a . . ."

"Cop," I said, and smiled gently at the hatred that suddenly shone in Miss Jorgens' eyes.

Paula Reid's fingers touched her smoke-blue hair, which wasn't one strand out of place, and her blue eyes had an arctic quality as she looked at me. "A police officer?" she queried coldly.

"Lieutenant," I explained. "I wanted to see you, but your secretary's been trying to stall me. Says you're too busy to be bothered with the police."

I saw the look of relief in Miss Jorgens' eyes.

"Oh?" Paula's voice was flat. "Why did you want to see me?"

"You've been threatened about your show," I said. "Frankly, it's not the possibility of you being murdered that worries us, it's all that publicity your murder would get."

"You're honest, anyway," she said. "I can give you five minutes but I don't think they will do you much good. You'd better come to my suite."

She turned toward the door and I followed her.

"Lieutenant!" Janice Jorgens said urgently.

"Yes?" I turned and looked at her for a moment.

"Don't . . . er . . . keep Miss Reid too long, will you?" Her eyes were asking all sorts of questions.

"That depends on Miss Reid," I said and smiled sweetly at her, the moment before I closed the door.

We went into the suite next door.

"Please sit down, Lieutenant," Paula Reid said.

I sank into a comfortable armchair and she sat opposite me. Her dark blue shirt rode a short way up her rounded thighs as she crossed her legs. Her blouse was of a paler blue and clung to the bold thrust of her boobs with a sort of smug satisfaction.

"Well, Lieutenant?"

"What about these threats?"

"There have been threatening phone calls," she said, "quite a few of them. But I'm used to that kind of thing, I don't take them seriously."

"How about Miss Brown—does she take them seriously?"

"No, she's hidden away quite safely. No one could find her."

"That's a sweeping statement."

"It's true."

"Don't you think it would be better if we gave you police protection—until after your show, anyway?"

"No, it's not necessary."

"Do you have any idea who's making the threats?"

She shook her head. "The caller doesn't give a name, of course. It's the same husky voice each time, sounds like a woman but I'm not sure. I don't think its important. A good publicity gimmick, that's all."

"You aren't being much help, Miss Reid."

"Did I ask you for any help?"

"I guess you didn't," I admitted. "What exactly is Georgia Brown going to say Saturday night?"

She smiled momentarily. "Why don't you watch the show and find out?"

"She's going to name names?"

"I don't know," she said lightly. "We don't work to a script and the show isn't rehearsed, not the actual interview, at least. It goes over better that way, it's more authentic. The viewers like that."

"But you must have a pretty good idea what you're going to ask her."

"Surely," she said. "I'm going to ask her the truth about Lee Manning's death and the people associated with him at that time. And I think she'll answer by telling me the truth."

"O.K.," I said, "I quit."

I got onto my feet and looked down at her.

"You're a wise man, Lieutenant," she said. "Good afternoon."

"Good afternoon, Miss Reid," I said. "If you wake up

THE BLONDE 9

dead one morning, I hope you won't blame the Sheriff's office."

I stopped at the desk downstairs and showed my shield to the clerk and told him who I was. He wasn't impressed. He started to fidget. I could see he thought that if I stayed around too long they'd have to knock five dollars a day off the price of their suites.

"How many people are with Miss Reid exactly?" I asked him.

He consulted his book. "She has a suite of her own, so does her secretary and her producer," he said. "There are three others with them, and they have rooms of their own. Six in all, Lieutenant."

He closed the book with a bang and looked at me hopefully but I didn't move.

"Anybody called on her since she arrived?"

"The reporters were here to meet her," he said. "There have been no other callers. . . . Excuse me." He turned to greet the man who had walked up to the desk and stood beside me. "Yes, sir?" the clerk said politely. "You have a reservation?"

The man was tall, wearing a dark-blue Brooks Brothers suit and a white carnation in his lapel. He had an ascetic's face and his carefully waved gray hair had recently been given a blue rinse.

"No," he said in an English accent, "I don't have a reservation. I would like to see Miss Reid."

"I'm sorry, sir," the clerk looked faintly regretful. "Miss Reid has given strict orders that she will see no one."

"But it's most important that I see her." He brushed the side of his head, fingering the wave into place. "Would you call her and say that Norman Coates——"

"I'm sorry, sir," the clerk said firmly. "I have strict orders——"

"You don't understand!" Coates said. "My business with Miss Reid is urgent and——"

"Quite impossible!" the clerk said and pointedly turned his back on him.

Coates hesitated for a fleeting moment; even the Brooks Brothers suit had an air of uncertainty. Then he turned and walked slowly away from the desk.

The clerk glared at his departing back for a moment, then turned to me. "Really!" he said. "Some people!"

"You got to expect all types when you're running a flophouse," I said, and left him impersonating a goldfish suddenly removed from its bowl.

I went out of the hotel to the car parked at the curb and drove over to Lake Street. It was a nondescript street and the nearest lake was about ten miles north. It consisted mostly of apartment buildings and they all had the same wilted look as if they'd been waiting too long for something to happen and had finally given up.

I stopped outside 1105 and got out. I walked up the steps to the front entrance and found that 4-A was on the second floor. I went up the two flights of stairs and then down the corridor to the door at one end. I knocked gently on the door—three times—and waited.

Nothing happened. I knocked again and said in a guarded voice: "Miss Jones? Miss Jorgens sent me. Miss Jones?" I wondered if she'd be wearing a false beard when she opened the door.

Some twenty seconds went by without my seeing them. I though I heard a movement inside the apartment but I wasn't sure. Maybe she was allergic to knocks? I could try the buzzer for a switch in technique.

I put my thumb against the buzzer and pressed.

The door leaped out of its frame and hit me over the head. I was flung backwards about ten feet down the corridor with the noise of the explosion still ringing in my ears.

I sat up slowly and shook my head. "That's one hell of a way to answer the door," I said to nobody in particular.

Blue smoke drifted from the open doorway and I could see part of the way into the apartment. I could see the plaster floating down from the ceiling and the splintered matchwood which had once been a chair. A tongue of flame licked from the center of the carpet.

The front door lay in the corridor a couple of feet away from me. I looked down at it and slowly realized I must be looking at the inside panels, which were also splintered. But the handle was intact.

Attached to the handle was a human hand. I noticed vaguely that the nails were a bright carnation-pink.

Chapter Two

Dr. Murphy came out of the wrecked apartment, rubbing his hands together. "Got a matchbox?" he asked.

I took my lighter out of my pocket and offered it to him.

"You know I don't smoke," he said. "Disgusting habit!"

"Then why ask for a matchbox?"

"It'll save the meat-wagon a job," he said.

"You ghoul," I said. "It's a wonder they don't save you for Halloween."

He shrugged his shoulders. "She was blonde, I can tell you that much; we found some hairs on one wall."

"Thanks."

"Saves an autopsy, anyway," he said and walked away whistling.

MacDonald, the explosives expert, came out along with Sergeant Polnik.

"Find anything exciting?" I asked him.

"You pressed the buzzer and the whole lot went up," he said. "That right, Lieutenant?"

"That's right."

"You were lucky—the bomb was rigged to blow inwards, if it hadn't been, you wouldn't be here now."

"What else?"

"Whoever set it up knew what they were doing," he said. "They wired it through the buzzer circuit. As soon as anybody pressed the buzzer they completed the circuit—and blooey!"

"How big was the bomb?"

"Not very big, I'd say the whole package would be around a foot square, maybe smaller. It didn't need a timing device and they're the things that take up the room generally."

"Anything else?"

"I've got a few bits and pieces to take back to the lab with me," MacDonald said. "Give you a report on it just as soon as I can, Lieutenant."

"Thanks," I said.

"Fixed the woman all right." His face was a couple shades paler than normal. "I wouldn't want to see something like the inside of that apartment too often—not and sleep nights, that is!"

He walked off down the corridor, and he wasn't whistling. But then MacDonald was a human being, which was the difference between him and Doc Murphy.

Polnik looked at me hopefully. "What do we do now, Lieutenant?"

"Scream," I said.

"Huh?"

"Sheriff Lavers particularly wanted me to look after the woman who was in there," I explained.

Polnik gulped. "You mean it was you blasted her?"

I lit myself a cigarette carefully. "Are the rest of the boys still working inside there?"

"Sure, Lieutenant."

"Stay here till they're finished," I said. "Seeing that I looked after the woman so well, Lavers gave me a bonus. This is now the Sheriff's homicide, as well as Homicide's homicide."

"You going to confess to yourself, Lieutenant?"

"I'll think about it," I said. "When the boys are through, check the rest of the apartments in the building. Find out if anybody knew her, if they saw her at all, if she had any callers—you know the routine."

"Whatever you say, Lieutenant."

"I'm going over to the Starlight Hotel," I said. "When you're through here, follow me over. Ask for me at the desk."

"Sure, Lieutenant." He blinked at me. "You were kidding about the Sheriff wanting you to take care of her, weren't you?"

"Why no," I said. "I thought I did it rather well—it went over with a bang."

I walked away, hearing the rasping sound as Polnik scratched his head. I went downstairs and out through the entrance hall. I pushed my way through the gaping crowd on the sidewalk and got into the car and drove away.

Fifteen minutes later I knocked on the door of Paula Reid's suite. She opened it right away. She had changed into a pair of dark blue, snugly molded slacks and didn't look pleased to see me.

"Really, Lieutenant!" she said. "I can't afford to waste any more time talking to you. I have to work on the show and——"

"There won't be any show," I said. "So you've got all the time in the world. Get Miss Jorgens in here, will you? It will save me repeating myself."

I walked past her into the suite and saw Miss Jorgens was already there. Her eyes grew wider as she looked at me.

"Hello, Lieutenant," she said nervously. "Nothing wrong I hope?"

"Nothing a jury can't fix," I said.

Paula Reid slammed the door shut and glared at me. "If this is a sample of the manners of Pine City Police Department I'm going to complain to the——"

I lit myself a cigarette. "Miss Jorgens was worried about those threatening letters," I explained. "She asked for our help, unofficially."

"You . . ." Janice Jorgens stopped, trying to think of an adequate word.

"So I talked to her," I said. "And she gave me the address where you were hiding Georgia Brown."

"Janice!" Paula glared icily at her secretary. "What right had you to——"

"You can go into that later," I interrupted her. "She told me that only two people knew that address, one was herself and the other was you. Is that right?"

"It was right!" Paula said. "Now, I suppose you've told the papers or something equally stupid!"

"When did you last see Georgia?"

"I don't see what——"

I closed my eyes for a moment: "I'm having a long, hard day—don't make it any harder."

"About three days ago," she said. "I came here incognito to see her."

"Better than flying?"

"If you're asking me a serious question . . ."

"I am," I said hastily. "Three days ago. You haven't seen her since then?"

"I haven't had the time. We only arrived here this morning, you might remember."

I looked at Janice. "How about you?"

"I saw her this morning," she said. "Paula wanted me to check she was all right."

"And was she?"

"Of course," she said in a puzzled voice. "She was still there when you called, wasn't she?"

"She was still there," I agreed.

"What have you done with her now?" Paula asked briskly. "If it's public knowledge where she is, that apartment is too dangerous for her now. You didn't leave her there, did you?"

"In a sense," I said.

"Will you stop being mysterious!"

"I knocked," I said, "but there was no answer. So I pressed the buzzer. That completed a circuit which blew up a bomb inside the apartment."

They both stared at me for a moment, open-mouthed.

"Georgia," Paula said shakily, "is she . . ."

"The doctor said she was a blonde," I told her gently. "He found a few hairs on the wall to prove it."

Paula Reid's face suddenly dissolved into tears.

"Oh," she said faintly. Then she crumpled into a chair.

"Get her a drink," I told Janice. "You could get me one too," I added hopefully.

Janice poured out three drinks, which proved she was more sensible than I thought. By the time Paula had got halfway through hers, she had recovered a little.

She dabbed her eyes gently. "If I hadn't publicized the fact she was appearing on the show . . ."

"If she was ready to talk, she would have talked anyway—your show was only coincidental," I said. "I want to ask you some questions."

"Of course," she nodded. "I'll do my best to help you, Lieutenant."

"Why did she want to appear on the show?"

"To clear her name," Paula murmured. "She was tired of living in obscurity. She had run out of money, so she wanted to get back into film business."

"Were you going to pay her to appear on your show?"

"Five thousand."

"I should be a cop," I said regretfully. "How did you find her?"

"She found me," Paula went on. "We did the show from San Francisco six weeks back. She came to my hotel there one night and told me who she was..."

"How much did she tell you about the Manning suicide?"

"Not a great deal. She was... well, a little cagey. I suppose she didn't trust me entirely. She thought if she told me too much I mightn't need her on the show at all and she wouldn't get the money."

"She must have told you something."

"Please, Lieutenant!" Janice said earnestly. "At a time like this! Do you have to keep on with these questions? Can't you see Miss Reid is all——"

"She's in much better shape than Georgia Brown right now," I pointed out mildly. "Why don't you do something useful like pouring us all another drink?"

She came over and took the glass out of my hand, nearly taking a couple of my fingers along with it.

"The Lieutenant is right, Janice," Paula said. "Georgia has been murdered and he's got to find the murderer, and I've got to help him."

"She must have told you something," I said. "What about names? Did she mention any names?"

"Yes, she did. She said she was prepared to tell the truth about the circumstances surrounding Lee Manning's death, and that would involve a number of prominent people. She also said she could prove her statement if necessary and she'd take full responsibility for any accusations made on the show."

"Fine," I said patiently. "What were the names?"

"There were four," she said. "Hilary Blain, Kay Steinway, Norman Coates and Kent Fargo."

"Fargo?" I said. "I know he's been mixed up in most of the rackets, but I didn't know the film business was included."

"He did back a number of films at one time," she said. "But it was kept very quiet. Coates produced most of the films he backed."

"That makes Coates a producer?"

"You're so sharp, Lieutenant!" Janice said.

"Kay Steinway is the girl who can't sing but everybody loves watching her try," I said. "I saw her last musical. And Blain is *the* Blain, the financier?"

"That's right," Paula agreed.

"Only those four names?"

"They were the only ones she mentioned. But they're all famous names, one way or another, Lieutenant. Enough to boost my Trendex another five points at least!"

I glanced at her contoured silk shirt. "It doesn't need boosting from where I sit," I said admiringly.

"Trendex," Janice said coldly, "is a rating service. A scientific measurement of a show's popularity."

"I'm disenchanted," I confided.

"That's all I can tell you, Lieutenant," Paula added.

Janice handed me the new drink and I took it gratefully.

"It's a start," I said to Paula. "Now I'll have to find out where I can get in touch with these people."

"I can tell you that," she said. "Georgia was frightened to death that someone might kill her to stop her appearing on my show and, after what's happened, she was obviously right. I checked on where those people were only a few days ago."

"You're getting to be a help," I said.

"Give the Lieutenant a list of those addresses, Janice," she said.

Janice went out of the suite and came back half a minute later with a typed list which she handed to me. I thanked her and put it into my pocket.

"Is there anything else you can tell me?" I asked Paula. "Anything at all you think might help?"

She shook her head. "I'm sorry, I can't think of anything right now."

The phone rang and Janice lifted the receiver. She looked across at me a moment later. "It's for you, Lieutenant."

I took the receiver from her and said, "Wheeler," into the mouthpiece.

"Polnik, Lieutenant. I'm at the desk."

"Wait there, I'll be down in a moment." I replaced the phone on the cradle. "Thanks for your help," I said to Paula. "I'll let you know any developments."

"Thank you," she said dully. "This is a tragedy, Lieutenant!"

"Try not to think about it," I suggested. "Try and forget Georgia Brown ever existed, for a while."

"Georgia Brown!" she wailed. "I'm not worrying about her. . . . What am I going to do for a show Saturday night!"

Polnik smiled at me as I came up to the desk.

"Hi, Lieutenant! What's new?"

"My thirst," I said. "Let's go into the bar and get a drink."

I ordered Scotch on the rocks, with a touch of soda. Polnik let his head go and ordered a beer.

"What did you find out?" I asked him.

"I checked all the other tenants like you said, and the janitor. He helped her in with her bags and that was the only time he ever saw her. Said she was a blonde, not a bad looker, but she didn't say much."

"What about the other tenants?"

"They never saw her at all, she never went out."

"What about callers?"

"Two. Both women, both had class. One was a redhead—she was there this morning—and the other was . . ." he hesitated for a moment, "well, so help me, Lieutenant, this is what they say . . ."

"She had blue hair and was dressed in blue," I said.

"You know?" Polnik looked disappointed. "They were the only two, Lieutenant."

"They were the only two with legitimate reasons for calling on her," I said. "You sure there was nobody else?"

"There's an old woman lives in the apartment opposite and she told me for sure there weren't any others. The janitor said she's the nosiest old woman he's ever met and he's got forty years' experience in the business. If she says the blonde don't have any other callers, then she don't."

"It makes a depressing picture," I said.

The bartender served the drinks and Polnik looked worried until I paid for them.

"So she got bored, sitting around doing nothing," I said broodingly. "So she made herself a bomb and wired it into the buzzer circuit, then sat around waiting for somebody to press the buzzer."

"Suicide!" Polnik said admiringly. "Maybe you got the whole case sewed up already, Lieutenant!"

Chapter Three

The style was twentieth-century Spanish in white stucco. "My adobe hacienda," they used to sing once and this was the place they sang about. It had a walled courtyard and six palm trees that weren't good for a date between the lot of them.

I tried the front door and got no answer. I walked back toward where I'd left the car on the driveway and heard a splashing noise from somewhere inside the courtyard. I stopped for a moment and heard a voice singing. A husky voice crooning gently, "Lover, come back to me."

It was off-key and Kay Steinway.

The courtyard had a door which was closed. I tried the handle and found it wasn't locked, so I opened it and stepped inside.

There was a swimming pool shaped like the sign of a bass clef. At the far end I caught a flash of whiteness, then there was a splash. I lit a cigarette and waited patiently.

She swam three-quarters of the length of the pool with a powerful crawl stroke before she noticed me. She stopped swimming suddenly and trod water.

"This is private property," she said in that husky voice. "Or didn't you notice?"

"You're Kay Steinway?"

"Get out of here!"

"I'm Lieutenant Wheeler, from the County Sheriff's office," I said. "I wanted to talk to you."

"Oh," she said, and swam in to the tiled edge of the pool, and as I watched her legs scissoring through the clear water, I could see that she wasn't wearing a swimsuit. Reaching the steps, she grabbed the railings and pulled herself up out of the water.

THE BLONDE

Her dark hair clung wetly to her head, and as she emerged from the water, her long shapely body beaded with crystal drops, I couldn't help but stand in open-mouthed admiration. Her body was sleek, and tanned a light bronze all over. She was completely unself-conscious and natural in the way she moved, as if she were unaware of my presence altogether. She was like Aphrodite rising. She was magnificent. Her breasts were full and proud, the dark pink nipples standing erect, her hips rounded and her thighs firm and not too fleshy, with, between them, the drops of water glistening like tiny diamonds on the dark, damp delta of her pubis.

She moved across to a chair, and picking up a white bathrobe which had been draped across it, shrugged herself into it, then pulled the belt tight around her waist.

"Let's go into the house," she said. "I need a drink."

We skirted the edge of the pool, then crossed the white-flagged patio and went in through the open glass doors.

The living area was furnished modern style with a bar at one end. Kay Steinway walked around the serving side of the bar counter and looked at me. "What will it be?" she asked.

"Scotch," I said, "on the rocks, with a little soda."

I watched her as she poured two. She looked as good in real life as she did with a head twenty feet square on widescreen.

She had an elfin face with gray-green eyes that she must have traded from a small demon. Her lower lip was full and sensuous, and I guessed she knew how to use it to maximum delicious effect. The robe was open over the inner rise of her breasts and fell away down one long, bronzed thigh.

She handed me a glass and raised her own. "Here's to the Police Department," she said. "I was getting bored being on my own tonight."

I remembered her dripping body rising from the water. "You don't strike me as being a boring person," I remarked.

She smiled at me crookedly. "So you saw me as I really am. A girl with no secrets."

"I'm longsighted," I told her.

"Looking ahead. Into a crystal ball. What do you see?"

"If I wasn't here on business," I said, "this would be a pleasure."

"You should combine the two," she said lazily. "Maybe you have an expense account."

"Enough for a beer and a sandwich," I admitted. "Do you know Georgia Brown?"

"I did once, vaguely," she said. "Isn't she going to be the new star of television come Saturday night?"

"Not any more. When did you last see her?"

"It must be three years ago now," she grimaced. "The day the coroner gave his decision on Lee Manning's suicide. She was in court. I didn't see her after that. I didn't know anybody had seen her since then, excepting Paula Reid."

"I saw her this morning," I said. "Somebody exploded a bomb in her apartment and blew her into small pieces."

She finished her drink and then topped the glass up with neat Scotch. She drank it down without a tremor disturbing the smoothness of her face. "That's tough," she said.

"She was going to tell the truth about why Manning committed suicide," I said. "She was going to prove her own innocence and she was going to name names."

Kay Steinway gurgled with laughter. "You kill me!"

"Did I say something funny?"

"That bit about Georgia and innocence. Georgia's about as innocent as an actress trying out for a part in a porno flick."

"One of the names was yours," I said.

"That's crazy," she said evenly. "I knew Manning—who didn't? I was a nobody then. I'd had a speaking part, a oneliner. The band stopped playing and the camera cut to a close-up of me. 'Solid!' I said and then they cut back to the band. They left the close-up on the cutting-room floor."

"Tell me some more about Georgia Brown," I said.

She poured herself a third drink, but without the urgency this time. "Should I see my lawyer, Lieutenant?"

"I'm only looking for information. There were other names she was going to mention. I haven't talked to their owners yet. I just happened to pick yours first."

"Why?"

"Call it a hunch, coupled with the fact that yours was the only female name on the list. I'm glad it was," I said, studying the rising contour of her breasts.

"Who are the others?"

"I have to keep some secrets."

"Why? I don't have any from you now. You're a slow drinker, Lieutenant . . . Lieutenant? Do I have to keep on

THE BLONDE

calling you that all the time I'm baring my soul to you. I've bared everything else already—can't we be friends?"

"Call me Al," I said.

"Al," she said. "Short and sweet. Very macho. I like it. Is it short for anything?"

"Never mind," I said firmly. "How about Georgia Brown?"

"She was a friend of Manning's," she said. "I don't suppose you ever knew Manning?"

"No."

"He was a first-rate louse, and believe me, in Hollywood it's hard to qualify, the competition's so keen!"

"So?"

"He liked girls, lots of girls, but they all had a few things in common—they were young and innocent, they had ambitions, and no contracts. His I-can-get-you-into-pictures routine was better than most, because he was in pictures and everybody knew it."

"It doesn't sound original."

"But it was effective. He'd have weekend parties with anything up to half a dozen young hopefuls out at his place—and I do mean young, barely into their teens, some of them not even properly developed. Very supple and eager to please, ready to learn. Coke-sniffing and group sex, movies and mirrors, you name it. He had this thing about barely developed kids. They turned him on. They got younger all the time."

"You were one of his party girls?" I asked.

She shook her head: "I was too old for him even then," she said. "When I first met him I was all of nineteen."

"He liked them really young."

"And innocent. I didn't qualify on either count."

"Sounds like a nice guy."

"He treated them rough, too," she said. "You could say he was one of the nicest perverts you could meet any place. I wouldn't say he was queer, either—just depraved."

"But with a setup like that, he committed suicide," I said incredulously. "All he needed was some vitamin tablets."

"It was a little more complicated than that," she said. "Norman Coates was his producer at the time and he was making independent films. The money came from Hilary Blain—you know, the financier?"

"I've heard of him," I said.

"Lee Manning picked the wrong girl finally. I guess it had to happen sooner or later. She was a kid from Arkansas or Tennessee or someplace, with all the qualifications necessary for someone with jaded tastes like Lee's. She came out to one of his weekends parties, which meant the usual thing, being screwed by any guy who had the inclination. Maybe she had a weak heart, or maybe they played it a little too rough, but she died there."

I finished my first drink and she absently refilled my glass.

"The police started digging," she continued, "and they found out just what type of party it had been; then they found out the girl's true age. They were going to hit Lee with half the statute book. Drugs, sex with minors. He was no Roman Polanski. He didn't skip the country, though only Christ knows why he didn't."

"That was one of the troubles with Coates' being an independent—he didn't have the sort of big organization that could hope to hush it up. It was a first-class scandal about due to hit the headlines. Then Lee grabbed the headlines for himself . . . he always was a scene-stealer."

I offered her a cigarette, lit it for her and one for myself. "How did Georgia Brown fit into it?"

"Georgia introduced the girl to Lee. She introduced a lot of girls to him. There's a word for it, isn't there?"

"Procuress?"

"Something like that. It's not something they give Oscars for."

I nodded. "I can remember the headlines about Manning's suicide, and the stories about orgies and drugs, but there was nothing definite. Nothing about a young girl."

"After Lee was dead, they managed to hush it up," she said.

"How?"

"Well, Lee was dead anyway, so they couldn't bring a case against him. I think they sold it to the authorities on that and there was the angle that it wouldn't help the girl's family any to have her name dragged through the mud."

"Thanks," I said. "Any more?"

"Not that I can think of, Al. Why don't you stick around and relax a little?"

"I'd like to, but I have to keep on working, you know how it is."

She shook her head. "No, tell me."

"Some other time I'd enjoy it," I said sincerely.

I finished my drink and walked slowly toward the glass doors. She caught up with me on the white-flagged patio.

"You're sure you wouldn't like to stay a while longer, Al?"

"Not right now," I said. "But I'd like to come back soon."

"Come back tonight, why don't you?" she suggested. "I'm having a party. Some interesting people will be here. Paula Reid for one."

"She won't come now after what's happened," I said.

"She'll come," Kay said confidently. "I hate to say it myself but I'm Kay Steinway, remember? The biggest name in musicals since Ginger Rogers. Paula wouldn't dare refuse my invitation!"

"If I have time, I'd like to be there," I said, "and thanks."

"It'll be a very intimate party," she said. "I hope you make time to come, Al."

We walked toward the courtyard gate.

"How do you know so much about what happened that weekend at Mannings?" I asked her.

"I was there," she said. "Georgia took me down with her, but Lee took one look at me and right away that was the end of it. I was too old and had too much experience for him. Besides, I'd left school!"

"Didn't the same apply to Georgia?" I asked. "What was she doing down there?"

"She was always there for his parties," Kay said coolly. "I guess she had a personal interest; after all, she got the girls for him. I guess she liked to study their performance. It was more fun than a day at Santa Anita for Georgia."

"She sounds like fun herself," I said.

"Like a black widow spider!"

I pushed the gate open. "Thanks again, Kay. I'll really try to make that party. I'd like to see you again soon."

"Even sooner than you think, maybe," she said casually. "I'm hot again. If I didn't have this pool, I'd go crazy in the summer."

She undid the belt of her robe and shrugged her shoulders free. The robe dropped to the flagstones and she turned to me, her lower lip pouting a little.

Her body was dry now, and the tips of her finely sculpted breasts still taut. The dark curling hair of her delta was still damp, and through it I could see the line of her slit. She ran her hands slowly down her flanks, then she turned and moved back to the edge of the pool, her buttocks meshing gently together as she walked. I was aware of a vague, wistful stirring in my loins, then as she dived expertly into the water, I told myself this was neither the time nor the place to allow my imagination to wander. There was work to be done.

I stood for a few seconds watching the splash, then stepped out of the courtyard, closing the door behind me.

I walked back to the car with the clarion call of duty ringing derisively inside my head. The rocks moved over and made room for it.

Chapter Four

Norman Coates opened the door of his hotel room and the uncertain smile on his face vanished when he saw me.

"Yes?" he asked in a high-pitched voice.

I told him who I was, and that I wanted to talk to him.

"Perhaps you'd better come in," he said doubtfully. He stood there for a few seconds longer, then sighed deeply and led the way inside.

I followed him in, closing the door behind me. He wore a Paisley silk dressing gown, the color of a seasick Picasso dove of peace, and a lavender scarf tucked carefully around his neck.

"I've seen you before, Lieutenant," he said, a smile appearing and reappearing on his face like a nervous tic. "As I remember it was this morning?"

"And you didn't appreciate my talent, Mr. Coates," I said regretfully. "At house parties my impersonation of a bystander is a riot, straight out of Runyon, they say."

"I didn't stay," he said, fluttering his hands in front of him. "I thought the situation was becoming too absurd. I only wanted to contact Miss Reid to see if she could tell me where I could find Miss Brown. And that desk clerk . . . Well, he upset me. You do understand, Lieutenant Wheeler, don't you?"

"What difference does it make," I said. "Why did you want to see Georgia Brown?"

"Well," his hand patted the wave deeper along the side of his head, "I understand she's going to rake up all that old stuff about Lee Manning on Paula Reid's program, and I'm hoping I can persuade her not to. It won't do anyone any good, you know. It's just like that Reid woman to think up something like this. I don't mind these interview programs on television but, really! This Reid woman is nothing but the end! Don't you agree, Lieutenant Wheeler?"

"I have good news for you, Mr. Coates," I said. "The program won't go on Saturday night."

"Really?" His face brightened a little. "You're sure, Lieutenant."

"Quite sure—Georgia Brown is dead."

"Dead?" His face sagged as he repeated the word and two years' facials went down the drain. "I . . . Excuse me, I must sit down."

He groped his way to a chair and eased himself into it carefully.

"Forgive me," he said, "it's the shock. Death always disturbs me, Lieutenant."

"It disturbed Georgia, too," I said. "She was blown to pieces inside her apartment. All we found was——"

"Please!" He shuddered and closed his eyes tight. "I can't bear to think about it."

"She was murdered," I said. "My guess is she was murdered by someone who didn't want her on that program, someone like you, maybe?"

He opened his eyes wide: "You can't think that I . . . why, it's preposterous!"

"She was going to blow the works about Lee Manning's suicide. Tell the stories about his weekend orgies and the kid with the maybe weak heart and how you managed to hush it up, wasn't she?"

He dabbed his lips with a silk handkerchief. "I will admit that if she had spoken of those things it could have been embarrassing for me. Embarrassing, Lieutenant, but no more. I wanted to see her and appeal to her not to do it. I hoped I might reason with her. But kill her! The whole concept is ridiculous, Lieutenant. I couldn't hurt a fly!"

"Somebody put that bomb in her apartment," I said. "You had a good reason for killing her. Who had a better one?"

"How on earth should I know!" he said petulantly. "It's your job to find the guilty person, Lieutenant, not mine."

I looked at him with the poker face that everyone else says is just my normal blank expression. He shifted uneasily in his chair, glanced at me, then turned his eyes away quickly.

"I can't think of anyone who would want to kill her," he said finally.

THE BLONDE

"What about Hilary Blain?"

"Blain?" He shook his head. "He had no reason."

"What about Fargo?"

"Who is Fargo?" he asked blankly.

"Kent Fargo," I said. "Don't tell me you haven't heard of him? His name must have penetrated even where you live."

"You mean the racketeer, Fargo?"

"I don't mean Wells Fargo."

"If he had any reason to murder Georgia I'm sure I know nothing about it."

"Didn't Fargo back your pictures starring Manning when you were working as an independent?"

"No, it was Hilary who backed me." His hand brushed the side of his head again unconsciously. "Hilary was always . . . well, terribly nice about money. I'm sure I could never have worked with a gangster!" He shuddered as he said the word.

"O.K.," I said, "that's your story and I'm stuck with it for now. You staying in Pine City long, Mr. Coates?"

"A few days."

"Fine," I said. "That means I don't have to ask you to stay, doesn't it?" I took out a card and scribbled on it. "If you think of anything that could help us, Mr. Coates, I'd like you to call that number. If I'm not there, I've written my home number down. Anything at all, however trivial, I'd like you to call me."

He took the card. "Of course, Lieutenant. Certainly—anything you say."

I opened the door and stepped out into the corridor. The delicate scent of roses stayed with me till I reached the car.

Half an hour's drive got me to Hilary Blain's house. A butler opened the door and looked at me with polite inquiry in his eyes.

"I'm Lieutenant Wheeler," I told him. "From the County Sheriff's office. I want to see Mr. Blain."

"Good afternoon, Lieutenant," he said gravely. "Mr. Blain is at home. I shall inform him of your presence."

"I'd beware of the presence," I said, equally grave, "for all you know, I might be a Greek."

"Indeed, sir," he said and left me standing on the doorstep.

He came back and looked at me somberly with all the cheerfulness of a bloodhound that has just lost its mother.

"Mr. Blain will see you in the library, sir. If you'll follow me?"

I followed him into the library and Hilary Blain got up from the chair behind his desk to greet me. He was a short, thin man with the last of his hair sitting on the crown of his head and a pair of gold-rimmed glasses sitting on his nose. He looked worried and the deep lines on his face pointed up that he'd been worried ever since he'd been born and had to rely on other people.

"Sit down, Lieutenant," he said abruptly, "what can I do for you?"

I sat down in a comfortable, leather-padded chair and lit a cigarette. He sat back carefully onto his own chair and looked at me with a pinched expression.

I couldn't think of an original gambit so I gave him the one about Georgia naming names and his being one of them, and about her being dead.

"I see, Lieutenant," he said.

He took off his glasses and polished them thoroughly with his pocket handkerchief, then replaced them on the bridge of his nose. The reflected light as he looked at me gave his face a peculiarly blank expression.

"Well, of course, I was connected with her at one time." He thought about that for a moment. "That is, we were associated for a time—it was purely business of course."

"You were backing Coates when he was making pictures starring Lee Manning," I said. "Georgia played in a few of them, too, didn't she?"

"Quite so," he said, "quite so. Though I fail to understand why she should mention my name in connection with her revelations about the Manning affair. I have nothing to hide."

"I've heard the story about the young girl who died," I said, "how it was hushed up after Manning suicided."

"Unfortunate!" he said sharply. "Most unfortunate. At the time if there had been any publicity given to the girl's death it would have been, well . . ."

"Unfortunate?"

"Quite so! But now?" he shrugged his thin shoulders. "I no longer invest money in films made by Mr. Coates. In fact I no longer invest in films at all. So why I should worry about my name being mentioned in connection with——"

"I understand it wasn't actually your money, Mr. Blain," I

said. "The way I hear it, you were only a dummy—the hard cash belonged to Kent Fargo."

He hesitated for a moment. "I neither deny nor affirm that statement, Lieutenant."

"Supposing, for the moment, it is true—*if* Georgia Brown had mentioned that in a television interview, wouldn't you have been embarrassed."

"I don't see why," he said abruptly.

"It could have embarrassed Fargo."

He whipped off his glasses and held them up to the light. With a small grunt of triumph he detected a minute smudge and polished it off vigorously.

"Why don't you ask Mr. Fargo about that?" he said cautiously.

"I will," I said. "Mr. Blain, I don't think we're being quite realistic about this. A woman has been murdered. Before she died she gave the names of the people she intended to denounce on Paula Reid's show. Your name was one of the four. Fargo's was another. It makes you both prime suspects, along with the other two. I'm looking for your help and you're not giving me any."

He glared at me for a few seconds. "Sincerely, Lieutenant," he said finally, "I can't help you. I wish I could. My own personal opinion is that Georgia Brown needed money badly, so she approached this woman interviewer with an invented story about being able to lift the lid on the scandal surrounding Manning's suicide. And her only reason for so doing was to make money from it.

"I think if the interview had taken place it would have been a complete anticlimax. There was only one person who had anything to fear if all the facts concerning Lee's death were made public!"

"Who's that?"

He grimaced. "It was Georgia Brown herself. I don't know how much you've learned of the circumstances, Lieutenant, but I gather it's a good deal from what you've said. You must surely know the role that Georgia Brown played!"

"I'd like to hear your version," I said politely.

"She was nothing better than a pimp!" he said. "She sought out the girls, the young girls that were Manning's weakness. She persuaded them that he could start them on the road to stardom, and inveigled them to his weekend parties. It was she who found the girl. She knew her true age, but it didn't stop Georgia."

"Georgia sounds like she was a homey girl," I said.

"Lieutenant," he said in a low-pitched voice, "Georgia Brown was an evil woman! A truly evil woman, and the world is well rid of her!"

He sat back in his chair and clasped both hands to his vest. "Now I suppose you'll arrest me?"

"I think you're voicing the majority opinion about Georgia Brown," I said. "I don't think that's a crime. Is there anything else you can tell me, Mr. Blain?"

"No," he said. "I've probably said too much already."

"Thanks, anyway," I told him.

I got onto my feet and walked toward the door.

"Lieutenant," he called.

"Mr. Blain?" I looked back at him.

"Whatever Georgia was, she wasn't a fool. I would say she picked out the four names she mentioned to Miss Reid very carefully, choosing the names that would have maximum publicity value—to increase her fee, if nothing else. If Georgia had known her comments about any one person might endanger her own life, she wouldn't have made them. She placed too high a value on her own skin to risk it knowingly."

"You mean—those four names mean absolutely nothing?"

"Absolutely nothing!" he repeated firmly.

I closed my eyes and counted up to ten.

"Why did I ever have to talk to you?" I moaned, and tottered out into the hallway.

The butler met me at the front door. He didn't look any happier. He bowed slightly and opened the door for me. "Never mind," I said cheerfully, patting him on the shoulder, which made him wince and take a step backward. "If the roof caves in, let me know. I could always find you a job in the morgue. You'll like it. It's a bundle of laughs."

Chapter Five

It was a nice bright night for a party. A three-quarter moon riding up into a cloudless sky, and it was warm without being uncomfortably hot. That was the way I felt when I knocked on Kay Steinway's door.

The door opened and the sound of music and people's voices came flooding out.

"Well," Kay said, "this isn't a surprise, but it's nice all the same."

"I just happened to be passing," I said, "it was only ten miles out of my way..."

"Come on in," she said.

She wore a low-slung black gown that came all the way down to her ankles and clung so lovingly to every curve of her body that I wondered if there was any room for her to have anything on beneath it. Her breasts moved with an independent life of their own, and having seen them in their natural state, I knew they didn't need anything in the way of support. The black gown was smooth over her pelvis and thighs, dipping slightly in between them.

"If I had known this was formal," I said, "I wouldn't have dressed."

She turned away, and I noticed with admiration the way her buttocks shifted loosely beneath the gown. "Come and meet the other guests," she said.

I followed her into the living room. There was a haze of blue smoke, a din of voices, a blur of faces—maybe a dozen people in all. Kay introduced me around. I didn't remember the names; it didn't matter, they didn't remember mine. Then there were faces I recognized.

"You taking time off, Lieutenant?" Paula Reid asked. "Or do you call this working?"

"Yes," I said, which seemed the easiest answer right then. I looked at her appreciatively. She wore a blue gown every bit as tight as Kay's, with a neckline that plunged beyond the cleavage and could have only been supported by hope alone. Beside her, Janice Jorgens looked almost pure in a high-necked white sweater.

"I'll get you a drink, Al," Kay said. "Scotch on the rocks?"

"With a little soda," I said.

I made a threesome, along with Paula and Janice, but not for long. Norman Coates joined us, a lurid-colored cocktail in his delicate hand.

"Nice to see you again, Lieutenant," he smiled at me.

Kay Steinway returned and handed me my drink. "Thanks," I said.

"Georgia's death must be quite a problem for you." Coates smiled at Paula. "I mean, what will you do for a show on Saturday night?"

"I'll manage," she said tersely. "You don't have to look so pleased about the whole thing, Norman!"

"Me—pleased?" He looked suitably sympathetic. "I'm very sorry for you, dear, I really am."

"I can imagine!" she said.

"I think it gives you a golden opportunity, darling," Kay purred to Paula. "Why don't you interview yourself?"

"Maybe I should interview you, darling," Paula smiled sweetly at her. "But my program's never been faded off the air yet, and I wouldn't want to spoil a record."

"I still like my original idea," Kay said. "That way you'd get more dirt than you've ever got. And that is the point of the program, darling, isn't it? To dig as much dirt as possible."

"Why don't we just go home?" Janice pleaded with Paula.

"Nonsense," Paula said tightly. "I'm just beginning to enjoy myself. Tell me, Lieutenant, have you asked Kay about Georgia Brown yet? She was very close to Lee Manning, I've heard. About as close as you can get even if you're married, which they weren't."

"We've talked," I said. "Kay told me she was too old for him."

"You don't have to convince me of that!" Paula laughed shortly.

THE BLONDE

"I was nineteen at the time," Kay said tightly. "If you'd been around he would have called you Mother!"

"Such a delightful sense of humor," Paula said. "She's the original anything-for-a-laugh girl. Have you heard her sing, Lieutenant?"

"Paula's the original blues girl, too," Kay smiled. "And don't believe those rumors about her hair being gray originally, Lieutenant. It was white."

"Why, you——" Paula took a quick step toward her, but Janice caught her arm quickly and pulled her back.

"Remember your manners, darling," Kay said. "Or at least try. I know it might be difficult, but do try to remember that the people here have class. They're quite out of your league, sweetheart, so maybe, if you keep your eyes open, you might learn something."

"So when does the swapping start?" Paula inquired with a purr in her voice.

"Get fucked, darling," Kay said sweetly and walked away with a lazy seductive swing of her buttocks.

Paula took a deep breath, which parted her enough from the blue gown to make it all worthwhile.

Coates laughed nervously: "Nothing like the casual conversation between two stars in their own right for good clean fun!" he said brightly.

"One of these days I'll . . ." Paula turned away. "Get me another drink, Janice."

"Don't you think you've had enough?" Janice asked nervously.

"I pay you too much to be a secretary," Paula snapped, "not a nursemaid!"

They both moved away toward the bar, leaving me with Coates. He took his pocket handkerchief out and dabbed his forehead with it. "It certainly gets warm when those two get together," he said.

"If not hot," I agreed. "Kay was telling me earlier about Manning."

"Lee?" he cleared his throat. "He was quite a . . . character."

"A guy who knew what he liked," I said. "He must have run the most original finishing school in the country."

"A character," Coates nodded. "Not that I agreed with his . . . amusements, you understand, Lieutenant."

I looked at him for a long moment: "I'll believe that," I said finally.

"Most unfortunate," he said. "But what could one do? I mean, at that time, he was a star, a great star, Lieutenant. He was box office."

"That meant he could get away with murder?"

"There was some doubt, you know," Coates said quickly. "I mean, the girl had a weak heart, that is, she could have had a weak heart. I mean . . ."

"I get your message," I said. "Wasn't Fargo worried about it, after it happened?"

"I really don't know," he said. "If you'll excuse me, Lieutenant, I must really go and get myself another White Lady."

"Help yourself." I looked around the room. "You've got a wide choice."

"I mean another cocktail, of course," he said.

"Of course," I agreed, but he was already on his way to the bar.

I finished my drink and stood looking at the empty glass for a moment. I really didn't have too much time; I had to call on Kent Fargo before the evening was through. I went across to the bar and by the time I reached it Coates had disappeared. The only other person there was Paula Reid.

"Having yourself a time, Lieutenant?" she said.

"There seems to be a lot of interesting people here tonight," I said.

"Interesting?" she smiled thinly. "I suppose they are, particularly when you know them as well as I do."

She turned her back to the bar, surveying the rest of the people in the room. "There's an interesting character for you, Lieutenant. Over there, in the corner. You recognize him, of course?"

"Jackie Slade?" I said. "Sure, the blue jeans are a dead giveaway."

"The current teenage rebel," she said. "He's guaranteed to rebel against everything, except the money his studio pays him. The fading blonde beside him isn't his mother."

"No?"

"No, she taught him everything he knows, particularly about women. That's why she looks so haggard that even the beauty parlors pass her up now. I guess Jackie would like something more his own age, but she picked him up out of the gutter and owns fifty per cent of his contract. He's got more chance of becoming an actor than he has of getting rid of her. And he'll never be an actor!"

"Tough for Jackie," I said.

"He's young," she said, "but then he's a slob, too. You put them both together and all you get is a young slob. See Carol Hart over there?"

I looked at the willowy brunette with the urchin-cut and the large, soulful eyes. "She's worth looking at," I said admiringly.

"You have no chance, Lieutenant," she said. "She's shopping for a new husband right now. Anyone will do just so long as he has a million dollars, preferably plural. She's playing very hard to get at the moment—until the million comes along. Then she'll melt so fast they'll need a drip tray to catch her. I see she's drinking again."

"That's unusual?"

"She's been on the wagon while she's husband-shopping, but tonight looks as if it's too much for her. Four drinks and she strips at a party—I thought everybody knew that."

"I didn't," I said. "I wonder if she needs another drink yet?"

"Don't worry," she said. "It's as sure as death and taxes."

I found I'd finished the new drink so I poured myself a newer one. "You seem to be well informed," I said.

"I should be," she said expressionlessly. "I've been digging dirt—as Kay so charmingly put it—for the last two years. Show me a celebrity and I'll show you a stinker."

"Introduce me to Paula Reid," I said gently.

She smiled thinly: "I left myself open for that. Let me introduce you to someone else, Lieutenant. The short man over there, the one with the cigar and the bald head. That's Emile Brocales."

"The producer?"

"The most versatile producer of them all. Standing on his right is his current girl friend; on his left, his current boy friend."

"He has time to make pictures?"

"He has to make pictures. How else would he meet all his blackmail payments? You see the blonde with the impossible front?"

"You mean improbable," I corrected her.

"Impossible!" she said tersely. "Believe me, I know! I walked into her shower one morning just to check up. She graduated into pictures from a house in Mexico City. It took them a year to cure her of the habit."

"Dope?"

Paula shook her head. "Every time a man said good-bye, she'd insist on shaking hands with her palm up."

I lit myself a cigarette. "There must be some ordinary people in this business? Normal people, no better, no worse than average?"

"Here's Carol, right on schedule," she said.

The willowy brunette walked slowly into the center of the room, a dreamy look in her eyes. Someone started to whistle "All of Me," softly, and there was the sound of laughter around the room.

Carol didn't seem to hear it. She swayed slowly, her eyes closed, and then she peeled off her gown, which left her only in a black bra and black lace briefs. She reached up behind her, and unclipping the bra, flung it away from her. Then she hooked her thumbs into the waistband of her briefs and began to peel them down over her thighs. Her hips wiggled and she was doing a crazy sort of dance. Her hands came in across from her hips to the edges of her dark vulva, her pelvis thrust forward, and then, suddenly, the floor seemed to give way beneath her, and she gracefully collapsed to a heap on the floor. The hum of conversation renewed as everyone lost interest in her now the act was over.

Carol lay where she was, bottom uppermost. A redheaded chick in a hurry to speak to someone on the other side carefully stepped over her on her way across.

"You were saying?" Paula asked.

"Isn't there anybody normal in this business?"

"Sure," she nodded. "There's me, for example—and you, Lieutenant."

"And Kay Steinway?"

Her lips stretched in that thin smile again. "Well now, I wouldn't really classify Kay as normal. She has too much vitality, I've always thought. It is a fact that she's the only girl who's had to chase a producer three times around the casting couch before she finally caught him. Kay lives for men, you know, Lieutenant. The doubt is, just how long her men manage to keep alive."

"It can happen to anybody," I said. "You keep on eating that breakfast cereal and before you know it . . ."

"She always reminds me of the Black Widow spider," Paula said. "Isn't that the one that eats its mate after——"

"Don't spill any of that acid on my carpet, darling," a cold voice interrupted. "I happen to have paid rather a lot for it!"

Kay Steinway was standing directly behind Paula, a look of cold fury on her face.

"Hello, darling," Paula said easily. "I was just telling the Lieutenant about the men in your life and how you always seem to take the life out of your men." She looked at me and smiled. "Of course, it's not that Kay is so beautiful, just so accessible!"

Kay Steinway moved between us. "I need a drink," she said tautly. "This one will do." She took the glass out of my hand and threw the contents into Paula's face. "You dirty-mouthed, lying old hag!" she said loudly. "You——"

I heard the trumpet sound Retreat, and retreated quickly across the room, then out into the fresh air. I walked out onto the flagstoned patio beside the pool. I saw a shapeless silhouette in front of me.

"Can I get you a drink, I hope not," I said.

Janice Jorgens turned around and looked at me slowly. "It's you, Lieutenant. No drink, thanks. I don't drink much at all, really."

"You sound as if you have the blues," I said. "That figures."

"That's strictly Paula's gimmick," she said.

"Anyway," I added, "she's still a very attractive young woman."

"I wouldn't be too sure about the young part," Janice's lips curled down at the edges. "Haven't you noticed those little scars under each ear?"

"Someone bit her?"

"Plastic surgery," she said.

"I remember the story about the broad who had her face lifted so many times she——"

"Maybe I will have that drink after all," Janice said quickly.

"Sure," I said.

"Do you drive that green Sigma parked out front?" she asked.

"Sure, why?"

"I heard you arrive. It needs a tune, the carburetors are out of sync."

"How do you tell?" I asked in a hushed voice. "All I know about it is there's a hole in the rear end where they put the gas."

"I've got a mechanical knack, I guess," she said listlessly. "And I like cars. You should get it tuned—it's a waste of an automobile otherwise."

"Thank you for those words of wisdom," I said. "In return I will go get you a drink."

I'd taken three steps toward the living room when it happened. The glass door flew outwards violently and two figures burst out onto the flagstones, locked in a savage embrace.

It took me a couple of seconds to realize that Kay and Paula weren't embracing—they were fighting. They swayed and struggled their way past me toward the pool. Paula had one hand locked in Kay's hair, while Kay was trying desperately to pummel her opponent's face.

They reached the edge of the pool and Kay suddenly reversed her tactics. She grabbed the top of Paula's blue gown and jerked her hands sharply downward.

The gown and Paula abruptly parted company, leaving her naked to the waist. The sudden exposure of her white pointed breasts left her looking curiously defenseless. They were still quivering with the sudden movement. It didn't worry her opponent.

Kay caught hold of Paula's left arm and turned away, bending double from the waist, forcing the arm down across her shoulders. Paula shrieked wildly as she catapulted up over Kay's shoulder in a wild arc. A moment later she hit the pool with a resounding splash and sank out of sight.

"That's something you don't see very often," I said.

But Janice wasn't listening. With a thin wail of horror she was running toward the side of the pool, ready to fish her employer out when she surfaced.

I walked over and took Kay's arm and led her away gently from the side of the pool. Her gown had been ripped away right down one side, and her hair hung over her eyes.

"You need a drink," I said.

"That bitch!" she said passionately. "I'll teach her to——"

THE BLONDE

She relaxed suddenly and leaned against me. "You're right, Al, I do need a drink, but not in there. Take me around the back of the house."

I walked her around the back of the house and she opened a side door that wasn't locked. I followed her into what was obviously her own room. She sank down onto the bed, her shoulders still heaving.

"Light me a cigarette," she said softly.

I lit two and gave her one. She dragged smoke down into her lungs, then exhaled slowly. "Thanks," she murmured. "There's some Scotch in that cabinet over there. Don't worry about the ice."

I found the Scotch and the glasses, and poured two drinks. I handed her one and she drained it instantly then gave the glass back to me.

"Give me another," she said. "Christ, I need it."

I fixed her another drink and handed it to her. She pushed her hair out of her eyes and looked at me. "You know I feel good," she said. "That bitch had it coming to her. Shit, she's got everybody in the whole business so damned scared of her muckraking program, they fall over her. Well, I showed her."

"You certainly did," I agreed, and handed her the second drink.

She drank it a little more slowly, then tossed the empty glass onto the floor. It hit the thick rug and didn't bounce. She stood up slowly.

"I feel better," she said, "a whole lot better. In fact, I feel wonderful!"

"That's fine," I said and checked my watch. It was a little after nine-thirty. "I have to be going. I've still got some work to do."

"You don't have to go yet," she said. "Stay for a while."

"I really must go," I said.

"Nothing I can do to stop you?" she asked.

"Nothing, honey," I said. "It's been a wonderful party, never a dull moment."

She got onto her feet slowly and looked down at herself. "This gown cost me three hundred," she said. "First time I've worn it."

She undid the zipper and let the tattered remnants of the gown fall to the floor. All she had on beneath it was a pair of flimsy black briefs, so small and so tight that the bulge between her firm thighs was clearly outlined even to the slit to which the thin material adhered. Her proud breasts rose and fell with her breathing, the nipples still rising tautly from the puckered pink areolas.

I took a step toward her and she laughed huskily. "I thought you were in a hurry to get someplace, Al."

"I was," I said. "I still am. I just changed direction, that's all."

"Good old Al." Her eyes dropped briefly to my groin, where there were obvious signs of the effect her body was having on me. "I can tell." She peeled off her briefs and kicked them across the room. The racket from the living room beat faintly around my ears.

"What about your party?" I asked, and my voice was just as husky as hers. Between my legs, my engorged yard was throbbing violently.

"They'll never know I'm missing," she said. "Anyway, isn't *this* going to be a party?"

She stepped closer to me and suddenly swung her right fist so that it connected painfully with my solar plexus. She was panting slightly.

"Hit me!" she cried in a muffled voice. She backed away until she stopped against the wall where she stood, her shoulders against it, the lower part of her body thrust forward, her legs parted, and her sex pink and distended with the small protruding outline of her clitoris showing between the labia.

That fist in my stomach hurt. I was still hard, my raging desire beginning to play havoc with my senses. There was a misty out-of-focus look in her eyes as she watched me fumble with my trousers, unfastening them and letting them fall so that my prick reared upward at an angle from the base of my pelvis. I moved across to her, and raising one hand, brought it down hard against the side of her face with a resounding, echoing slap. She looked up at me and smiled. A dull red flush was spreading across her cheek.

"That's better, Al," she murmured dreamily. "That's what I like." Then reaching forward, she took hold of my straining weapon, and parting her legs even more, rubbed the bulbous tip of it against the lubricated lips of her vulva.

Tautening my buttocks, I lunged forward, strongly, and my prick slid easily through her guiding fingers upward into her moist, receptive passage, right to the hilt. She strained hard

THE BLONDE

against me as I slammed her against the wall with each powerful stroke. She clung to me tightly, her tensed thighs gripped me, and her fingernails dug into my back. Her moans rose in intensity, and her breasts flattened against my chest. I drove against her relentlessly, not relaxing the onslaught until with one last vigorous stroke between the clamping muscles of her vagina, we attained a mutual, shattering climax that held us transfixed against the wall for a long, shuddering, ebbing moment that stretched into a small velvet-cased eternity. And even then, as we drifted slowly back to earth, she wouldn't let me go.

Chapter Six

The offices of Fargo Enterprises were located on the twelfth floor of a midtown office block. Fargo lived in the penthouse above.

It was just after eleven-thirty when I rode the elevator to the penthouse. Maybe it was late to go calling, but not too late for calling on a racketeer, even if he was retired. I pressed the button and got chimes. I lit a cigarette and waited for the door to open. I nearly swallowed the cigarette when it did open.

A girl with silver-blonde hair stood there, looking at me with nothing more than idle curiosity. Her dark eyebrows were arched in perpetual surprise, and her mouth was open. All she was wearing was a thin yellow sweater, which barely brushed the tops of her sleek rounded thighs, and nothing else.

Her nipples made small but distinct impressions against the material of her sweater.

"It's hot," she said in some sort of explanation.

"Yeah, sure," I said.

"So what are you selling?" she asked suspiciously.

"I'd like to see Mr. Fargo," I said.

"He doesn't see anybody outside of office hours," she said. "Even then he doesn't see anybody, mostly."

I showed her my shield. "Lieutenant Wheeler is the name."

"A cop?" Her eyebrows got more surprised. "They get wackier every day."

She turned her head and called out, "Hey, Kent! There's a cop out here wants to see you. A lieutenant no less." She turned to face me again, shrugging her shoulders gently. "I've got to find out—maybe he won't talk to anybody except captains, you understand?"

"Bring him in!" a voice bellowed from somewhere inside. "You'll catch cold standing out there!"

She smiled at me encouragingly. "Kent says it's O.K. for you to come on in. Don't let him scare you, he always bawls people out when his ulcer's kicking him around."

"He has an ulcer?"

"Why sure—he's an executive!"

I followed the insouciant swing of the girl's rounded behind into the entrance hall. As she walked, the sweater rode up slightly over the smooth cheeks of her buttocks and the powder-blue briefs that clung precariously to their lower extremities, and were caught in the reverse cleavage. From the entrance hall we moved into the living room.

There was a row of brightly lit fish tanks along one wall and even brighter tropical fish swimming around inside them. Fargo stood looking out of the massive plate-glass window at the panoramic view of the city.

He turned around and looked at me. "What do you want?" he asked wearily.

"Some questions," I said.

"O.K.," he said. "But make it quick, will you." He looked at the girl. "So screw, sweetheart. You're only a distraction around here."

She shrugged, and the sweater lifted a fraction over the blue V of her briefs. "Anything you say," she said, then turning, moved out of the room, her cute behind swinging in the charming carefree manner I had admired so much out in the hall.

"You like a drink?" Fargo asked me.

"Very much," I said. "Scotch, a little soda."

"Sure." He went over to the bar and switched on the panel lights on either side of it. I turned my head away as the dazzling brilliance of chromed metal hit me.

I watched him as he poured the drinks. He was short, with wide shoulders and long arms. He had crisp, black hair, crew-cut and flecked with gray at the temples. He had a thin nose and a tight mouth. His eyes, I saw as he walked back with the drinks, were a bright, pale blue.

"Thanks," I said as I took the drink.

He waved his hand toward a chair and sank into another beside it. I sat down and drank some of the Scotch; it was a very good Scotch.

"Questions," he said, "what about?"

"Georgia Brown."

"What about Georgia Brown?"

"She got herself murdered this morning." I told him the story briefly.

"Why tell me? I read about it in the evening papers."

I mentioned Manning's suicide, Georgia's appearance on Paula Reid's show, the threatening letters. He wasn't impressed.

"None of my business," he said and yawned loudly.

"The way I hear it, it is," I said carefully. "She was going to name names on that show, and your name was one of them."

"You're crazy," he said, "or somebody is. Why me?"

"That's what I thought you might tell me."

"It's always the same," he said. "Look, Lieutenant, I'm clean. I retired out of the rackets a few years back, I run a legitimate business now. You know that, every cop in town knows that. But soon as anything happens, somebody's got to toss my name around!"

"But you were mixed up with Manning at the time he killed himself," I said.

"Me?"

"You were backing his pictures through Hilary Blair."

He sat up straight in his chair. "Who told you that?" he asked softly.

"I heard it," I said.

"I'd like to know where," he said. "You want another drink, Lieutenant?"

"I'd prefer some answers. You've asked all the questions so far and that isn't the routine I had prepared."

I heard the outside door open and close. A moment later the living-room door opened and a character walked in.

"Kent!" he said. "I talked to Joe and he said Steve's been out of town for . . . sorry, I didn't know you got company."

"This is Lieutenant Wheeler," Fargo said coldly. "This is Charlie Dunn, he works for me."

Dunn was a tall, thin young man with an expressionless face. "Good evening, Lieutenant," he said.

"Sure," I said.

"I go and come back, or I wait around?" Charlie asked.

THE BLONDE

"You wait around," Fargo said. "Toni's watching television—go and watch with her, but not too close!"

"My income bracket keeps me at a distance," Charlie said, and went looking for the girl who I thought was just the company I would pick to watch television with.

Fargo relaxed in his chair. "All right, so I was backing his pictures—that's legitimate."

"Sure," I said. "It's only Georgia Brown's murder that's illegitimate, so far."

"You want me to give you an alibi?"

"You've six guys who'll swear you never made a bomb in your whole life?" I asked him gently.

He glared at me for a moment then he grinned sourly:

"O.K., so you don't want an alibi, what do you want?"

"Georgia was going to tell the truth about Manning's death," I said. "She——"

"What do you mean—the truth about Manning's death!" he said coldly. "He committed suicide, didn't he!"

"The circumstances that made him kill himself," I corrected myself. "The young kid with the weak heart—I've heard the story. You were around at the time, so maybe you could tell me who'd have a good reason for not wanting Georgia to speak her piece?"

He thought about it for a little while. "I guess there were quite a few people around at the time who wouldn't want it talked about," he said, "but murder!" He shook his head. "I don't see any of them going that far!"

"Nobody does," I said sadly, "that's the trouble. You don't, Coates doesn't, Kay Steinway doesn't, Blain doesn't. I wouldn't believe it myself—if Georgia Brown wasn't dead."

I was watching him as I tossed the names into mid-air. If he caught them, he gave no sign they meant anything in particular to him.

"Sorry I can't help you, Lieutenant," he said. "Was there anything else?"

I finished the drink and got onto my feet. "I don't think so. Thanks for your time, Mr. Fargo."

"Any time," he said expansively.

He walked with me to the front door.

"Georgia was a good-looking kid the last time I saw her," he said reflectively. "That would be about three years ago.

She was a blonde with the best figure I'd ever . . . I guess I'm morbid, Lieutenant, but how did she look?"

"Your guess is as good as mine," I said. "What they scraped off the wall wasn't photogenic."

He put a cigarette into his mouth and lit it. The fingers that held the match trembled slightly.

"You bastard!" he said softly.

That finished the interview on a conclusive note. I let myself out and went back to the car. I drove away from the curb at a leisurely pace and reflected that I did see life even if I wasn't going to live to an old age.

The lights were still burning in the Sheriff's office when I parked outside. I walked in past Annabelle Jackson's empty desk and regretted the Southern indolence that kept her from working twenty-four hours a day the way her boss did.

Lavers looked up from his desk and grunted as I came in.

"I bring you greetings," I said politely and sank into a chair.

"The only thing you ever bring me is grief," he said. "What did you find out, if anything?"

I gave him a condensed rundown on who I'd seen, what had happened. It didn't really sound like much—even to me—but then, of course, I hadn't told him the most exciting part.

"Fargo?" he said. "That's interesting. I'd like to tie something on his tail."

"It would be a crime to let that girl of his go to waste," I said, spreading my hands in mock horror. "She needs a home, a future, something to live for. Could she go back to the sleaze, to being a short-time hooker with a heart of gold? Live porno shows. Is that fair?"

"Shut up, Wheeler. I'm beginning to yawn."

"You've got a heart of stone."

He lit his pipe. "The news is still running hot over the wire services. This murder is going to be front-page news throughout the country in the morning."

"Yes, sir," I said.

"We need to crack it fast," he said. "I spoke to Inspector Martin. I told him I felt it was better if you had a free hand and he said you always do anyway! Captain Parker is handling it from their end. He gets anything, he passes it on to us. We get anything——" He stopped and looked at me for a

THE BLONDE 47

moment. "Ah! what's the use of me talking! What are you going to do?"

"I thought I might take a run down to Laguna Beach first thing in the morning," I said.

"Laguna Beach!" His face reddened. "You think this is a good time to take a vacation?"

"Any time is a good time to take a vacation—but that's where Manning killed himself."

"Three years ago!" Lavers thundered. "You think you're going to turn up anything now that the police didn't when it happened?"

"I'd just like to get the feel of it," I said. "And that reminds me about the story about the star and the new French wife who couldn't speak any English. She——"

"Get out of here!" he said resignedly. "I don't need you—I've got an ulcer already!"

"Yes, sir," I said.

I went back to the car and drove myself home. It was close to one-thirty when I got inside the apartment. I poured myself a drink and put something thoughtful on the stereo. I thought Carole Bayer Sager was a fair enough choice.

I was just settling down when the phone rang. I grabbed it and held it at arm's length until the first track had finished. Then I put it to my ear and said: "This is the morgue here. What was your husband's name again?"

There was a short silence then a voice said dubiously: "Is that Lieutenant Wheeler?"

"It certainly is," I said brightly, because a feminine voice always has that effect on me.

"This is Janice Jorgens," she said. "I got your home number from the Homicide Bureau. I hope you don't mind me calling you?"

"I'm hoping it will be a pleasure," I said. "Are you lonely, bored with life? Has Romance passed you by? Just dial Wheeler for the whirl of a lifetime and——"

"Lieutenant, please!" she said coldly. "It's late and I'm tired, Paula is a nervous wreck after that shocking——"

"So if this is strictly business," I said equally coldly, "you have exactly ten seconds left to explain why the hell you called me in the middle of the night!"

"I'm sorry," she said. "I'm upset, I guess. I just wondered what progress you were making. I thought if you had anything definite on the murderer, the news might cheer Paula up a little."

"Nothing yet," I said, "but tomorrow is another day."

"You stun me, Lieutenant."

"I'm going down to Laguna Beach in the morning," I said. "Something big might break down there."

"Your leg?"

"I might just find the one piece of evidence I want," I lied with the ease of long habit. "The one thing I need to clinch the whole deal."

"It sounds exciting," her voice had thawed a little.

"Say!" I made it sound like a brand-new idea. "If you're not doing anything vital tomorrow morning, why don't you come with me for the ride?"

"No thank you," she said firmly. "I have a fair idea of what a ride with you would involve, Lieutenant."

"But it wouldn't . . . well, maybe it would, but——"

"Good night, Lieutenant," she said and hung up.

I put down the phone and picked up my drink. Carole Bayer Sager was still giving out with the thoughtful domestic messages, and I raised my glass in a silent toast. "You got it, baby," I muttered. "You sure got the answers. I only wish I knew what they were myself."

Chapter Seven

I was lucky when I reached the Laguna Beach police headquarters. The guy who'd handled the Manning case three years ago was on duty. His name was Lieutenant Monro, and he was short and gray-headed, with a face that had been chiseled out of rock.

"Sure, Lieutenant," he said, after I'd explained more or less why I was there. "Be happy to help you. But I don't know that I can."

"How exactly did he kill himself?" I asked.

"Threw himself over a cliff-edge," Monro said. "About a two-hundred foot sheer drop down onto the rocks—it was messy."

He thought about it for a moment. "What exactly is it you're looking for?"

"I don't know," I admitted. "The Georgia Brown killing ties in with the suicide somewhere."

"I'll take you out there if it'll help," he said.

"I'd like that," I said, "thanks."

We drove out there in my car. We left the car on the road, and walked across the brown grass to the cliff-edge. I looked down cautiously. It was exactly as Monro had said, a sheer drop for a long, long way. I watched the waves breaking over the jagged rocks below for a few moments, then turned away.

"He couldn't have picked a better spot."

"He sure couldn't," Monro agreed.

We got back into the car and drove about a quarter of a mile down the road. There was a split-level with the paint peeling and a general air of decay about it. Behind the house, the ground sloped gently down to the beach.

"That's where he lived," Monro explained. "You want to take a look?"

"I guess not," I said. "He left the house, he walked up to the top of the cliff and jumped over?"

"Yeah," Monro nodded. "They didn't miss him for a couple of hours—there was a party going on inside the house at the time."

"They?"

"Some of his friends were there. Maybe it wasn't exactly a party, but they'd been drinking pretty heavily. One of them saw Manning go out the back about midnight, but they thought he was just going for some air. It was around two o'clock before they started worrying about him not coming back."

"Sounds like it was a party."

"I guess it was. Manning had a reputation for throwing good parties," Monro said dryly.

"You remember who was there?"

"Only a few people," he said. "It wasn't very long after the girl——" he stopped abruptly.

"I know that story, too," I said. "The young kid who had a bad heart—maybe."

He looked at me for a long moment, making up his mind: "You're well-informed, Lieutenant."

"I guess I am at that, Lieutenant," I said. "Who was there at the party?"

He thought for a few moments. "It was a long time ago now. I remember that producer—the one who always gave me the creeps—he was there."

"Coates?"

"That's him, Coates. And the financial brain, Hilary Blain."

"How about Kent Fargo?"

"Sure, I remember now, he was there. And the female you're worrying about—Georgia Brown."

"How about Kay Steinway?"

"You mean that overblown singer who can't sing?"

"Fullblown," I corrected him. "Was she there?"

"No," he said firmly. "Only the five of them, including Manning."

"Nobody else?"

"I'm sure, Lieutenant!" he said curtly.

I took a last look at the house and then started the car rolling again.

THE BLONDE

Monro lit a cigarette and relaxed a little in his seat. "Anything else, Lieutenant?"

"The girl," I said. "Tell me about her."

"It could be a sore point," he said cautiously. "Me, I'm just a cop—you know how it is."

"Sure," I said. "I know the whole thing was kept quiet after Manning jumped over the cliff. I'm not asking just for the sake of asking, Lieutenant."

"There's a bar on the next block," he said. "Why don't we stop off there?"

"I wondered what was worrying me," I said. "It's my thirst."

We stopped at the bar and sat in a booth. Monro drank rye and I drank Scotch.

"Her name was Geraldine Morgan," he said slowly. "She came from Louisville, in Kentucky. She looked a lot older than she was; we found out after it happened that she'd run away from home. A kid with a yen for the bright lights—she had ambitions. She wasn't original."

He drank some of his rye. "I got a daughter," he said. "She's going to be a nurse. She was the same age as the Morgan kid when it happened. It can scare you, thinking about what can happen to a kid when she's on the loose. There are so many traps, and in most cases there's no way they can win. They got only one thing they can sell, and that's their body. Christ, sometimes I feel like throwing up just thinking about it."

"I can imagine," I said.

"Her mother was dead," he went on, "her old man worked a night shift. There was an elder sister—around twenty, but she wasn't home often. The kid would come home from school most nights to an empty house. There wasn't much money around, the old man hit the booze, too. She got tired of it, so she quit."

He finished his drink. "So she comes to sunny California and she's going to work in pictures, but meantime she's broke. So she gets herself a job as a waitress, and that's where Manning found her."

Monro laughed mirthlessly. "It's a story so old nobody even wants to hear it. The big-time star, the young hopeful. In no time at all, Manning got her out at his Laguna Beach house every weekend. She quit her job as a waitress on his say-so and then she's his housekeeper. She even wrote home to the sister, telling her all about it—or most of it.

"She really believed that Manning was going to give her a break, going to arrange a screen test for her, and if it was O.K. she'd have a part in his next film. She said if her family tried to do anything she'd kill herself. This was her big chance and she was going to take it."

"So they didn't do anything?"

He looked at me somberly. "They didn't have a chance. Four days later she was dead. I was on duty when the call came in. I went out there and found Manning in a robe and still stinking drunk. The kid was stretched out on the bed—he hadn't even thought to throw a cover over her. He didn't care about the kid—he just didn't want any publicity!"

"They tell me it was her heart," I said.

"Yeah," he nodded. "The doc said it was heart failure all right. But she had bruises all over her. Maybe the way Manning played it put an extra strain on her heart and it just quit. I asked the doc about it, when there wasn't anybody around to listen to his answer. 'You know why everybody dies,' he said, 'because their heart stops beating. That's why she died.' You know what I would have called it?"

"I guess so," I said. "Murder?"

"But me," he said, "I'm only a cop, not a politician. When it comes to an indictment, they don't ask me. Anyway, how can you indict a dead man?"

"You didn't like Manning," I said.

"I hated his guts," Monro said quietly. "And I didn't even know him until that night. You figure how the people who did know him must have hated his guts!"

"Was Georgia Brown his panderer?" I asked. "The way I hear it, she used to line up the girls for him—young and innocent, the way Geraldine Morgan was. Then she'd sit on the side and watch."

"I wouldn't know anything about that," he said. "All I know is what I saw that night."

"Lieutenant," I said, "you ever think what you might do if you had so much money it didn't matter any more—and people around you who'd pander to your each and every whim?"

"You figure he was maybe no worse than anybody else would be in his position," he said coldly. "But you didn't see the kid's body the way I did. A kid just hitting puberty. It could have been my own kid lying there."

"Yeah," I said, "I see what you mean. But I'm still glad it was me that pressed the buzzer."

"Buzzer?"

"The one that blew Georgia Brown into little pieces," I said. "Shall we go, Lieutenant?"

It was afternoon when I got back to Pine City. I stopped outside the Bureau and found my way into Captain Parker's office.

"The big Wheeler himself!" Parker said jovially as I walked in. "I bet you got the whole case wrapped up, Al. Give me a break and tell me whodunit."

"I'll tell you how it's been," I said. "Yesterday I got some place, today I'm about back where I started. If somebody exploded that bomb again, we could start even."

"You disappoint me," he grinned. "You, the unorthodox cop, and the County Sheriff's white-haired boy. I can't wait to tell Lieutenant Hammond about this, he'll enjoy it."

"Break it down into words of one syllable before you tell it," I suggested, "otherwise he won't understand."

I sat on the edge of his desk and lit a cigarette. "What have you got?"

"Nothing much," he said. "That bomb fixed things all right. MacDonald says the bomb was a simple mechanism that anybody could make—a sort of homemade contraption. There's a report on it," he flicked a typewritten sheet on his desk.

"A blow-it-up yourself project?" I said. "Well, that helps a lot."

"I double-checked on Polnik's round of the other tenants and the janitor," Parker went on. "Nothing new, they all had the same story. Lavers tells me you've been chasing the Manning suicide angle down in Laguna Beach. Come up with anything exciting?"

"No," I said.

I gave him the broad outline of what Monro had told me, and added the gist of the interviews I'd had with the four people Georgia Brown had named.

"A nice guy, this Manning!" he said.

"It's a wonder he lived so long," I agreed. "But like Blain says, Georgia was even nicer."

"Yeah." Parker lost his grin. "This is starting to get under my skin, Al. We start off with a whole lot of facts and end up with nothing."

"You've got it," I agreed. "Well, I quit for the night—see you in Traffic."

"I wouldn't mind being called Sergeant again," Parker said earnestly. "It's just that you lose so much money, too!"

I shuddered. "I wouldn't like to be called Sergeant again, not with Hammond still a lieutenant."

I left the Bureau and drove back to the apartment. It was just on six when I got there. I felt I should do something energetic, something positive, live aggressively, but I didn't know where to start. If I had a next move, nobody had told me about it.

I put a Dore Previn cassette into the player, but it didn't give me the mental inspiration I needed right then. The words just seemed to wash right over me. Then the phone rang.

For sure it was Lavers and I was in no mood for Lavers. I picked up the phone and said: "We're sorry about that, sir, we can't understand just how he came to sit up. He was lying down all right when we put him into the hearse——"

"I want to speak to Lieutenant Wheeler!" a high-pitched voice said. "Tell him I must speak to him at once. It's . . . terribly urgent!"

I closed my eyes and could see the wave in the blue-rinsed hair being patted carefully into place.

"This is Wheeler speaking," I said. "That's Mr. Coates?"

"Yes!" he said. "I'm so glad I found you. You told me to call you if anything happened."

"What's on your mind?"

"I need protection," he said breathlessly. "I must have protection, I demand it!" His voice held a rising inflection of fear. "My life has been threatened! They're coming here! You must come straightaway, Lieutenant Wheeler! At once! You understand."

"Take it easy," I said. "What's it all about? Who's been threatening your life—who's coming there?"

"I can't tell you over the telephone," his voice dropped to a low whisper. "But you must come at once! I want police protection, you hear!"

"I'd need to be three blocks away before I didn't," I said. "Eardrums aren't replaceable."

There was a click in my ear as he hung up.

"You ham!" I said into the dead mouthpiece, then dropped the phone back onto the cradle.

I poured myself a drink and thought about it. I had nothing better to do, I might as well go over there and see what it was about. Maybe he was drunk or . . . a million maybe's. . . . There was one easy way to find out. I finished the drink and went out of the apartment and down to the car.

It took me five minutes to find a parking space and then it was a block away from his hotel. I walked toward it, thinking the least Coates could do when I got there was to buy me a drink.

I walked through the foyer and rode an elevator up to his floor. I went down the corridor to his room and knocked on the door. Nothing happened. I knocked again and waited and still nothing happened.

I began to feel glad there was no buzzer so I wasn't tempted to push the button. One bomb in one lifetime is enough. Then I had a flash of brilliance and tried the handle—the door opened quite easily.

I stepped inside the room and fumbled for the light switch. My fingers found it and flicked it down. The room suddenly came to life. There was only one exception.

That was Norman Coates.

He lay sprawled across the bed, his eyes wide open but not seeing the overhead light. I walked slowly across to the bed and looked at him. He had been shot twice through the chest and the Paisley silk would never look the same again.

I walked across to the phone and got all orthodox as I lifted the receiver with a handkerchief. I dialed Homicide and asked if Parker had left. He hadn't. I wondered idly for a moment, while they connected me, what it would be like to have a conscience.

"Parker," he said heartily in my ear.

"Al Wheeler," I said. "I'm in Coates's hotel room. He's been shot." I gave the room number, the name of the hotel.

"When did it happen?"

I checked my watch. "It couldn't have happened more than half an hour ago. He rang me about six-fifteen."

"What did he want?'"

"Police protection, *they* were threatening him, *they* were going to kill him—that's why I came over here."

The only sound was a faint humming noise in my ear.

"You still there?" I said.

"I was just wondering, Al, why didn't you give me a call right away. We could have had a couple of the boys down there in ten minutes."

"He sounded as if he was drunk," I said. "I didn't take him seriously."

"That's too bad, Al," he said heavily.

"I guess it is," I said coldly. "Send somebody out to take care of things, will you?"

"Right away. You'll wait there and take over?"

"I won't be here," I said.

"But——"

"Somebody murdered Georgia Brown to stop her talking," I said quickly. "I guess they murdered Coates for the same reason. They could have a couple more murders on their mind. If I'm right and I move fast I might be able to stop one of them, anyway."

"Al!" he roared. "What in hell are you talking about? What do you think we got a Homicide detail for! You think you're a one-man——" I hung up on him while he was still talking.

I took a last quick look around the room. The drawers had been emptied, their contents still sprawled across the floor. The wardrobe was wide open; the two suits hanging there had been slashed almost to ribbons. The three suitcases were empty and torn apart. I wondered if the murderer had found what he was looking for.

I took one last glance at Coates. He looked back at me unseeingly. The blue-rinse wave was now permanently out of place.

Chapter Eight

I didn't bother with the front entrance this time. I went straight to the door of the courtyard and listened for a moment. There was a splashing noise coming from inside. I tried the door; it was still unlocked.

I walked into the courtyard, closing the door behind me and locking it. Then I headed toward the pool.

I was about three seconds too late. She was out of the pool, knotting the robe tightly around her waist. Even so, the flanges of her magnificent boobs pushed outward from the deep opening of the robe. She looked pleased to see me.

"I thought you might be back, Al," she said. "I keep thinking back to the other night and it still gives me tingles."

"How have you been?" I asked. "Lonely, I hope."

"Just swimming," she said. "Come in and I'll pour you a drink."

We went through the open glass doors and down to the bar. The robe brushed lightly off the rounded orbs of her buttocks, and remembering the other night and the quick but highly satisfying encounter against the wall, I was beginning to have tingles myself.

"Scotch, as I remember, Al," she said.

"With a little soda." I watched the way her breasts moved in the opening of her robe which also fell away from her thighs as she bent slightly forward to fix the drinks. I was beginning to experience another brief, agitated flurry in the region of my groin.

She walked around the corner of the bar and stood in front of me, her lower lip drooping a fraction, her eyes soft and misty. The tip of her tongue flicked lightly over her lower lip. "I'm beginning to think you're losing interest in me." She sounded a little disappointed. "I mean, I would have thought after that night you would have been so aroused you would have grabbed me, bent me over that chair there, and slaked your pent-up lust."

"That I can manage," I said huskily.

Her eyes dropped briefly to my groin. "I know you could," she purred. "I have the utmost faith in you."

Her fingers loosened the belt and the robe fell open to reveal her naked body in all its vibrant glory. The hair of her pubis sworled thickly over her slit. Then, suddenly, the phone rang.

"Damn!" she said and walked over to the phone. I leaned against the bar and picked up my drink.

"Yes?" she said in a low voice. "Yes, this is *the* Kay Steinway. Who? . . . Oh, how are you? You what? . . . I didn't call you. . . . But . . . I swear I didn't! I wouldn't do a crazy thing like that. . . . I don't know anything about . . . You've got to listen to . . . Hello?" She joggled the cradle for a few seconds, then gave up

She walked back toward me slowly, a worried look on her face. "He hung up," she said dully.

"Who was it?"

"A wrong number, I guess," she said. "I need a drink!"

She picked up her drink. "Where were we?"

"You were talking about the faith you have in me."

She pouted. "And you still have your clothes on."

"Soon remedy that," I said, my fumbling fingers beginning to unbutton my shirt.

"Afterward we can have a swim," she suggested.

I had my clothes off in no time flat, throwing them everywhere on the floor around me, and we stood facing each other, full of quivering expectation. My prick was ramrod hard and twitching just a little as she walked slowly toward me, with a soft grind of her pelvis, and took hold of it between her cool fingers. She squeezed it gently, then without a word, she dropped to her knees on the thick carpet in front of me and with her lips and tongue began to caress my throbbing, straining organ. Her lips closed around it, and her tongue as it gently laved the glans was deliciously cool. With my hands on her shoulders, I tensed and eased myself forward, pushing myself deeper into her mouth. The sensation stirred thickly beneath the sacs she was gently manipulating with her clever fingers. With my organ in her mouth she angled her head slightly and smiled up at me with her eyes. Her fingers traced a tingling line back from my balls and insinuated upward between my tensed buttocks.

Then we were both lying on the floor and she was straddling me with her knees pressing down on the carpet to either side of my upturned face so that I was staring up at her gaping pink vulva, watching it as in a long swooping movement she brushed it across my face and I could taste the faint sourness of it. Then she was pressing it down on me, enveloping me with its exciting moistness while her own head was busy between my legs, her lips moving expertly around my smooth, thick column.

She was orchestrating the whole affair, and I didn't mind in the least. All I needed to do was hold myself back so that I didn't come too soon and spoil it all for her—and it was quite some effort to achieve this, as she sure knew what she was doing, particularly when she brought herself round to face me, and still straddling me, lowered herself down onto my yard, which she held upright between her fingers, locking me into the snug smoothness of her gently palpitating sheath.

At first she moved slowly, riding me in a long, circular motion, her muscles clamping the length of my staff as she brought herself up to the very tip, so that it was almost in danger of breaking loose, then lowering herself on it until it had disappeared inside her to the hilt. Then, as she brought herself toward an all-consuming climax, her movements accelerated, and I was finding it more difficult to hold myself back. Her head was arched backward, and she was making deep warbling sounds in her throat.

Her movements quickened even more. Her thighs clamped me and I thrust up hard against her from the floor, relaxing my control as she drew closer to her climax. And then we came, simultaneously, and as the milky fluid spurted strongly up into her, her body went rigid, she shivered and gave a long, strangled cry, then seemed to melt on top of me.

A short time later, after we had dressed and we were having another drink, I thought of something I had meant to ask her before the immediacy of our physical needs took over.

"Who was that on the phone? The wrong number that wasn't?"

"A creep. It's an unlisted number but I still get them. One

of the hazards of displaying my charms on wide screen. They think there's enough to go round for everybody."

"Norman Coates was murdered tonight," I said. "Not more than an hour ago."

Her glass tilted sideways suddenly and good Scotch formed a pool on the bartop.

"You're kidding!" she whispered.

"No," I said flatly. "I think he had a phone call before it happened. He rang me afterwards for protection but I got there too late. *They* were coming, he said, *they* were going to kill him."

Her hand brushed her throat. "I don't believe it. It's some kind of trick." She looked at something over my shoulder and her pupils widened into the same look I'd seen in Coates's eyes as he stared up at the ceiling of his hotel room.

"He's right sweetheart," a harsh voice said. "And you set up the whole deal with that lousy call."

The .38 in its holster, strapped around my waist under my coat, felt heavy—and useless. I turned around slowly, keeping my hands on top of the bar counter.

Kent Fargo stood there, a gun in his hand, and beside him was the thin young man, Charlie Dunn, who also had a gun in his hand.

"I phoned from just around the corner," Fargo said. "I figured you wouldn't expect me to call right away." He looked at me for a moment. "I see you got company."

"Kent," Kay said nervously, "I never called you. I don't know what you're talking about."

"Don't give me that," he said impatiently. "You picked me for the fall guy and I don't like it. You got maybe one chance. Where is it?"

"I tell you," she said, "I don't know!"

Fargo hunched his shoulders: "O.K., you want to play it the hard way, it's all right with me. You ever seen Charlie's fingers up close?"

Dunn extended the fingers of his left hand in front of him. His eyes glittered with excitement. The fingers were long and thin, almost delicate.

"Charlie's an artist," Fargo said. "Just the guy to knock a tune out of a Steinway! But sing the right notes, my sweet. You get off-key and they'll be playing your theme song on an organ!"

THE BLONDE

Dunn slipped his gun back to his pocket and walked leisurely toward Kay Steinway. She backed away until she came up against the wall behind the bar and couldn't go any farther.

"This is a free performance, Wheeler," Kent said, "but remember you're only the audience. Try to get into the act and I'll put you into the morgue instead."

"I should be a hero," I said, "with two months' insurance premiums not paid yet?"

"That's right," Fargo grinned, "be sensible and you got a chance of staying alive."

"You don't mind if I pour myself another drink? Screams make me feel nervous."

"Why not?" he said expansively.

Dunn reached the edge of the bar and looked at Kay. He licked his lips absently. "I'm remembering how you are now, honey," he said gently, "you won't look the same again."

Kay moaned softly, her eyes shining, polished by fear. "Why won't you believe me?" she whispered. "I'm telling you the truth."

"That's what Coates said," Fargo sneered contemptuously. "Look what happened to him—and he was telling the truth! You're luckier than Coates, you still got a chance."

Dunn moved around the other side of the bar and closed in on Kay. His back was toward me as I reached out for the Scotch bottle.

His fingers twisted into the lapels of her robe, ripping it open all the way down the front. He looked at her wonderingly for a moment: "And Kent pays me for this!" he said. Then his fingers started to work and Kay screamed in sharp agony.

My fist closed around the neck of the bottle and I threw it in Fargo's direction, jerking myself backwards off the bar stool at the same time.

I rolled a couple of times as soon as I hit the floor, dragging the .38 out of its holster, hearing the blast of Fargo's gun at the same time.

A sliver of wood sliced my cheek as the slug plowed into the floor a foot away from my head. I came up onto my knees, rammed the heel of my right hand into my solar plexus to steady the gun, and fired.

Fargo dropped his gun and reeled backwards, his left hand

clutching his shoulder. I heard another scream from Kay Steinway and jerked my head around toward her.

Dunn had slammed her back against the wall and was facing me, his gun in his hand. We fired simultaneously. Something slammed the top of my head, switching out all the lights. This time the dive to the floor was painless.

I opened my eyes and looked into the limp gray eyes that showed no trace of green.

"For a moment I thought you were dead," she said tremulously.

"So did I," I muttered. I managed to sit up, feeling the top of my head gingerly; my fingers came away sticky.

"I think the bullet just scraped the top of your head," Kay said. "I've been bathing it, it's not bleeding much now but the doctor should be here any minute."

"Should I see the other guy?" I asked her.

"Him!" she shuddered. "He's dead, I think. You shot him right between the eyes, Al! Did you mean to?"

"I wasn't really particular," I said. "I always figure you hit anything with a .38, you're lucky. What about Fargo?"

"He ran out," she said. "You hit him with that first shot and he started running then." Her lower lip curled slightly. "I didn't know he was yellow like that underneath."

"That's something nobody could accuse you of being, anyway," I said.

I got onto my feet. The room tilted for a moment, then decided to behave itself and steadied down.

"I rang the police," Kay said, "they're on their way."

"How long was I out cold?"

"About five minutes, I guess."

"Did the Scotch bottle break?"

"There's another. You want a drink?"

"Amen."

She stepped over to the bar and poured me a drink. She took good care not to go around the other side. I walked around and found out why.

Charlie Dunn was there, taking up the space. He'd slipped down onto his knees and his head leaned against the inside of the bar. I tugged the collar of his jacket gently and he fell backwards and lay on the floor, giving me a faintly surprised look. Kay was right; I had shot him between the eyes.

I went back the other side of the bar and picked up the

THE BLONDE

drink Kay had poured me. I was two-thirds of the way through it when the boys arrived, headed by Sergeant Polnik. Behind him was Doc Murphy, who grabbed my ears and pulled my head down.

"Hah!" he said. "Like I thought—cast iron! The slug hit and bounced off."

"There's a corpse around the other side of the bar," I said, freeing myself of his painful grip. "Why don't you go insult him—he can't talk back."

Murphy started on his way and stopped suddenly, pointing at my glass. "Is that whisky?" He downed it in one gulp and nodded. "I thought it was."

"I'm glad you're O.K., Lieutenant," Polnik said. "The Captain is still over at the hotel with the Coates deal. He said he'd get over as soon as he could."

"Put out a general alarm for Kent Fargo," I told him. "For Coates's murder and the attempted murder of Kay Steinway."

Polnik gulped. "You sure, Lieutenant? I mean, that crease you got across your skull, maybe——"

"I'm as rational as you are," I said, "not that that's any recommendation. Do it!"

He moved across to the phone as Murphy's head appeared suddenly above the bar.

"That's the first time I've seen a mobile corpse," I told him.

"I'm not that stiff I couldn't use a drink," he leered and lunged for the open bottle.

I lit a cigarette and waited until Polnik had finished the phone call.

"I'm going over to Fargo's place," I said, "he may have gone back there. When Captain Parker arrives, tell him where I've gone. And tell him to leave a stake-out here in case Fargo decided to come back."

"Whatever you say, Lieutenant."

I walked toward the glass doors and Kay Steinway caught up with me as I reached them.

"I should say thank you, you saved my live," she said softly.

"Next time you call a cop," I said, "call anybody but me."

"Come back when you've got Fargo," she said, "then we can take up where we left off. You and I, we just seem to click. You've got something I like, and frankly, I want more of it."

Her eyes were changing from gray to green again. When she was finished with pictures she could always get a regular job as an off-beat traffic signal.

"My mother told me about girls like you," I said. "I used to lie awake nights worrying I wouldn't meet them."

Chapter Nine

I listened to the chimes and stood to one side of the door, the .38 in my hand.

The door opened, and Toni with the silver-blonde hair stood there. This time, the sweater—the one she wore with nothing else and reached the tops of her thighs—was turquoise. Otherwise, nothing had changed.

She looked at me and saw the gun. Her eyes widened a fraction. "What are you trying to do, scare me?"

"Is Fargo inside?"

"He's been out for the last three hours," she said. "Did you want to see him or something?"

"Or something," I said. "I'll wait."

She looked doubtful. "I don't know whether Kent will like that."

"I would," I said. I moved my hand casually so the gun was pointing at her defenseless midriff. "You're going to be a good girl, aren't you?"

She gulped. "It'll be a switch," she said nervelessly, "but who am I to argue with a cop when he's got a gun in his hand?"

She backed off smartly into the entrance hall and I followed her, closing the door behind me carefully. I checked through the place—the enormous living room, the dining room with the built-in color television, the automatic kitchen, the bathroom which could have inspired even Nero to fiddle his time away, the two bedrooms, and the room Fargo used as an office.

Fargo wasn't anywhere inside the penthouse.

I came back to the living room and found her at the bar.

"I told you he wasn't here," she said. "Do you want a drink or something?"

"I'll settle for a drink," I said. "And I'll wait for Kent."

"He won't like it," she said. "Would you like a martini?"

"Scotch, thanks," I said, "a touch of soda."

She poured the drinks, then looked at me over the rim of her glass. "What did he do?" she asked.

"Who—Fargo?"

"Don't kid me," she said. "You're trouble and I know it. He's done something. He was crazy-mad when he went out of here, and he took that Charlie with him!" She shivered. "That Charlie, he's not right in the head."

"He's O.K. now," I told her.

"How's that?"

"He's dead."

She choked on the gin that was only perfumed with vermouth.

"Dead?"

"He got into an argument," I said. "Fargo's on the run, he's wanted for murder. Don't be on his side, honey, there's no percentage in it."

"Damn him," she said coldly, "now what am I going to do?"

"I don't know," I said. "I think you're out of my league, honey."

"Toni is the name," she said absently.

"Toni, sure," I said vaguely. "Look, if Fargo comes back here, you'll open the door to him and I'll be right behind you with a gun. O.K.?"

"He has his own key."

"We'll put the chain on the door so he'll have to ring," I said. "I could do that right now."

I went to the front door and hooked the chain into position. I came back and watched the tropical fish. They were smarter than people—they weren't going any place either, but they didn't hurry about it.

"That Fargo!" Toni said. "He said he was retired and I thought he meant it."

"Maybe he couldn't retire," I suggested. "Maybe something, or somebody, wouldn't let him."

"He was crazy down inside," she said. "Not vicious really,

like Charlie, but crazy all the same. Imagine anybody carrying a torch that long!"

"What torch?"

"He never got over that cheap actress running out on him. Imagine! He nearly burst out crying after you'd gone last night—when you told him about it."

I turned away from the fish and looked at her. "You mean Georgia Brown?"

"Who else?" She was pouring herself another martini, not worrying about the vermouth this time.

"I didn't know he was that way about her."

"Half the time he wasn't sure himself," she said. "One time he'd be calling her all the names you could think of and another time he'd be moping around looking at her picture and everything, he wouldn't even see me! I used to tell him to make up his mind. One minute she was a lousy, double-crossing broad, and the next she was the only one he'd ever really cared for. It made me sick!"

I picked up my drink and finished it. "I'm going to take a look around his office," I said.

"Help yourself," she shrugged her shoulders.

"You'd better come with me."

"What for?"

"I could get lonely—and you just might take that chain off the hook."

"Me?" she shook her head. "For Kent Fargo? You think I'm a girl Friday or something?"

"You can hold my hand," I said.

"All right." She picked up her glass in one hand and the gin bottle in the other. I let her go first. It was the second time I had seen her rump playing peekaboo beneath the upriding sweater, and I knew I hadn't overvalued it at the first viewing.

We got into Fargo's office and I sat down behind his desk. Toni slumped into a chair facing me, and crossed her long, nicely curved legs. She was going to be a distraction, for which I was grateful.

I started with the top drawer of the desk and worked my way down to the third, without finding anything really interesting. I opened the bottom drawer as the doorbell sounded.

Toni's glass hit the thick-piled rug, the gin leaving a widening stain.

"What if he's got a gun?" she said hoarsely.

"Don't worry, honey," I consoled her, "I'll be right behind you."

"So he'll have to shoot through me to get at you!" she moaned.

"Let's go answer the door," I said. "You wouldn't want him to wait so long he lost his temper, would you?"

She got up from the chair and walked in front of me on stiff, jerky legs. We reached the front door and I stood to one side of it and motioned with the .38 for her to open it.

Toni took the chain off the hook as the chimes sounded again impatiently. Then she closed both eyes tight and opened the door.

"I want to see Lieutenant . . ." The voice that had started off crisply, tailed off into silence. "Are you real?" he croaked.

"Come on in, Polnik," I said, and put the gun away.

The Sergeant stepped inside and Toni closed the door again, hastily putting the chain back into place.

Polnik took another look at her, then he looked at me. "I'd like to put my old lady into an outfit like that," he said, "and have her walk around the block just once."

"So everybody could admire her?"

"Maybe she wouldn't come back," he said simply. "I got a message from the Captain, Lieutenant."

"O.K.," I said, "but right now, I'm busy. You stay here and keep an eye on Toni."

"This is Toni?" he pointed his thumb in her direction."

"That's Toni," I agreed.

"Don't hurry, Lieutenant," he said. "Take all night if you got to."

I went back to Fargo's desk and the fourth drawer. I took the contents out and put them on the desktop in front of me. I lit a cigarette and opened the top folder. Maybe I'd hit the jackpot; I'd found something interesting at least.

The folder contained a bundle of newspaper clips concerning Lee Manning's suicide three years back. I read through them carefully. After the first one, they were mostly repetitive. I didn't read anything new.

As I finished the cigarette and was lighting another I heard a gentle cough and looked up. Polnik stood in the doorway, apologetically.

THE BLONDE

"Sorry to bother you, Lieutenant. I just remembered the Captain said it was urgent."

"What was?"

"He said he was going back to the Sheriff's office, and for you to go there right away. He said to tell you it was Lavers' idea and he figured you'd better go along with it."

"Thanks," I said.

He hesitated: "Toni, she asks me if I want a drink."

"Do you?"

"Well," he licked his lips, "I figured I should talk to you first."

"It's all right by me," I said, "you can bring me one."

"Thanks, Lieutenant."

He came back a minute later with the drink and put it on the desk in front of me.

"You figure Fargo will come back here?" he asked.

"Not now," I said, "but we'd better stick around to make sure."

"You're right, Lieutenant," he said happily. "Toni here is a most interesting person. She has a wealth of stories to tell."

"I would never have guessed," I said gravely.

"She has met a great number of celebrities."

"I bet she has," I said dryly "You'd better get back out there. You wouldn't want to miss any of it, would you?"

"You're right, Lieutenant," he said vehemently. "You know something, Lieutenant? I like working with you. You meet so many interesting people, like Toni out there. I feel sort of lousy about you getting canned."

"Well, thanks," I said.

Then I looked up at him. "What?"

"That's what the Captain says," he stopped suddenly and looked unhappy. "There I go, shooting off my big mouth again."

"Just what did the Captain say?"

"He says if you did the right thing—you'll pardon the expression, Lieutenant—that Coates guy wouldn't have got knocked off. And then he says if you'd told him where you was going, he could have staked out the Steinway broad's place and picked up Fargo with no trouble on his way in."

"The Captain might be right," I admitted. "Why don't you go ask Toni if she ever met the Happy Hooker, or something useful like that?"

"I sure will, Lieutenant." His eyes glistened. "Maybe she did at that."

"Maybe even worked with her," I suggested.

"Lieutenant," he said, awestruck. "You open up new horizons."

When he had gone I went back to the last remaining clips, and a couple of minutes later I did strike something new. A write-up on the death of Geraldine Morgan, the kid with the maybe weak heart.

The story had been published a week before Manning's suicide. There was no reference to Manning, or the fact that she had died at his house. It was a one-column story on page five, probably written by a woman, playing the human interest angle.

She'd handled it well. The hopes and aspirations of the small-town kid who'd come to the Dream-Maker's City to make good. And Death had cheated her right at the beginning. The story quoted excerpts from the two letters she'd written home to her eldest sister, showing how wonderful Life had looked to her in Hollywood. The letters were what you'd expect from a starry-eyed kid—an organized tour of the bright spots. One mentioned she had spent the weekend at Laguna Beach but there was no reference to whom she had spent it with.

I finished reading the story and picked up the glass. My throat jerked spasmodically as I swallowed. It was my own fault, I realized—I should have named my drink. Polnik had brought me one of Toni's martinis—straight gin.

I turned over to the next clip and saw it was from the same day's paper as the story on Geraldine Morgan. It consisted simply of two smudged photographs, clipped from a page of pix of "People in the News."

The small head read: DEATH CUT SHORT HER DREAMS. The caption under the first photo told me that it was the girl herself, and for the story I should turn to page five, column five. The caption under the second photo read: "Mandy Morgan, elder sister of Geraldine."

I stared at the second photo for quite some time. The more I looked, the more familiar that face got. I folded the two clips and put them into my pocket. Then I walked out, into the living room.

Polnik sat comfortably in an armchair, a large glass of gin

THE BLONDE

in one hand, an even larger cigar in the other. There was a look of pure bliss on his face.

In front of him, Toni wavered gently, the hem of her sweater only just managing to cover her crotch. "Then, you see," she said thickly, "there was the great bust of seventy-six, and Christ, you should have seen the shit hitting the fan. Maybe you read about the Senator."

"I hate to break this up," I said almost sincerely.

Polnik looked at me, blinked a couple of times, then got onto his feet hastily. "Lieutenant?"

"I'm going," I said. "You'd better get a permanent stake-out set up here and wait till it arrives."

"Yes, sir, Lieutenant!" he said enthusiastically. "You going down to the Sheriff's office now?"

"I don't think so," I said.

"But what do I say if the Captain rings?" He sounded worried.

"Tell him . . . maybe not."

I looked at the fish tanks. I'd had a feeling something was different from the moment I came back into the living room. I realized what it was—the tropical fish weren't swimming anymore.

"What happened to the fish?" I asked.

Toni giggled loudly. "I put 'em to sleep," she said, and gestured toward the empty gin bottle standing on the bar. "They made me dizzy, whizzing around like that!" Her eyes were suddenly cold. "Fargo was crazy about them!" she added bleakly.

Chapter Ten

It was ten-thirty when I parked outside the Starlight Hotel. I went up to Janice Jorgens' suite and knocked on the door. She took a while to open it. When she did, she wasn't pleased to see me.

"Don't you ever give up!" she said in an exasperated voice. "What do I have to do—get myself police protection?"

"You've been holding out on me," I said reproachfully, "haven't you . . . Mandy?"

She pulled the robe tighter around herself, her eyes suddenly dull. "I don't know what you're talking about," she said.

"Let me in and I'll explain," I said, not very brilliantly.

She turned away from the door and walked back inside the suite. I followed her. She stopped beside the desk and turned to face me.

"This must be your off-beat technique," she said. "You don't amuse me any more, Lieutenant."

I took out the newspaper clips and showed her the two photos. She looked at them for about fifteen seconds, then lifted her head slowly.

"Mandy Morgan—Janice Jorgens," I said. "The names are different, but not that different."

She turned away and walked over to the window, pushing it open wide as if, suddenly, there wasn't enough air in the room. She stood with her back to me, without saying anything.

"When did you change your name?" I said. "Right after your sister died?"

"I don't know what you're talking about," she said faintly.

"I can recognize you as Mandy Morgan from a lousy newspaper photograph, three years old," I said wearily. "If you want to play dumb on it, all right. It won't be hard for us to find somebody in Louisville who will identify you, somebody like your old man, for instance."

"He's dead," she said in a sullen voice, "he died two years back. Hit and run; he was drunk of course."

"That's better," I said. "You are Mandy Morgan?"

"Yes," she turned away from the window and walked back toward the desk, "I'm Mandy Morgan."

"Why bother to change your name?"

"I was sick of everything," she said. "Sick of living in Louisville, sick of the old man being drunk all the time . . . and then Geraldine was murdered! I wanted to make a new start; I didn't want anything that belonged to the past, not even my name. So I went to New York and became Janice Jorgens."

I sat down in the nearest chair and touched my forehead gingerly; it was still faintly sticky around the hairline.

"Tell me some more about it," I said.

She sat down behind the desk and lit a cigarette. "What is there to tell?"

"I'd like to hear it, even if it isn't exciting."

Her fingers touched the typewriter keys idly for a moment.

"I'd taken a secretarial course, and I had a job in an advertising agency for a time. They were the people who finally found a sponsor for Paula's program. I got to see quite a bit of her, one way and another. She was always in the office, or phoning in. When the series was definitely set, she offered me the job as her secretary. The money was better, it would be more interesting—I took it."

I looked at the clippings again. "Just how did a Los Angeles newspaper come to quote Geraldine's letters to you?"

"One of the police officers connected with the case came to Louisville and talked to me about it. I showed him the letters and he took them away with him. He must have told the paper, I suppose."

"You remember his name?"

She thought for a moment: "He was a Lieutenant, a nice man . . . Monro, I think."

"He told you how your sister died?" I asked gently.

"He told me how she was murdered," she said flatly. "He told me about Lee Manning and his weekend parties at Laguna Beach. That was another reason for changing my name. It made me feel dirty, every time I thought about it."

"It caught up with Manning," I said. "He suicided a couple of weeks after your sister died."

"I know."

"But it didn't catch up with Georgia Brown."

"What do you mean?"

I got up and walked over to the desk. I stubbed the cigarette in the silver ash tray and looked down at her. "You know what Georgia Brown was, don't you?" I asked.

"She was a star," Janice said, without looking at me. "Everybody knows that."

"But everybody doesn't know the connection between Lee Manning and your sister. And everybody doesn't know just exactly what Georgia Brown was. She was worse than Manning in a lot of ways. She dealt cold-bloodedly in girls, girls like your sister, not even for cash—just for kicks. Monro knew it and if he told you about Manning, he told you about Georgia."

"You don't make any sense to me, Lieutenant," she said stiffly.

I would have liked a drink. "I was talking to Monro this morning," I said. "All I have to do now is to phone him. He'd remember whether he told you about Georgia Brown or not."

"All right!" she said tautly. "So he did tell me about Georgia Brown! What difference does that make?"

"There's a cop's handbook somewhere," I said, "and it gives certain fundamental rules. Things like looking for motive and opportunity in crime. Paula told me those names that Georgia Brown had mentioned to her, and that gave four people a strong motive for killing Georgia. So I started chasing around, because I had four hot suspects with a strong motive. I didn't think about opportunity."

"If you must give a lecture, do you have to pick me as an audience?" she asked tiredly.

"Right now I do," I said. "But it won't take very long. If I'd thought about opportunity earlier I could have saved myself a lot of trouble. I should have remembered that both you and Paula told me you were the only two who knew where Georgia Brown was."

"Are you trying to prove something?"

THE BLONDE

"I think I am proving it," I said. "I should have thought then that both of you had the opportunity to murder Georgia Brown. So next comes motive. What motive would Paula have? She was relying on Georgia's appearance on her show to boost her rating—the last thing Paula would want would be her non-appearance.

"But *you* had all the motive anybody could want. Georgia had been indirectly—or even directly—responsible for your sister's death."

Janice lit herself another cigarette: "You're out of your mind, Lieutenant!"

"You don't like men," I said. "You've got good reason not to like them, remembering what happened to your sister. You have a mechanical knack—I remember you mentioned my car needed tuning. The murderer had to be somebody Georgia trusted. Somebody she would let into that apartment without a question. Somebody who could stay there long enough to hook that homemade bomb into the buzzer circuit. I should have realized she would never have let any of those four people inside the apartment for a second."

She pushed the chair back and got onto her feet and walked over to the window again. "It's a very interesting theory, Lieutenant, but you can't prove any of it."

"Not right now," I said, "but I will. Even if you made that bomb out of old tin cans, you still had to buy the explosive for it. Georgia first approached Paula in San Francisco, then you came here. You had to buy the explosive either in 'Frisco or Pine City. There aren't that many places you could buy it; we'll find out where you bought it. Add that to the motive and opportunity we can already prove and the State's got a good case."

The door opened suddenly and Paula Reid walked in. She wore a powder-blue housecoat which accentuated more than concealed the suppleness of her body, and her eyes were surprised to see me.

"I'm sorry," she said. "I didn't know you were here, Lieutenant. I hope I'm not intruding."

"Come right in," I said unnecessarily. "While you're here, I'd like to check a couple of points with you. How many people knew where Georgia Brown's hideout was, did you say?"

"Just the two of us," she said, "Janice and myself, as far as

I know, Lieutenant. Though obviously the murderer must have found out. How, I don't know."

She looked at me uncertainly, then across at Janice. "Is everything all right?"

"Just fine," Janice said. She smiled at me, tiredly. "I congratulate you on your technique, Lieutenant! You had me fooled. The only thing I thought you were really interested in was women."

"Fundamentally you're right," I agreed.

"Lieutenant Monro did tell me about Georgia Brown," she said. "After Manning killed himself I read about her sudden disappearance and I read all the stories in the magazines. Then it became stale news and I'd almost forgotten about her. But I could never forget Geraldine."

"Geraldine?" Paula said blankly. "Who was Geraldine?"

"Janice's sister," I said. "She died at Manning's Laguna Beach house a couple of weeks before he threw himself over that cliff . . . it's a long story."

"Oh?" Paula said, even more blankly.

Janice ignored her. "Then Paula told me about Georgia approaching her and saying she wanted to tell the truth about what happened at the time of Manning's death. Paula explained to me Georgia had said she was innocent, and I knew then that she wasn't going to tell the truth. How could she, and reveal herself for what she was? She only wanted to get onto the program to smear other people!"

"So you killed her?"

"Not for that, for what she did to Geraldine, for what she must have done to a lot of other girls. . . . It was quite easy, really. I bought the explosive and packed it tight into a small canister and wired it up. The morning we arrived here, I called on Georgia. She knew I was Paula's secretary so she opened the door to me, then went back to her bath . . ."

"That was when you hooked the bomb into the buzzer circuit?"

She nodded. "It only took a couple of minutes. Georgia was still in the bath when I left."

"Then you rang Lavers and asked for some protection for Georgia and Paula?"

"That's right," she said calmly. "I thought it would help divert any suspicion."

"So when you gave me the address, you knew that when I

went out there and pressed that buzzer I was going to blow Georgia Brown into little pieces?"

"The thought did occur to me, Lieutenant."

"You!" Paula croaked suddenly. "You killed her!"

"I would have thought it was obvious by now, even to you!" Janice said coldly.

"I . . . I can't believe it!" Paula exclaimed, then sat abruptly down on the sofa. She stared wide-eyed at Janice. "Tell me it isn't true!"

"You better get dressed," I told Janice. "I'll wait here."

"I don't think I'll bother," she said. "Good-bye, Lieutenant. I can't say it's been nice knowing you."

She stepped up into the windowsill and then stepped straight out through the open window into space. Paula screamed and sprang up onto her feet.

I reached the window in time to see Janice hit the awning over the hotel front. She hit and bounced off, then landed on the sidewalk. Blood spread out like a glistening red cape from beneath her broken body, and the screams of a couple of women close by reached me faintly. Motioning Paula Reid to silence, I walked back to the desk and made the necessary phone calls. White-faced, Paula Reid stared at me helplessly.

"I still don't believe it," she whispered.

"Don't worry about it," I told her. "I'll get us a drink. We both need one."

I moved over to the cupboard and got out a couple of glasses.

"This is dreadful," she breathed. "She's been with me since the show started, and this"—she shook her head—"oh shit, it's too much. These things happening. Oh." Suddenly there was a look on her face as if she just remembered something. I looked at her inquiringly.

"I'd almost forgotten," she said. "She gave me something yesterday, she asked me to keep it for her . . . I suppose I should hand it over to you now?"

"What was it?"

"I don't know. I mean, it was a sealed envelope and she said it was valuable and she was frightened of losing it, so I offered to put it in my strongbox."

"I'd better have it," I said.

"I'll get it." She got up from her chair and went out the door.

I drank the four fingers of Scotch neat, then refilled the glass. I'd added ice to both drinks by the time she came back and handed me a heavily sealed envelope.

She took the drink from me gratefully and sank down into the chair again. "I still can't believe it," she muttered, "Janice!"

I ripped the seal open and shook the contents of the envelope into the palm of my hand. It was a negative, about an inch by an inch and a half in size. I held it up to the light and looked at it. There were three figures carrying something, but that was all I could make out; the negative was too small to see any more detail. I replaced it in the envelope and put it in my pocket.

I looked up and saw the curiosity quivering in Paula's eyes. "Something interesting, Lieutenant?" she asked in what was meant to be a casual voice.

"I don't know yet," I said. "But I'll find out."

Chapter Eleven

I walked into the Bureau at eleven forty-five. I bumped into Polnik on his way out, just inside the door.

"Lieutenant!" he said hoarsely. "Where you been?"

"Out," I said. "Did something happen?"

"They waited for you in Lavers' office till eleven," he said. "Then they came back here. They're in Parker's office now. They're about ready to put out a general alarm for you!"

"Maybe I'd better say hello, then." I said.

He shuddered: "I think you're going to need to say more than that, Lieutenant; a whole lot more!"

I went into the lab and found Kaplan there. He grinned at me over the top of his steel-rimmed glasses.

"The guy who makes with the bangs!" he said. "I hear Murphy did his quickest autopsy ever! He only had half a torso and a pair of legs to work with!"

I gave him the negative. "Look, do me a favor, Kap. Make a blowup of this right away for me, and bring it up to Parker's office as soon as it's through. Don't worry much about it being wet."

"Coming right up!" he said.

I went out of the lab and along to Parker's office. I opened the door and put my head inside. "Surprise!" I said brightly. "Where is your wandering boy tonight? Fear no more, for I am here. Bring out the fatted calf and——"

"Come inside and close that door, Wheeler!" Lavers said thickly. "I wouldn't want any junior officers to hear this!"

I stepped into the office and closed the door behind me gently. Parker looked through me stonily. Lavers massacred a good cigar into shreds between his teeth.

"You," he said finally, "are finished! This is the last time, Wheeler, that you ever——"

"Would you like me to dictate Janice Jorgens' confession now, Sheriff?" I asked him finally. "Or will I wait till you've finished whatever it is you're going to say?"

His mouth worked for a few moments: "Janice Jorgens' con——What the hell are you talking about!"

"She made a complete confession, before she jumped out of her hotel window," I said. "I thought you knew?"

"How would I——" He made a gigantic effort. "All right, Wheeler, let's hear it!"

"She made a confession to you, then killed herself?" Parker asked coldly.

"That's right," I agreed.

"Just you? Nobody else heard it?" The sneer was in his voice if not his face.

"Paula Reid was there, too," I said. "She heard it."

"Uh," he sounded almost disappointed.

Lavers clapped a hand to his face and squeezed the jowls cruelly. "All right," he said finally, "tell me!"

I told him the story as it had happened. I took the clips out of my pocket and both he and Parker stared at them, disbelievingly. I lit a cigarette when I'd finished.

Lavers and Parker looked at each other for a long moment, then they both scowled at me.

"It still leaves a hell of a lot unexplained," Lavers grunted. "Why did Fargo kill Coates, and then threaten to kill the Steinway girl?"

"Not forgetting of course," Parker added gently, "that if Wheeler had handled things properly, Coates probably wouldn't have been killed and we would have picked up Fargo before he got inside the Steinway girl's house!"

"I'm not forgetting those things for one moment," Lavers growled, "and neither is Inspector Martin."

"Have you picked up Fargo yet?" I asked.

"No," Parker said morosely. "And it's not going to be easy, either. He knows too many people in this town. There'd be dozens of them glad to give him a hideout."

There was a knock on the door and Kaplan walked in.

"Here it is, Al," he said and put a dripping wet eight-by-six print on Parker's desk in front of me. "O.K.?"

"Thanks, Kap," I said.

"Think nothing of it," he said and went out of the office, closing the door behind him.

THE BLONDE 81

I looked closely at the print.

"What's that?" Lavers asked.

"Janice Jorgens gave Paula Reid a sealed envelope yesterday," I said, "and asked her to mind it for her, so Paula gave it to me. There was a negative inside—this is the print from it."

They crowded in on either side of me to look at it. It wasn't a very good picture, but it was good enough. It showed three people holding a body. Coates and Hilary Blain had an arm each while Kent Fargo held the legs.

"What does it mean?" Lavers said. "Some sort of horseplay?"

"Some sort of murder, Sheriff," I said. "You recognize the guy they're holding? That's Lee Manning."

"Manning?" he peered closer at the print. "So it is—Manning!"

"I recognize the spot where this shot was taken," I said. "It's the top of the cliff above Manning's Laguna Beach house."

"But that's where he . . ." Parker stopped abruptly.

"You're so right, Captain," I agreed. "We've got a new switch. He didn't jump, he wasn't pushed, he was thrown."

Lavers straightened his back painfully. "That means the three of them are equally guilty of Manning's murder."

"That was the thing that worried me," I said. "It was so convenient, Manning's suicide I mean. With Geraldine Morgan's death, the lid was ready to blow right off. The scandal would have ruined all of them—Manning himself and, along with him, Fargo, Blain, Coates and Georgia Brown. But then Manning generously tossed himself over a cliff so they could all live happily ever after."

"I'd like to know who took this picture," Lavers said slowly.

"Georgia herself," I said. "Who else? How would Janice Jorgens have gotten hold of it otherwise? She must have found it in that apartment when she took her bomb and went calling. This photo is what Fargo was looking for, and the reason why he killed Coates."

"Why would he think Coates had it?"

"Somebody must have told him so. Janice Jorgens could have called him and said Coates had the negative. But she obviously wouldn't say who she was——" It hit me suddenly.

"She must have said she was Kay Steinway. Coates was producing her films now. Fargo would know that there was a tie-up between them."

"Why would Janice Jorgens say she was Kay Steinway?" Parker asked skeptically.

"Kay and Paula Reid had a fight at her place the other night," I said. "I don't think Janice liked Kay. It might be her way of hitting Kay. After Fargo killed Coates and couldn't find the negative, he thought he'd been double-crossed by Kay, so he phoned her. I was there when she got the call. The first thing Fargo said when he came into the room was that she'd set up the whole lousy deal with that phone call."

"Fargo is a little, shall we say, headstrong?" Parker said gently.

"We all know what Fargo is," I said. "And he always had a soft spot for Georgia Brown. He'd figured whoever had that negative had killed Georgia to get it. He killed Coates and found it wasn't him; so then he thought it must be Kay Steinway, because he believed Kay had given him the false lead to Coates."

"Makes sense," Lavers admitted gruffly.

"That Janice," I said. "What a cozy little character she was!" I smiled politely at Parker. "I hope you don't feel quite so bad about Coates's death now, Captain? After all, it only saved the State an expense."

Parker glared at me: "I'm beginning to realize why Hammond feels the way he does about you!" he said slowly.

Lavers' lips twitched for a moment. "We still aren't finished with this, anyway. Blain's got to be brought in and booked for Manning's murder." He tapped the print with his knuckle, "We've got all the proof we need right here."

"I'd like to ask a favor, sir," I said. "Could I take Polnik with me and bring him in?"

"Don't worry, Al," Parker said. "You'll get your picture in the papers, anyway."

"All right, Wheeler," the Sheriff said. "But if you lose him on the way, I'll . . ."

"Thank you, sir," I said. "You don't mind if I take this with me?" I lifted the photo from the desk. "The lab is holding the negative, so it doesn't much matter what happens to a print."

"Don't take too long about it," Lavers glanced at his

THE BLONDE

watch. "We've still got time to make the morning papers, but I want Blain safely on his way back here before I give the story to the reporters."

"I'll hurry," I said.

I went out of the office and found Polnik. "Big deal," I told him. "You're coming with me."

He blinked. "Are you still a lieutenant, Lieutenant?"

"I was the last time I looked," I said. "There are times, Polnik, when I feel you don't have faith in me."

"It's not that, Lieutenant," he said earnestly. "It's just that I get a feeling sometimes that it's too good to last. One day you'll just disappear," he snapped his fingers, "like that! and take all those beautiful women with you!"

"So long as I don't leave them behind," I said. "You had me worried for a moment there."

We drove out to Blain's home in a prowl car. It was one-thirty when we reached the house and parked on the driveway. Polnik came with me up the front steps.

"What do we do now, Lieutenant?" He looked at the house hopefully. "What new surprises do you have in store. Another broad with an interesting past? A society chick who's having it away with the gardener or anyone who comes within reach? So surprise me, huh?"

"You know something, Sergeant," I said as I pressed the bell, "when you get home, I think your old lady's going to be surprised."

I kept on pressing and finally a light came on in the hallway. A few seconds after that the door opened and the butler stood there, blinking at me. He was wearing a faded green flannel dressing gown; the moths had dined from the edges.

I looked at it slowly. "You should see someone about getting a raise," I suggested. "Or is it just the shabbiness of the genteel?"

He took a deep breath, then exhaled slowly. "Mr. Blain has already retired for the night."

"Then tell him we're putting him back into active service," I said. "We'll wait in the library."

"The library yet!" Polnik said in a hushed voice.

The butler gave up. He moved to one side to let us pass, then closed the front door. I watched him plod slowly up the stairs, then I led the way into the library, switching on the lights when we got there.

I lit a cigarette and sat in a chair while Polnik looked around.

"Lieutenant," he said, "what do people buy books for?"

"To read, I guess."

"Don't they have television?"

"I'll ask him," I said.

He shook his head wonderingly. "The things people spend their money on—it never ceases to amaze me. All these books, and how ever could he find the time to read them all?" He grinned wolfishly at me. "Say, that Toni was really something, huh?"

"Something," I agreed.

"A woman of the world."

"Come on," I said, "you're supposed to be a hard-bitten cop. You're not supposed to be impressed."

"Yeah." He nodded slowly. "And this guy buys books," he said in wonderment.

The door opened and Blain walked in. He was fully dressed, and he didn't look happy.

"Really, Lieutenant!" he said coldly. "I hope you can justify this intrusion into my household at this time of night!"

"I think so," I said. "I won't take much of your time, Mr. Blain. I just wondered if you could identify any of the people in this photograph?"

I put the print down on his desk and he came over and peered at it. He straightened up slowly, took off his glasses and began to polish them vigorously.

"You'll have to come with us, Mr. Blain," I said.

"On what charge?"

"Murder."

"I demand to see my lawyer!"

"You can call him to meet you down at the Bureau, if you want," I said.

His fingers shook as he replaced the glasses on the bridge of his nose. His hand reached out toward the phone, wavered for a moment, then dropped to his side.

"It was Fargo's idea," he whispered. "He talked us into it, he made us do it!"

"Why don't you tell me about it?" I said. "Coates is dead, Georgia Brown is dead, and Fargo is on the run, wanted for another murder. There's really only you left, Mr. Blain. You could make it easier for yourself."

THE BLONDE

He walked around his desk stiffly and lowered himself into the chair behind it. "I'd like a drink," he said.

"Sergeant," I said to Polnik, "pour Mr. Blain a drink." I corrected myself hastily. "Pour all of us a drink."

"Sure thing, Lieutenant!" Polnik followed his nose to the liquor cabinet.

Blain sat staring dully at the desk top in front of him.

"Manning invited the four of us down to his place for the weekend," he said in a low voice. "I went because I had nothing else to do and I was worried like the rest of them. The death of that young girl was going to cause a scandal that would ruin all of us."

"I know all about the girl and the scandal," I said. "It's the murder I want to hear about." I leaned over and tapped the photo with my index finger to emphasize the point.

"That was the Saturday night," he said. "We were just sitting around, drinking, without saying much. There didn't seem to be anything to say. We knew the coroner's court would be held the following Wednesday, and that would be the end of everything."

Polnik put a drink down in front of Blain and then handed me one. I noted the level in his own glass was an inch higher than in either of the other two. Blain drank some of the Scotch, then put the glass back onto the desk.

"Lee went over to the bar and Fargo poured him a drink," he went on. "They talked for a time while Manning finished his drink, then he suddenly collapsed to the floor. Fargo told us he had drugged the drink and Manning would be unconscious for at least another three hours. Then he made his proposition."

"To murder Manning?"

"He said it was our only hope. With Manning out of the way, there would be a chance we could kill the story about the young girl's death. Fargo argued that there would be nothing left to blame if Manning were dead and the story would be hushed up for the sake of the girl and her family. It made sense."

"So you all agreed to help murder, Manning?"

He winced. "Not all of us, Lieutenant. Georgia was enthusiastic immediately, but Coates and I weren't. Yet there seemed no other way out."

"Why did so many of you have to get into the act?"

"That was Fargo's idea," he said. "Fargo maintained we all had an equal stake and if we shared the guilt it would stop any one of us ever telling the police how Manning had really died."

"Symbolic act—or something?"

Blain nodded. "Something like that. Finally Coates and I agreed, so that was what happened."

"And Georgia Brown?"

"She was Fargo's strongest supporter, as I said before, Lieutenant. But she sprained her ankle getting out of the car. It was very convincing," he laughed mirthlessly, "she certainly fooled both Coates and myself. She lay on the grass, apparently sobbing with pain, while the three of us men carried Manning to the edge and threw him over."

"So it was Georgia Brown who took the picture?" I said. "Didn't the flash tell you what was happening?"

"She didn't use flashlight photography," he said. "She used another process—infrared, I believe they call it."

"You mean she just happened to have that sort of equipment with her?"

Blain finished his drink and looked up. "If you don't mind, I'd like another drink?"

"Polnik," I said, and held out my own empty glass just in case he overlooked it.

"You aren't making sense," I said to Blain. "You told me that Fargo suddenly sprung this idea on you out of the blue, and—at the most an hour later—you took Manning up to the cliff and threw him over. Yet in that time Georgia suddenly acquired a camera with infrared plates!"

He shook his head tiredly. "We only found out about the camera later, Lieutenant. That was when the blackmail started."

I grabbed the new drink out of Polnik's hand. "I really needed this," I told him.

"You see," Blain laughed, this time with almost genuine humor, "it was what you would call a put-up job, Lieutenant. Fargo and Georgia planned it between them. She had the camera already hidden in the car. Fargo had to actually help us throw Manning over, to stop us becoming suspicious of him. But why should we have been suspicious of Georgia's ankle?"

"So afterwards they blackmailed you—and Coates?"

THE BLONDE

"For three years we have been paying," he agreed. "I have been bled white over that period!"

"Then why did Georgia disappear immediately after the coroner's court?"

"She couldn't have been honest with anyone," Blain said. "It wasn't in her. She cheated on Fargo. She held the negative and she ran out on him, still holding it. Don't you see, Lieutenant? Fargo was in that picture *himself*. She forced him to collect the blackmail money for her, and more than that, to pay up as well!"

Polnik had a look of open admiration on his face. "What a setup!" he said. "You have to hand it to her!"

"Even if she did get herself blown to bits," I agreed.

Blain finished his second drink and got onto his feet. "I don't think there's anything else, Lieutenant. I'm ready to go now."

We went out of the library and down the hallway to the front door. The butler opened it for us and I let the other two go first. I stood and watched while Polnik put Blain in the back seat of the car and got in beside him.

There was a gentle cough from behind me.

"Excuse me, sir," the butler said, "but when can I expect the master to return?"

"Not in your lifetime," I said truthfully and walked out to the car.

Polnik took care of the formalities when we got back to the Bureau. Lavers was still in Parker's office when I went in. He was looking almost happy. I told him Blain's story about the Manning murder.

He grunted when I'd finished. "I had Miss Reid down here," he said. "She just left. She made a statement which corroborates your story about Janice Jorgens' confession to Georgia Brown's murder. It's all wrapped up now. You can come down sometime tomorrow morning and dictate a formal statement. All we have to do now is find Fargo and everybody will be happy, including me."

"Yes, sir," I said. "You mind if I leave now? It's been a long day and a long night and now it's starting to be a long day again."

"Twenty-four hours' work and it kills you!" he said contemptuously.

"One thing about being a Sheriff," I said. "You don't ever have to ride herd with the posse."

"Get out of here before I challenge you to a draw, partner!" Lavers said jovially.

"You feeling all right, Sheriff?" I asked him anxiously. "You just made a joke."

I reached the door and stopped.

"Go on, Wheeler!" Lavers said irritably. "You made your exit line!"

"There's just one thing I don't get," I said. "Georgia Brown had a perfect blackmail setup—it was making her a fortune. Yet she came to Paula Reid and volunteered to appear on her show and tell the truth about Manning's death. Why would she want to throw away everything like that?"

"Maybe she was crazy!" Lavers snarled. "Who cares why she did it! The case is finished, Wheeler. You *do* need a rest!"

I went out to the car and drove back home to my apartment. I saw the dawn break but the dull thud inside my head was migraine.

I wearily turned the key in the lock, pushed open the door and walked inside the apartment. The lights were on in the living room. I tripped over a suitcase which wasn't mine and fell headlong.

Then I lifted my head slowly and surveyed the bulging overnight bag I had fallen over, which certainly wasn't mine. Then I climbed back onto my feet and saw a leopard-skin coat spread across the couch.

I felt my jaw sag as I watched the silver-blonde head rise slowly above the coat.

"You're late!" she said coldly.

I glared at her.

"The janitor let me in," she said defensively. "He said what difference did one more make."

"What in hell did you come here for?"

"I was frightened of the reporters," she said. "And I was frightened that Kent might be mad at me. I couldn't think of any other place that would be safe."

"What makes you think you're safe with me? That's an insult to my reputation."

"I don't mean that sort of safe," she said casually, "I mean real safe."

The migraine neatly sliced off the top of my head, filled it with red-hot rivets and replaced it with a sharp slap.

"Never mind," I croaked. "Can you cook?"

Her eyes widened with disbelief. "You mean food and stuff like that?"

"Can you make coffee?" I pleaded.

"I could mix you a martini," she said brightly.

I shuddered. "I've tasted your martinis. Try the coffee, it's not really hard."

"If you say so."

She got up onto her feet and I saw she was wearing a tight shirt unbuttoned about half the way down that was barely able to contain her full curves; and a pair of cream slacks that looked as though they had been spray-painted on her. She was definitely the answer to someone's prayer, and I only hoped she made a success of the coffee.

I went into the bedroom and collected a robe. Then I went into the bathroom, stripped off my clothes, and stood under the hot shower for about ten minutes; cold needle-sprays are for those men with sharp pointed heads. I toweled myself dry, wrapped the robe around me, and went out into the living room again.

Toni had the coffee made and on the table. I lifted the cup and sipped it cautiously. "That's not bad," I admitted grudgingly.

She was sitting with her legs crossed, compressing the bulge of her pubis into an even smaller wedge. "If I could stay here just for the night," she said. "I'm booked on a plane to Vegas in the morning—nine-thirty. I won't be any trouble."

"O.K.," I said, "but I sleep in the bed."

Her perpetually surprised eyebrows looked even more so. "I'm a reasonable girl, Lieutenant," she said archly. "I don't take up too much room."

Maybe it was the coffee, but right then the migraine vanished, and when she came across to me, gently easing open my robe and laying her head on my quickening genitals, I was as right as rain.

Chapter Twelve

"Honey," I said drowsily, "we must have something—I can hear bells ringing."

Then another layer of sleep peeled away and I realized it was the phone I was hearing. I got out of bed, staggered into the living room and picked up the receiver.

"Lady," I said, "we got three hundred acres and seventy thousand permanent residents at Peaceful Pastures. If we put your husband in the wrong plot, I'm sorry. You want we should dig him up again?"

There was a silvery tinkle of laughter in my ear.

"Lieutenant," a soft, feminine voice said, "you're awful!"

"I feel it, I look it, I admit it," I said. "Who is this?"

"I hoped you'd recognize my voice." She sounded vaguely disappointed. "This is Paula Reid speaking. I wonder if I could see you today. It's really very important."

"I guess so," I said. "I have to make a statement down at the Bureau this morning. How about this afternoon?"

"That would be wonderful," she said enthusiastically. "This place is chaos at the moment—could we make it somewhere else?"

"Why not my apartment," I said, and thought that would stop her kidding around.

"That sounds fine," she said brightly. "What time would suit you, Lieutenant?"

"Around four?"

"I'll see you then," she said softly into my once shell-like pink ear. "Bye now." There was the faintest click as she hung up.

"I have something she wants?" I asked myself out loud, feeling the stubble around my chin. I dropped the receiver back onto the rest and headed toward the bedroom.

THE BLONDE

I guess I should have looked where I was going. The next moment I was flat on my face. I picked myself up and made a face at the bulging overnight bag.

The bathroom door creaked slightly and then Toni walked into the room, her naked body still pink and steaming after her shower. Her pink nipples were taut and the hair of her pubis came to a small damp tuft between her shapely thighs. I could feel myself quickly becoming aroused again at the sight of her.

"Hi!" she gave me a dazzling smile.

"That thing you hear spinning is my mind, not a roulette wheel," I said coldly. I glanced at my watch, which read eleven o'clock. "I thought you were supposed to be in Las Vegas by now."

"I missed my plane," she said. "But there's another one. I made some coffee—it's in the kitchen."

"I have an appointment here at four this afternoon," I said.

"My!" her eyebrows tweaked. "We are a busy man, aren't we!"

"Do something for me," I said. "Get a plane before then, will you?"

"Of course I will," she said. "You don't think I want to stay here, do you?"

"I'd say no if I were sure you were sane," I said doubtfully.

"Are you going to take a shower?" she asked.

"I always take a shower," I said, wounded.

"Right now, I mean?"

"Yeah."

"Well, then, would you like me to do your back for you?"

"You've just had your shower."

"Then I'll have another. I don't mind."

"O.K. Sure, if you like."

"I like. Then you can do mine for me."

In the shower, the warm water streamed down on both of us, crowded into the cubicle so that there wasn't much room to move. Taking the soap, she gently massaged it over my back down from my shoulders to my buttocks, working down between them, then coming round to work a soft lather around my genitals which responded to the silky touch of her fingers. Her body was against mine; I could feel her breasts pressing against my back, her pelvis, her thighs, the faint sponginess between her legs. Her fingers moved dexterously, and I was becoming rigid. Her fingers stroked me in long sweeps, and finally I couldn't help but give in. Suddenly, grabbing her, I brought her down onto the floor of the cubicle, bending her right forward in front of me, my hands gripping her smooth buttocks and parting them as far as they could go, opening her wide. Then I brought my iron-hard staff in beneath her gluteal orbs, guiding it in between her labia, driving hard into her pulsing vagina, my fingers coming around to roughly massage her clit, which, by the sounds she was beginning to make, must have been exactly what she wanted. The water cascaded down onto my back as I slammed against her, compelled by the furious intensity of my lust.

Later, when we were dressed, I asked: "You have any bright ideas where Fargo might be holed up?"

Since we had emerged from the shower, she had been dreamy and distant. She had made a lot of noise when I brought her to a climax, and even when, with my fingers, I had begun to soap out the bruised battlefield.

"Poor Kent," she murmured. "He must be a worried man. Fargo enterprises won't be the same without him. He was a very keen executive, you know."

"It was my own fault," I said. "I asked. Just don't be here at four o'clock."

"You're kissing me off?"

"With roses," I told her.

I went down to the Bureau and dictated a statement about Janice Jorgens—Mandy Morgan. I waited for it to be typed, then signed it. I heard that Fargo was still loose. I left the Bureau around noon and drove over to the County Sheriff's office.

Annabelle Jackson lifted her head and looked at me over the top of her typewriter. "Well," she said to nobody in particular, "look who's here. The bleary-eyed bloodhound. Come to pick up your bone, Lieutenant, or wag your tail while the Sheriff pats your head?"

"I just walked in," I said to nobody in particular, "I didn't say nothin'."

"Having himself such a time," she said. "Pricey hookers and television stars. So you've got a nice scene going for yourself. O.K., Lieutenant," she said coldly. "The Sheriff is in his office. Go on in, and try not to trip and break your neck, because when I start laughing I sometimes find it very difficult to stop."

I nodded slowly. "I know. It builds up. Like hepatitis."

"Screw, Lieutenant," she said as I walked past her desk. "Do me that kindness."

"The way I'm feeling right now," I told her, "it's hardly the magic word."

I knocked on Laver's door, opened it and walked into his office.

"Glad you dropped in, Wheeler," he said. "Sit down, have a cigar."

"This sounds awful close to the kiss of death," I said suspiciously as I sat down. "You know I never smoke cigars."

"You think I'd offer you one if you did?" he said.

I felt a little easier—this was the Lavers I knew.

"Have you read the morning paper?" he asked.

"I haven't been out of bed long enough," I said.

"The whole thing went very well, very well indeed," he said complacently. "The credit shared nice and evenly between this office and Homicide."

"Congratulations, Sheriff," I said politely.

"There is a mention of Lieutenant Wheeler, temporarily attached to the Sheriff's office, having helped in the investigation," he said. "At least, there was in the first edition. . . ."

"I'm glad they took it out," I said. "I get any more press clips I'll have to rent another apartment to live in. There just isn't room for both of us."

"When they pick up Fargo, it'll be all over," he said. "Maybe he's in Florida by now."

"Maybe," I said. "Can I go back to Homicide? I like the life there, they have nice complicated cases like a wife stabs her husband then phones in and tells you where to collect both of them."

"I used my influence on your behalf," Lavers said benignly. "You have a free weekend. You don't report back to this office until Monday."

"Thanks," I said, stunned.

"Anyway," he sort of leered at me, "I guess you'll need some time between now and tomorrow night to practice."

"Practice?" I repeated blankly.

"Maybe not," he said, "there's quite a lot of ham in you already."

"If it's not a rude question," I said, "what are you talking about?"

"You mean you don't know?"

"I'm trying hard to understand," I said, "but I only speak English."

He slumped back into his chair and began to laugh. Then he guffawed, he couldn't stop. He thumped his fist down on the desktop and the calendar was suddenly airborne.

"I won't spoil it for you!" he stuttered helplessly. "I wouldn't dream of spoiling it for you, Wheeler! Have a nice, quiet weekend."

"The only thing that appeals to me about this is you'll probably have a coronary any second now," I said stiffly. I got up from the chair and walked out of his office, the sound of his laughter following me all the way.

I stopped beside Annabelle Jackson's desk on my way out.

"Did you say something funny in there, Lieutenant?" she asked coldly. "Or maybe he just looked at you?"

"What have I done to deserve this treatment?" I asked helplessly. "Did I set fire to you and not remember?"

"You don't have to stop and talk to me, Lieutenant," she said. "I'm not a fan!" Her typewriter rattled furiously. I shrugged my shoulders resignedly and walked out.

I bought myself a lunch I couldn't afford and reflected that today was Friday and I was free all the way through to Monday.

I got back to the apartment just after three. I let myself in cautiously and sighed happily when I saw there was no bulging overnight bag on the living room floor. I checked each room to make sure, but I didn't find a girl with silver-blonde hair in any of them.

Then I got to work making the place look presentable for my next date, who maybe was only coming to ask my advice about getting a new secretary, cheap. After I had cleaned up the place, I pulled out a selection of cassettes which I thought might help set the mood, chipped some ice, and polished some glasses—well, two anyway.

The buzzer went at four o'clock precisely and the Wheeler apartment went to battle stations with the ease of long-practiced routine.

THE BLONDE

I opened the door and she smiled warmly at me. "Hello, Lieutenant, it was nice of you to ask me over here."

"Come on in," I said, and held the door open wide. She walked past me into the living room. I closed the front door and followed her.

"I like your apartment," she said, "it has an intimate atmosphere."

"That's the aim," I said modestly.

"Do you mind if I call you Al?" she said. "I feel we know each other much too well to persist with the formalities, don't you?"

"I certainly do, Paula," I agreed. "Won't you sit down?" I maneuvered her so she had no choice but the nearest couch.

"Thank you," she said, sat down and crossed her legs.

I looked at them with respect. She wore a sapphire-colored dress that plunged recklessly at the neckline to reveal about six inches of cleavage. I traced with my eyes the line of the thigh that was crossed over the other right up to the curve of her buttock.

"I'll get us a drink," I said. "Your usual?"

"How do you know what's my usual?"

"It has to be gin and tonic," I said. "The color harmonizes."

"I take that as a compliment, Al," she said slowly, giving me a lingering look.

I poured the drinks while she got up and riffled through the cassettes I had selected to help set the right mood. By the time I got back with the drinks she was sitting on the couch again.

"You like music?" she asked.

"Sure," I said. "Shall I put something on?"

"Fine."

I went over to the window and pulled down the shade. "All that sunlight," I explained, "it's bad for the eyes."

I crossed to the player, switched it on, and slipped in a cassette. "Music for you, Paula," I said.

"My usual?"

"Of course," I said. "What else but the blues?"

The sound of the cornet rose and fell plaintively around us as I sat down beside her on the couch. I was very aware of her closeness to me, the subtleness of her perfume.

"Al," Paula said earnestly, "I came to ask you a favor, a very great favor."

I looked at her and took a deep breath. "I'm sure we can make a deal, honey," I said.

"You know my show for tomorrow night was ruined when Georgia Brown was murdered?"

"Sure," I said sympathetically.

"Well, Kay Steinway agreed to come on the show as my main guest. Much as I dislike her she's really news now since Fargo tried to kill her. But I feel it isn't quite enough. I need somebody else to really tie the story into shape."

I thought for a few seconds then gave up. "I'm sorry, honey," I said sincerely, "I can't think of anyone who would——"

"I can!" she said excitedly.

"Who?"

"You!"

I closed my eyes for a moment and thought I should have seen the slow curve coming before the fast break hit me. I heard again the sound of Lavers' raucous guffaw in my ears. Now it began to make sense.

I opened my mouth to tell her she was crazy if she thought I'd appear before her cameras and risk around five million people making rude comments about my ancestry. Then I closed my mouth again quickly before I said a word.

I suddenly remembered she was going to pay Georgia a fee of five thousand dollars for her appearance. I spent the fee in five seconds' rapid mental calculation. I thought of all the things I could pay and still have enough left over to afford a vacation this year.

"Will you, Al?" she asked urgently.

"Why, sure." I put my arm around her shoulder and let my hand fall to within an ace of her right breast. "How could I refuse you anything?"

"You're wonderful!" she said simply. "I knew you'd do it. If I tell you a secret, will you promise not to get mad at me?"

"I promise."

"Well, I thought I'd better clear any barriers before I asked you. And it's quite all right with Inspector Martin and the County Sheriff if you appear on the show."

"Fine," I said without any great enthusiasm.

"And they said naturally you couldn't accept any fee, so

I'm paying a thousand dollars into the police fund you have for widows and orphans."

"You're what!" I shouted.

"Al!" she said reproachfully. "You promised you wouldn't get mad."

"But I don't have any widows or orphans."

She laughed gently. "You always see the funny side of things, don't you, Al?"

"That's me," I said bitterly. "Laugh, clown, laugh!"

She turned toward me, her eyes glittering "You don't know what this means to me! I don't know how to thank you."

"I can think of a way," I said meaningfully.

"Now you're being basic," she said with a smoldering, heavy-lidded smile.

"Is there any other way?"

She leaned toward me. "You can kiss me if you like."

We kissed, and her lips, as they writhed against mine, tasted as sweet as honey. Then her tongue was pushing against mine, thrusting and diving into my mouth. She was one hungry woman. Our hands were everywhere.

"My needs are simple, Al," she gasped as we broke apart. "As I'm sure yours are. Two people reaching out, comunication, a fusing of the bodies—I really would like to show you how grateful I am."

"Then what are we waiting for?" I said huskily, bringing my hand down over her breast and gently squeezing it.

"You're a very attractive man, Al," she breathed, and then we were kissing again and pawing each other as our tongues danced a torrid fandango.

Then we were pulling off our clothes, and Paula was lying back on the couch, her legs drawn up and parted as I eased myself down on top of her, locking the thickness of my stem into the palpitating receptivity of her passage. We made love quickly, and strongly, my hands gripping the backs of her thighs, forcing them higher as I pushed myself against her with all my might. Our bodies rode together in perfect harmony to the gentle, almost hypnotic slapping of our flesh. Her head rolled on the cushions beneath me, her forehead puckered slightly in concentration. Her eyes were closed and she was biting her lower lip. Her body bucked beneath me as I drove into her even harder. And then, with a rush that made my head spin, we both reached the peak and toppled over into a warm black abyss, and I was only dimly aware of the sharp cry from the woman beneath me, echoing hollowly in my head as if everything had been drawn out from it with the quick spurting rush from my genitals.

Sometime later, after we had more or less got our breath back, and we had had another drink, Paula got up and dressed. "Thanks again, Al," she said, smoothing down her dress. "Could you get out to the studio around four tomorrow afternoon? We'll have a sort of rehearsal just to get you used to the cameras and the lights. I never work to a script, so you don't have to worry about learning anything."

She was already halfway to the door. "I can't tell you what this means to me. I really am grateful. Don't bother to get up, I know my way out. See you tomorrow at four then."

The door quietly closed behind her.

Chapter Thirteen

I got down to the Bureau a little before ten the next morning and went along to Doc Murphy's office. He raised his eyebrows as I came in.

"Ah, Wheeler!" he said. "They tell me you're playing the lead in an adult Western tonight. I told them not to be stupid, how could you ever qualify?"

"So many comics going to waste," I said. "Anyway, it's the horses that are adult. You can always get another actor, but a good horse takes years to train."

"I shouldn't rib you," he said. "You're my pal. You're the boy who's going to do away with autopsies entirely. No more bodies, just bits!"

"Did you ever think of running a funeral parlor?" I asked him. "You'd be a riot there."

"Don't need to," he said cheerfully. "My brother runs one. I'm his best salesman!"

"Supplier would be the word," I corrected him.

He cackled like something out of *Macbeth*.

"I was wondering," I said, "about that body. Was any formal identification made?"

"Are you crazy?"

"Well, did anybody try and make a comparative identification then?"

"If you know anybody who was on such intimate terms with Georgia Brown's left tibia and right fibula that they could identify them," Murphy said, "bring them along. I'd like to meet them."

"I just wondered," I said.

"You should go far, Wheeler," he said coldly. "You're just stupid enough to be made an inspector or a county sheriff one of these days!"

"Come the day and there'll be a new doctor around here," I said as I headed toward the door. "Make the most of things, Murphy, it's later than you think."

I left his office and went over to Missing Persons, to Captain Parsons' office. He was three years from retirement and he'd been carefully nudged into Missing Persons because Inspector Martin thought than any precinct captain who still had a spittoon around his office was outdated.

Parsons scratched his bald head and grinned at me as I came into his office. "If it isn't the white-headed boy himself! What are you doing—slumming?"

"I'm looking for a blonde," I told him.

"Aren't we all?" he said passionately. "The youngest female I've got in this office is forty-five, and her idea of fun is to have mustard on a hot dog once in a while."

"Tough," I said. "Do you have any missing blondes on your books, Captain?"

"I got any kind of female or male you want," he said. "This is a city of missing persons! What did you have in mind, specifically?"

"I don't have much," I said. "She would be a blonde, probably in her late twenties or early thirties. She would have been missing a couple of weeks, maybe a little less than that."

"I'll get the wheels of industry churning," Parsons said cheerfully and picked up his phone.

Ten minutes later we looked at the list. We had started off with six names and had them reduced to two.

"This one," Parsons jabbed his pencil point against the name. "Ella Scott. She was reported missing by her mother. The mother thinks she might have gone to San Diego with a sailor. She says Ella's always going away with sailors but she never stayed away this long before, so maybe this time she went farther."

"All the way to San Diego?"

"You could be right," he grinned.

I lit a cigarette and he grunted and pushed the bridge of his glasses further up his nose.

"That leaves Rita Tango," Parsons said.

"Rita who?"

"That's what she calls herself anyway. Reported missing by the owner of the rooming house where she lives. Been gone for three days before she was reported missing. That was ten

THE BLONDE

days ago—she hasn't turned up yet. Age twenty-nine, height ... you want the detail on the personal description?"

"I don't think so," I said. "I might run over there and talk to the owner. What's his name?"

"O'Shea," he said, "and it's a Mrs."

"Thanks, Captain," I told him.

"If you ask me," he grinned, "you're going about getting yourself a blond the hard way!"

"I have a feeling you could be right," I agreed.

Mrs. O'Shea was out when I got to the rooming house. A freckle-faced kid around thirteen who was lounging on the stoop told me she'd be out all day. She'd gone to see her brother and she wouldn't be back before six, she never was. I said it didn't matter.

The kid stuck his hands into the pockets of his jeans and looked me over slowly: "Who are you anyway?" he asked.

"My name's Wheeler," I said.

"You one of them skip-tracers or something?" he asked.

"Sort of," I said. "I'm not really looking for Mrs. O'Shea, I'm looking for Rita Tango."

"You're out of luck, mister," he said, "she's skipped again."

I lit myself a cigarette. "I guess I am, if that's the case," I said. "Did you know her?"

"Sure. Used to see her around all the time, she didn't work much."

"What did she do when she was working?"

"She was in pictures, she said." He shrugged his shoulders contemptuously. "I never saw her in any. Big deal!"

"Did she have an agent, do you know?" I asked.

"Sure, she used to go in about once a week to see him. I asked her about it once. I said how come this guy wasn't even in Hollywood if he was such a big agent, and she said it was only a branch office out here."

"You wouldn't remember the name of the branch office?"

His eyes were suddenly shrewd. "Just how much does she owe that finance company of yours, mister?"

"Ten bucks," I said.

"Ah! You wouldn't be wasting your time chasing her for a lousy ten bucks!"

"You're too smart for me, I guess," I said. "How much is it worth?"

He took a deep breath. "Five bucks?" he said hesitantly.

"It's a deal," I said.

I stood beside him on the stoop and stared down at him coldly, then I opened my coat a little so he could see the gun. His eyes widened as he looked.

"You ever heard of Kent Fargo, kid?" I said softly out of the side of my mouth.

"Yeah, s-s-sure," he gulped.

"Fargo's looking for her, kid," I said menacingly. "That mean anything to you?"

"Sure, sure, mister!" he said nervously. "The guy's name is Chuck Finley. He's got an office over on Mortlake Street some place."

"O.K.," I said.

He gulped again. "You don't need to worry about no five bucks, mister, I was just kidding!"

I took a five out of my wallet and gave it to him.

"We made a deal, kid," I said, then walked back to the car.

It was two-thirty when I walked into Finley's office. There was a dyed blond receptionist who looked like she had died a couple of years back but nobody had done anything about it.

"Name?" she said.

"Wheeler, I——"

"Save it!" she said. "He ain't doing anything—go right on in."

I opened the door of Finley's private office and walked in. He was sitting behind a desk littered with photos and the remains of his lunch. He was fat and bald and repulsive.

'My name's Wheeler," I said, "I'm a—"

He held up a hand. "Don't tell me, brother, I'll tell you." He looked me over carefully then shook his head. "No," he said, "I have to tell you, brother, you just don't have it!"

"I saw a doctor," I said, "he fixed it."

"You don't have the looks to get to first base on a big deal," he said. "Character playing?" He shook his head again. "I can see it from here, you just don't have the character for it! Extras, they can get them in Hollywood without paying the bus fare from Pine City. You can pay the receptionist on your way out, sorry."

"Pay?"

"Five bucks for a consultation," he said. "You wanted to

know whether you could get into pictures, didn't you? That's what you come here for, wasn't it? It takes my time, my expert knowledge—it cost me a lot of hard cash to be an expert."

"An expert what?"

"What do you——" his eyes narrowed. "Just who are you anyway?"

I showed him my shield, and his face suddenly looked thinner.

"I'm running a legitimate business here, Lieutenant. I'm sorry I shot my mouth off when you came in, I——"

"Shut up!" I said.

"Was I talking?" he said nervously.

"You've got a girl on your books here named Rita Tango. I want to talk about her."

"Anything you say, Lieutenant."

He got up from his desk and pulled open the top drawer of the filing cabinet.

"Rita Tango," he said, thumbing through the files. "Jesus Christ, what a name. No imagination. Unless maybe it's her real name, and that I don't forgive." He pulled out a file, dropped it onto his desk, and slumped back into the chair.

"Tell me about her," I said.

"She's registered with me," he said. "A bit-player. I get her parts here and there."

"You got a photo of her?" I said.

"Sorry, Lieutenant, I don't."

I took the file off his desk; he made a half-hearted grab for it, but I put the flat of my hand against his face and pushed him back into his chair.

I opened the file. There was only a sheet of paper that had her name, address, and phone number on it, and half a dozen photos showing her in nude, lascivious poses that made up in tawdry enthusiasm what they lacked in art.

"She takes a good photo," I said, dropping the file back onto the desk. "How does she look with clothes?"

He gestured vaguely with his hands. "Christ, it's the thing. They all take off their clothes sooner or later, bit of a come-on, lie there with their legs wide open, no hidden charms. You gotta show the merchandise if you want to get anywhere. That's the way most of them figure it, anyway."

"When did you last see her?"

"About ten days back," he said. "Two weeks, I'm not sure."

"Who gave her the job?"

He jumped. "Job? I don't know what———"

"She's dead," I said evenly. "You weren't in on that as well?"

He tucked his fingers inside the edge of his crumpled collar and pulled on it. "Dead?" he repeated hoarsely.

"Who gave her the job?"

"I got a phone call," he said. "A week-end party, maybe longer. I figured there was going to be some big names at the party and they wanted to make sure there wasn't any trouble. Rita was the girl for it, she just has a room in town, no folks, no strings. . . . Dead, you say?"

"Who made the phone call?"

"A woman."

"So she was a female, what was her name?"

"I'll get crucified for this," he said.

"You might," I said, "if you don't give me the name."

"O.K., O.K.! It was Kay Steinway."

"You'd done business with her before?"

He shook his head. "But she said Kent Fargo had told her to ring me, that was good enough reference."

"How did she pay off? Did she come in here, or did you go to her?"

"She put fifty bucks in the mail," he said. "Cash."

"All right," I said, and picked up his phone. I rang Johnson, the boss of the Vice Detail, and gave him the name and the address.

"Something exciting, Al?" he asked.

"You want to get into pictures?" I said. "Why not be an intimate entertainer instead? We have clients who'll pay fifty bucks for an evening—and the liquor is free."

"One of those!" he said. "I love those characters. I'll have a couple of guys over there in about ten minutes. Thanks."

"My pleasure," I said and hung up.

I walked over to the window and watched until I saw the car stop outside and two men get out and cross the sidewalk to the front entrance.

"Your last clients are on their way up," I said to Finley. I picked up the file from his desk. "You won't need this any more."

I walked out of the office closing the door behind me.

"Mr. Wheeler!" the receptionist said. "I got your receipt made out already. That's five dollars."

I shook my head sadly. "Honey," I said, "you aren't worth it."

Chapter Fourteen

"You feeling all right, Al?" Paula asked, glancing at her watch. "There's only fifty minutes to go now. You aren't nervous or anything?"

"Just thirsty," I said.

"We can take care of that," she said. "I'll have Lonny Hughes look after you while I'm changing. You sure you've got it O.K.?"

I looked at the battery of arc lights, the cameras, the trail of cables across the studio floor. "I think so, honey," I said.

"It won't be so tough," she said soothingly. "Just the three of us, Kay, you and myself, sitting around a table and talking. You remember the signs?"

"Sure," I said. "Speed up, slow down, two minutes to go. ... I remember them all right."

"That's fine," she said. "Then I'll have Lonny look after you while I go and change." She glanced down at the blue slacks she was wearing. "My working clothes," she explained.

"They suit you," I said.

"Wouldn't like people to think I wear the pants around here," she said with a chuckle. "That's what the crew believes, but I can be very sweet sometimes. Sweet and demure. Hey, Lonny!" she yelled suddenly.

A character with graying hair, who looked as if he should have been on Wall Street instead of television, came over to us.

"Look after Al while I get changed, honey," Paula said to him. "And I think he's thirsty."

"Sure," Hughes said. "I can take care of that right away. Follow me, Lieutenant!"

We finished up in someone's private office. Hughes opened up the built-in icebox and started making the drinks.

"What will you have, Lieutenant?"

"Scotch on the rocks," I said automatically, "with a little soda."

"A man after my own heart," he smiled.

He handed me the glass a few seconds later. "Here's to tonight's show," he said. "It should be a smash! You know, you're a lucky man, Lieutenant. You're getting the kindest treatment anybody ever got on this show!"

"How's that?" I asked him.

His grin broadened. "Well, every other time we're putting over a controversial subject—that means somebody who's got something to hide—Paula has a whole trunkful of gimmicks to make them come across."

"I don't get it," I said.

"She's a smart girl, that Paula!" he said. "That 'blue' gimmick has gone over big, you know. Everything blue—even to a blues musical theme." He shook his head and grinned. "But I was talking about getting people to open up, wasn't I?"

"I think so," I said cautiously.

"Paula always talks to them before the show," he said. "She always asks them if there's one particular topic they don't want to discuss, because if they tell her about it, she won't mention it on the show."

Hughes chuckled appreciatively. "You can guess what the first question is she asks them!"

"There's nothing like ethics, is there?" I said.

"You know how it is in this business," he said. "Dog eat dog. It'll be cat eat cat with Kay Steinway on tonight!" He sobered down a little. "Imagine Kay being mixed up with all these murders! That guy Fargo trying to knock her off!"

"You know Kay Steinway?" I asked him.

"Sure," he said. "I had her on the floor at the Excelsior."

"Nobody cared?" I asked politely.

He grinned. "Technical term, Lieutenant. Studio floor. I was a director with Excelsior at the time. That was the name of Norman Coates's outfit."

"I see," I said.

"Sure," he said. "When I think about how it was then! Manning was right on top—they must have made a fortune out of his pictures. After he died, the box office was even better. People take a morbid interest in seeing a star who's dead."

"Maybe Fargo thought of that," I said.

"I wouldn't be surprised," he said. "The only thing I'm sorry about is that Morgan kid, the elder sister, I mean. . . . Hell! Janice! It's easier to call her that after knowing her by that name the last two years. I'm sorry she walked out of that window. If you'd known Georgia Brown, Lieutenant, you'd agree with me that Janice should have got a medal for killing her!"

"Is that a fact?"

"She used to line up the kids for Manning," he said. "And just for the kicks she'd get out of watching him go into action with them. Somehow it wouldn't have been so bad if she'd done it for money!"

"Yeah," I said.

"Another drink, Lieutenant?"

"I don't think so, thanks."

He checked his watch. "I guess we'd better get you over to make-up."

"Make-up?"

"Sure. Don't worry," he grinned. "We won't give you a false mustache or anything. Just a little pancake to take out the creases."

"Creases?"

"You're beginning to sound like a star already, Lieutenant!"

The time went fast. Ten minutes before the show was due to start Hughes brought me up to the table, where the other two were already seated.

Paula was wearing a low-cut deep blue gown which set her figure off to stunning perfection. Kay Steinway's gown was gunmetal in color and looked very elegant and expensive, as well as being cut a good two inches lower at the neckline than Paula's. She looked very cool and composed.

I sat down on the vacant chair between the two of them and Kay smiled at me slowly.

"I haven't seen you around lately, Al," she said huskily. "You must have been busy."

"Oh, he's been busy all right," Paula said easily. She gave me a heavy-lidded look. "Isn't that right, Al?"

"So you managed to get your hooks into him, too," Kay remarked sourly. "You disappoint me, Al. I thought you had better taste." She turned back to Paula. "Or is it because he

THE BLONDE

prefers older women with experience? Frankly, to me, it seems such a waste."

"Well, at least he knows I'm not a cheap whore," Paula said sweetly.

Kay chuckled softly. "Oh, no, dear. There's nothing cheap about you. Why, the going rate for a night must be all of fifty bucks with a bit of french thrown in for good measure."

"And where do you see yourself?" Paula asked. "In the bargain basement, on the remnants counter?"

Hughes came over to the table. "Five minutes to go, folks," he announced. "Everything O.K.?"

"Just fine," Kay said from between her teeth. "We're just one big happy family." She gestured gracefully with one hand in Paula's direction. "Have you met the skeleton in the closet?"

Hughes beat a hasty retreat, and I wished I could have gone with him.

A brooding silence set in and it lasted until the show opened. The second before the cameras became alive, the two girls broke into brilliant smiles.

It wasn't so bad once the show started. I could concentrate on Paula and almost forget the cameras and the brilliant lights. She handled it superbly. This was an on-the-spot show from Pine City, she told her audience. The city that had been stunned in the last seventy-two hours by two brutal murders, a suicide, the revelation that Lee Manning had been murdered three years before, and that even now a killer, Kent Fargo, was still loose within the city limits.

It was all good stuff. She built it up beautifully, then introduced Kay. She questioned Kay about the night Fargo and Dunn had arrived at her house.

Kay was equal to the occasion. She described the scene and you could see the fear shining out of her eyes as she faced Dunn again. She built me up into something more than a hero, using me carefully as a foil for her own part in the affair.

I glanced at my watch once and suddenly realized that twenty minutes of the show had gone already. There was a break for the commercial, and then Paula turned to me.

I told my story as quickly as I could. When I'd brought it up to the point where Blain had been arrested and told his story about the blackmail photograph, Paula smiled her thanks at me.

"It's a terrible story, Lieutenant," she said. "But a fascinating one. Is there any further comment you would like to make?"

"A couple of things happened today," I said. "You might like to hear about them."

"Of course, Lieutenant," Paula said. "Please tell us."

I went quickly over what had happened from when I talked to Murphy to the time Chuck Finley's business came to an abrupt halt.

Paula looked at me with a puzzled look in her eyes for a moment after I'd finished.

"I'm sorry, Lieutenant," she said, "but I'm not quite sure I get the full implication of what you have just told us. Would you please explain further?"

"It's basically simple," I said. "The missing girl, Rita Tango, is the girl who was blown to pieces in that apartment. *Not* Georgia Brown. The real Georgia Brown hired her as a decoy. She probably planned to murder the girl herself, but Janice Jorgens beat her to it."

"Wait a minute, Lieutenant!" Kay said tautly. "You said that man—Finley was it?—told you *I* called him and hired the girl? That's a lie!"

"Is it?" I said. "The one thing that worried me after hearing Blain's story was why Georgia Brown would want to throw away the perfect blackmailing setup she had. There could only be one reason—if she'd made enough money, not only out of the blackmail but maybe out of something else as well, she could want to retire. But if she stopped the blackmail there was always the danger that Fargo might catch up with her."

"I see what you mean, Lieutenant!" Paula said breathlessly. "If Georgia Brown died, then nobody would keep on looking for her. So she hired the Tango girl to impersonate herself, planning to murder her!"

"That's exactly right," I said.

"What you are really saying, Lieutenant," Paula faltered for a moment, "is that . . . Kay Steinway is really Georgia Brown!"

"I am not!" Kay screamed wildly.

"That's the way it looks," I agreed, ignoring Kay's out-

THE BLONDE

burst. "Fargo said it was Kay Steinway who called him and lied about Coates having the negative. Finley said it was Kay Steinway who called him and booked the Tango girl——"

"Lies!" Kay dissolved into a flood of tears. "All lies!"

"And if you remember," I went on talking to Paula, "as you told me in the first place, Georgia Brown was going to name names on your show, and she mentioned four. Fargo, Blain, Coates . . . and Kay Steinway."

"I do remember, Lieutenant!" Paula said excitedly. "Those were the four names she . . ." Her voice died away.

There was a sudden, deathly silence. Kay stopped crying and raised her head, her tear-filled eyes open wide.

"That's right," I said. "But it wasn't Georgia Brown who gave you those names—it was Rita Tango. And that's impossible—*she* couldn't have known any of those people. The only person who could have named those four people was the real Georgia Brown herself."

Paula shook her head faintly. "I'm . . . confused," she said. "The excitement, it's been too much."

"You were really very clever," I said. "You changed not only your appearance but your personality. You had your looks altered by plastic surgery. You built a whole new personality around this television show, with the accent on the color blue. Everything about you was blue—who would wonder why you had your hair dyed the same color? It fitted with the rest of the gimmick."

"You must be crazy!" she said.

"You were a good enough actress to imitate Kay Steinway's voice when you phoned Finley to hire Rita Tango," I went on. "And again when you rang Fargo and told him Coates had the negative. But Janice Jorgens pulled a fast one on you by killing Rita Tango. She thought she was avenging the death of her sister."

Paula bit down hard on her lower lip.

"After Janice walked out of that window," I said, "you played it real cool. You told me the story about Janice giving you a sealed envelope to hold for her, and said you'd get it for me. You walked into your own suite, sealed the negative in an envelope and brought it back to me."

"I won't listen," she said tautly. "I won't——"

"Didn't you notice the way I handled it?" I asked her gently. "How careful I was to hold it by the edges? We checked the prints before we made the photograph from it. There was only one set of fingerprints on that negative, Paula—yours!"

She slumped back into her chair and looked at me. Her eyes were suddenly tired. "All right," she said sullenly, "I'm Georgia Brown."

Chapter Fifteen

"You ham!" Lavers said bitterly. "That story about checking her prints on that negative. It's not true, is it?"

"No," I admitted. "But it seemed like a good clincher at the time. It was something I should have done, but I didn't."

"Supposing she still denied it?" he said. "What would you have done then?"

"How could she?" I grinned. "Like I said, Rita Tango couldn't have given her those four names, only the real Georgia Brown could have known them. She couldn't talk her way out of that."

"I'm glad she didn't try anyway," Lavers grunted. "I guess we'd better get her downtown and into a cell."

"Sometimes I'm not quite as bright as I could be," I said modestly. "I'm just remembering something someone once told me."

"What are you raving about now?" Lavers demanded.

"Let me play a hunch, Sheriff," I pleaded with him. "Let me take Paula up to Fargo's penthouse for an hour, no more. It won't make any difference to things as they are now."

"If you're suggesting I'd let this woman have a last fling with you, Wheeler!" Lavers face was apoplectic.

"I want to use her as bait," I said. "If she wants a last fling, she can fling herself out of the window the way Janice Jorgens did. I want to play a hunch and use her as bait for Fargo."

Lavers sneered contemptuously: "You don't think he'd be dumb enough to come anywhere near that penthouse of his! We've had a stake-out around that building since the night he killed Coates!"

"I said it's a hunch, Sheriff," I said patiently. "If I'm wrong, what have you lost—an hour. Nothing more."

He hesitated for a moment. "All right. Sometimes I think I'm as crazy as you are. One hour—no more, no less!"

"Thank you, Mr. Shylock," I said. "Shall we go?"

The Sheriff sat in the front of the car beside the driver. Paula Reid sat between me and Polnik in the back. She didn't say a word the whole way.

We stopped outside the building and Lavers looked at me.

"All right, Wheeler, this is your affair. You have one hour exactly. The Sergeant and I will wait for you here in the car."

"Thank you, sir," I said.

I took Paula's arm and propelled her across the sidewalk to the front door of the office block. One of the guys on permanent stake-out there came over and opened the front door for us. He gave me the key to the penthouse and then we went inside.

We rode the elevator to the top floor. I unlocked the front door of the penthouse, opened it and stood to one side to let Paula in first.

She walked in and I followed her, switching on the lights and closing the door behind me.

"Let's get this over with," she said shortly. "What's the idea of bringing me in here?"

"A hunch," I said. "Maybe it's no good. We'll find out."

"It's a pity that bomb didn't take you with it!" she said savagely.

"Make yourself comfortable," I said. "We're going to be here for an hour, anyway."

I walked through the other rooms slowly. The penthouse looked just the same as it had the last time I'd been here. I came back into the living room and saw Paula had opened up the bar and poured herself a drink.

"You can pour me one too," I said.

"You can go to hell!" she said. She took her glass with her and walked over to an armchair, then sat down.

I went over to the bar and got behind it. "If I have to pour my own drinks, I'm going to be barman and give my feet a break," I said.

She pointedly ignored the remark and looked out of the plate-glass window at the view. I took the .38 out of its holster and put it on the small shelf underneath the bar counter. Then I poured myself a drink.

THE BLONDE 115

The time seemed to drag by slowly. I finished the drink and poured myself another.

"You want another drink?" I asked her.

"You can go to hell!" she said.

"You said that."

She looked out of the window again. I sipped the second drink and looked at the dead fish floating on top of the water in the tanks. Maybe they were symbolic. Then I blinked. One of the tanks was moving of its own accord.

It moved quickly, swinging though an angle of ninety degrees, and a whole section of the wall behind the tank went with it.

And a moment later Fargo stepped into the room.

"Don't move, copper," he said. "I'd as soon let you have it first, anyway!"

I looked at the gun in his hand and shook my head. "I'm a statue," I said. "Just keep the dogs away from me."

Paula sat staring at him, her hands gripping the arms of the chair so that the knuckles showed white.

"Hello, Georgia," Fargo said softly. "You look different all right. I would never have picked you!"

"Where does the hole in the wall lead to?" I asked him. "Your offices downstairs?"

"I had the stairway built in when I bought the place," he said. "I thought it could come in useful sometime. There's a peephole cut in the wall there just behind the tanks."

"That's where you've been all the time? In your offices downstairs?"

"Sure," he said. "I've been coming up here when I felt like a drink. If you coppers were only half smart you would have noticed Fargo Enterprises closed down for business the day after you shot me in Kay Steinway's place. The only guy who goes in and out is the office manager, and he's a friend of mine!"

"Where did I get you?" I asked interestedly.

"In the shoulder," he said. "It was a lousy shot. I got it fixed the same night by a doctor. I got a lot of influence in this town!"

"I guess you have," I said. "You caught Paula's show on television tonight?"

"I watched it up here," he said, then added abruptly. "We've stalled enough!"

He half turned toward Paula and she shrank back into the chair.

"You got it coming, Paula," he said slowly. "For three years you made a monkey out of me. Then you really fixed me good. You told me it was Coates, and I had taken care of him before I looked for that negative. I would have taken care of Kay Steinway if it hadn't been for Wheeler over there. And it was all your idea."

"Kent!" she said in a low, imploring voice. "Kent, you know you were the only one I ever really—"

"Sure." He laughed harshly. "You were crazy about me! Oh sure. Well, now I'm gonna show you just how crazy I am about you!"

He pressed the trigger and the gun exploded into sound that re-echoed around the walls of the room. With half her head shot away and blood spattering everywhere, Paula's body slumped back in the chair. Fargo kept on pressing the trigger until the gun was empty.

The room was suddenly quiet. Paula was slumped against the ripped and bloodstained upholstery of the chair.

Fargo looked up at me and grinned, almost sheepishly.

"That's something I always used to tell Charlie," he said. "Never lose your temper, because you're liable to do something stupid!" He looked down at the empty gun in his hand. "I guess I did something stupid!"

"I guess you did," I agreed.

He tossed the gun onto the carpet and started to walk toward me slowly. "Well, that's it. You can take me in, copper!"

"Not this trip, Fargo," I told him.

I lifted the .38 clear of the counter and shot him carefully, twice in the chest. The impact of the slugs hitting him spun him around and he dropped across the chair on top of Paula's body.

I just had time to finish my drink before they arrived.

Lavers came to a stop in the middle of the room, staring down at the two bodies in the chair. Behind him were Polnik and the rest of them.

"What in hell happened!" Lavers gurgled.

I pointed to the opening in the wall behind him. "He came in through there—he's been hiding out in his own offices on

THE BLONDE

the next floor all the time. One moment there was just the two of us up here, and the next second, Fargo was here."

"What then?"

"It happened so quickly," I said. "Fargo had a gun in his hand. As soon as he saw her, he started pumping slugs into her. She was dead before I had a chance to get my own gun. As soon as I got my gun out, I shot him, of course."

"That was all?"

"I thought it was enough," I said.

"If it happened so fast, how the hell do you know that stairway leads to his offices!"

"We're on the top floor of the building now," I said. "Where else would it lead—Mars?"

"All right!" Lavers growled.

He bent down and picked up Fargo's gun and examined it.

"His gun's empty!"

"Is it?" I said carefully. "You mean, that he couldn't have shot me even if he wanted to, Sheriff?"

"I should have known better than let you play one of your so-called hunches!" Lavers said.

"Anyway," I shrugged my shoulders, "it saves the State an expense."

Lavers looked at me for a few seconds, his eyes thoughtful: "You keep on saying that, Wheeler," he said dryly. "Now I come to think of it, it makes an interesting sequence." He ticked them off on his fingers. "That first chick, the blonde, gets blown to pieces because you press a button. Coates gets murdered because you don't get over to his hotel fast enough. You shot Fargo's man and killed him. You exposed Janice Jorgens as the first girl's killer and she suicided. You exposed Paula Reid as the real Georgia Brown and she gets murdered by Fargo."

He glared at me. "Maybe we should call you Death-Watch Wheeler!"

"I'll try and stay out of your woodwork, Sheriff," I assured him.

He looked around the room again. "There's something here that stinks!" he said.

"The goldfish," I said. "They've been dead a couple of days."

"Maybe I should get smart," he said tiredly. "All right. I'll settle for the goldfish!"

"Can I go home now?" I asked him. "This is my free week end, remember?"

It was just after midnight when I finally did get home. I opened the front door of the apartment and saw the lights were on. I heard music. I took a step forward and fell flat on my face.

I climbed back onto my feet slowly and looked down at the bulging overnight bag. Toni was curled up on the couch, watching me with mild interest showing in her eyes. "You always do that," she said. "Maybe it's a conditioned reflex."

"How many planes have you missed now?" I snarled.

She smiled. "I lost count. I heard about you being on television tonight and I couldn't miss that, could I?"

"The janitor let you in again?"

"We're old friends now," she said. "He likes my mind. He says the instinctive grasp I have of important global and domestic issues stimulates him."

"I need a drink again," I said, and went about getting one.

"Did you find Fargo?" she asked.

"Yeah," I said. "It took me over twenty-four hours to get that crack of yours about him being so anxious about his office. You knew about that secret stairway?"

"I knew," she said. "What happened to Fargo?"

"I took Paula Reid up there with me," I said. "Fargo came in through that stairway and shot her."

"And what happened to Fargo?"

"He got shot, too."

"You shot him?"

"I shot him," I agreed.

"That figures," she said evenly.

I turned around and stared at her, the two glasses in my hands. "What do you mean—that figures?"

"You have a hero complex, Al," she said. "Didn't you know?"

"I never admit it," I said.

I handed her a drink and sat down beside her on the couch. "For a girl who was Fargo's plaything up to a couple of nights ago, you've got awfully smart all of a sudden."

"I majored in psychology,'" she said. "You know what it got me?"

"Tell me?"

"An office full of psychopaths," she said seriously. "So right then I decided to take advantage of the gifts bestowed upon me by Mother Nature."

She got up from the couch and stretched luxuriously so that the thin sweater she was wearing lifted up over her thighs and showed me that she was wearing absolutely nothing beneath it. I had a brief glimpse of a silver-blonde wedge between her lips. Her breasts lifted loosely upward as she stretched, then fell again when she lowered her arms.

"You have to admit that Mother Nature's been generous to me," she said contentedly.

"You never seem to wear anything much," I said. "Why did you really come back here?"

She came across to me, and sitting on my lap, squirmed around a bit until she had made herself comfortable. Beneath her smooth bare buttocks, my yard gave a leap and began to show signs of active interest. I laid one hand on her thigh and gently began to massage it.

"There's a plane at nine this morning," she said. "I could catch it."

"It so happens I have a free weekend," I told her. "So long as there aren't any interruptions."

The phone rang shrilly. Toni got up off my lap, and, with a slow upward grind of her superb behind, walked across to the table. She lifted the receiver and said crisply: "This is Mr. Wheeler's personal secretary. I'm afraid it's no use calling him this weekend. He's very busy. If you want the name of another good mortician, take a look in the directory." Then she hung up.

"You're getting to be quite an asset around here," I said admiringly.

She came back to the couch. "I can be even more of an asset," she said throatily, "if you'll just take those clothes off." Then she knelt down in front of me and took hold of the zip of my trousers. "Or do you want me to do it for you? Go ahead, enjoy your drink. Just let me do what I want."

Which is exactly what I did.

Girl in a Shroud

Chapter One

"It's a mortuary, right?" Sergeant Polnik said in a determined voice. "So where else would you find a stiff?"

"But it doesn't belong here!" The little man with the rosy cheeks and sunken eyes positively twitched in agitation.

"You real sure about that?" Polnik grunted skeptically.

"My God!" The pint-sized undertaker's voice suddenly cracked with despair. "You think I wouldn't recognize her if she was one of my own clients?"

A bright shaft of early morning sunlight seared my eyeballs painfully. My watch said it was only five of eight in the A.M.—and I always figured the only way they would get Wheeler into a funeral home at that hour was to carry me, feet first.

"Lieutenant?" Polnik's heavy eyebrows knit into a bristling hedge. "I figure this guy is a nut!"

"A mortician," I corrected him. "But then, I guess it's only a question of degree."

"Lieutenant Wheeler!" The little man swallowed hard. "Are you going to take a look at this unknown corpse someone sneaked into my establishment, or just stand around here all morning insulting me?"

"You sure make it a hard decision, Mr. Brenner," I said slowly, "but anything to get out of this sordid sunlight."

Once inside, we were enveloped in deep gloom, and I realized sunlight didn't have a hope in hell of ever penetrating Brenner's dark stained-glass windows. Neither did fresh air, I realized a few seconds later when my nostrils were assaulted by a combination of stale fug, formaldehyde, and something I could only hope was incense.

"In the display room," Brenner muttered, leading the way.

Polnik dropped back a couple of paces. "Lieutenant!" His

whisper rasped like a buzz saw jammed in knotty pine. "What they got on *display?*"

"Don't ask!" I said with a shudder. "Not before I've had breakfast, anyway."

Brenner held open a door and we managed not to drag our feet too much over the purple carpeting that led us through. The display room was immediately explained: caskets. There might have been a dozen in the room, of various styles and materials. About half of them were on trestles; the others were propped upright along one wall.

"It's in there!" Brenner pointed dramatically toward one gleaming casket that lay on a pair of trestles with its lid swung open at one end. "I knew something was wrong the first moment I saw that lid open—I'd never leave a casket looking untidy that way! When I saw what was inside—"

"You called the county sheriff's office," I said grimly. "I do so admire a man who gets an early start, Mr. Brenner. It was exactly seven A.M.—I'd had a whole three hours' sleep already!—when the sheriff called me—"

"Five after seven when the lieutenant called me!" Polnik rasped. He glared bitterly at the little man for a long moment. "What's bugging you, you got to start work at daybreak? Can't wait to find out who's died during the night?"

"Well, really!" The whole five-feet-two inches of mortician shook with fury. "I have never—never!—been so insulted in my whole—"

His voice was suddenly drowned by a sonorous clanging sound that exploded inside my head with all the brain-splitting finality of the Doomsday Bell. Before I had a chance to recover, it sounded again—and again—five times, before my reeling mind realized that the grandfather clock standing in one corner of the room was chiming the hour of eight. By the time the sound of the last chimes died away, the inside of my head felt like a soft, pulpy mass.

"What are you trying to do?" I snarled at Brenner. "Waken the dead!"

"—I'll complain to the mayor as well!" Apparently he was still threatening reprisals for that crack of Polnik's just before the clock chimed. "Furthermore, Lieutenant, I will—" He stopped suddenly and looked at me with a peculiar expression on his face. "What was that?"

"What?" I grunted.

"A kind of whispering noise." His voice had a strained quality, as if all his nerve ends were about to snap at the same time. "I heard it distinctly just then! It—" His eyes bulged as his trembling hand pointed toward the casket again. *"Look!"*

I looked and saw the lid slowly moving sideways across the top of the casket. Polnik and the mortician made a kind of whimpering sound in unison; I would have joined them only my vocal cords were suddenly paralyzed. Then the lid tilted and fell to the floor with a clattering sound. Faintly I heard the sound of footsteps coming down the hallway outside, and silently pleaded that whatever it was would open the door first—not just walk straight through it.

The corpse sat up in the casket, smiled brightly at the three of us and said, "Good morning!"

Brenner whimpered again and backed away, goggle-eyed as he stared at the smiling corpse, until he came up against the wall, where he leaned in a gasping catatonic state. Vaguely I wondered if his mind was about to become permanently unhinged the way mine was.

The smile slowly faded from the corpse's face. "Just what are you gentlemen doing in my bedroom?" she asked coldly.

"Chee!" Polnik said thickly. "A real live vamp!"

"In a casket?" I croaked. "You have to be kidding!"

"A female Dracula yet!" His face corrugated alarmingly with the immense effort of turning that rusty crank inside his skull. "You know something, Lieutenant?" His voice was a confidential whisper. "She's confused."

"She's confused?" I gibbered. "What the hell do you think I am!"

"Got her timetable all fouled up!" His whisper became conspiratorial. "You tell her, Lieutenant, that vamps is supposed to sleep in the day, and go get their transfusions at night!"

The corpse clambered awkwardly out of the casket, then stood facing us, her hands absently smoothing out the wrinkles from her black silk shroud.

"I don't understand any of this." Her voice shook slightly. "Will you please explain to me what it's all about?"

She was a slim girl with long dark hair, who would have been beautiful except for the air of confident authority bordering on arrogance which showed in her cold dark eyes and set her mouth in a petulent mold. The black shroud was of thin silk which clung tentatively to her body, to the ripe insolent thrust of her smallish breasts, hips, and thighs. Beneath it I could just discern the outline of a pair of abbreviated briefs. Her nipples prodded the black silk, making small, buttonlike indentations. Whatever else she was, I realized with a swift surge of relief, a corpse she wasn't—and obviously never had been.

"I'm waiting for an explanation!" she snapped.

Polnik peered at me hopefully. "You figure maybe daylight saving has gotten her confused, Lieutenant?"

"Ah, shut up!" I snarled. "I—" Then it was my turn to do likewise as I heard the door close firmly in back of me, and remembered those footsteps I'd heard coming down the hall.

"Good morning, Vicki!" A rich baritone filled the room. "Sleep well in your new bed?"

"Daddy!" The tension drained swiftly from the girl's face, and a look of warm adoration showed in her eyes. "I thought I must be having a nightmare!"

I turned around slowly and looked at the new arrival. A tall, lean man somewhere in his middle fifties, with the same air of casual authority about him the girl had. His face was striking, like a cruel, clever caricature of a real face. A thatch of wiry gray hair surmounted a high-domed forehead, and bushy black eyebrows arched satanically above his long aquiline nose. The heavy-lidded eyes seemed to hold an infinite understanding that had somehow long ago progressed beyond tolerance and now viewed the whole world with a darkly cynical contempt. The skin, stretched taut across the bone structure of his face, was covered by a fine mesh of wrinkles. I had a weird feeling it must be a hundred years older than the rest of him.

"And you, sir?" He boomed at me suddenly. "Obviously you don't belong to this singular establishment. The reverence is lacking, the smarmy dignity. No professional ghoul would dream of keeping his hands in his pockets inside his own mortuary."

He gave Polnik a momentary glance, then sneered. "This one is instantly betrayed by the inevitable combination of a custodian of the law. But you, sir? Could it be you are a body snatcher, a producer of pornographic movies checking out a new setting?"

GIRL IN A SHROUD

"Hey!" Polnik growled threateningly, boiling over with loyal indignation. "You can't talk to the lieutenant like that. He's easily hurt, particularly so early in the morning, when his defenses are down."

"A *lieutenant* of police?" He chuckled. "I can see I didn't set my sights low enough."

Brenner was still leaning back against the wall, moaning and holding his throat, his eyelids fluttering dramatically.

"This must be the ghoul himself." The rich baritone bounced off the four walls and hammered my eardrums unmercifully. "The sight of a corpse actively revolting against his shoddy merchandise was too much for the little man's flabby mind, I presume."

"Talk up a storm all morning if you want," I said coldly, "but sometime you have to come up with an explanation of just what, exactly, the girl was doing here, asleep in one of Mr. Brenner's brand-new caskets."

"I reluctantly accept your logic, Lieutenant," he said gracefully. "I am Max Landau, and the young woman you have been studying so carefully—with a purely official eye I'm sure, Lieutenant—is my daughter Vicki."

"Don't be so modest, Daddy," the girl said in a strictly partisan voice. "Doctor Max Landau, of the Landau Research Foundation, and—"

"It isn't relevant!" Landau snapped. "Frankly, Lieutenant, this is the result of a rather stupid practical joke that misfired. You see—"

"You mean," Brenner whimpered, "she wasn't dead at all?"

Landau looked at him like he was studying an unknown species of bug through a microscope. "My dear, sir, I do apologize," he boomed theatrically.

"If you hadn't panicked in the first place," I said, glaring at Brenner, "and had stayed long enough to check if your corpse was breathing—I could still be enjoying a peaceful night's sleep!"

"Entirely my fault, sir!" Landau beamed into the little man's stricken face, and gently patted his back. "I must make amends for my churlish thoughtlessness which has caused you all this emotional stress! Shall we say a hundred dollars—and my profound apologies?"

"Well—" a faint avaricious gleam sparked in Brenner's sunken eyes "—I guess there's no real harm done, is there?"

"A practical joke that misfired?" I repeated Landau's words in contemptuous disbelief. "Just what kind of a nut are you, Doctor?"

"Listen you!" Vicki Landau said furiously. "Don't you dare talk to my father like that! I'll have you know he's one of the top—"

"That's enough, my dear!" Landau snapped, with a touch of steel in his voice. "The lieutenant is quite justified in his attitude and you won't help matters by trying to impress him with my professional achievements. Right now I not only appear to be a half-baked idiot, I even feel like one!"

He turned toward me with a gentle smile on his lips, and his dark eyes were ruefully apologetic. I suddenly found myself smiling back at him, and realized just how powerful a force of personal charm he had when he chose to exert it.

"We are a somewhat eccentric family, Lieutenant," he said softly, "with a great weakness for practical jokes. My daughter is a very heavy sleeper and I have often joked about it, to a point where she claimed last night that the slightest sound inside her room would awaken her. I told her she slept like the dead and I could prove it, so she challenged me to do so."

"Daddy?" The girl stared at him blankly for a moment. "Are you sure you're—"

"Please, Vicki!" He held up his hand for silence. "It's my story and I should be the one to tell it. I thought about it, Lieutenant, and found Vicki's challenge irresistible. After she went to bed I waited an hour or so until I was sure she was sleeping soundly, then with the help of one of my associates, Kaye Allen, carried Vicki downstairs and into my car. This was the first private mortuary we came to, and the casket in this room seemed ideal." He shrugged. "So we put Vicki into it, made sure the lid was open at one end and she had plenty of air, then left. I came back about eight, as you know, intending to wake Vickie so she could see my proof positive for herself. Unfortunately, my good friend here—" he patted Brenner's back encouragingly "—had decided to get an early start, and that's how all the trouble arose."

I looked at the girl. "Let's hear your version, Miss Landau."

"I don't remember anything, Lieutenant, from the time I went to bed last night until I woke up this morning inside

GIRL IN A SHROUD 129

that—thing!" She nodded toward the casket. "I heard voices and thought someone was inside my bedroom, so I sat up to take a look—and I guess you know the rest." Her forehead creased momentarily, while the fingers of her right hand plucked at the silken shroud. "Daddy—I wasn't wearing this thing when I went to bed last night?"

"That was one of Kaye's inspired suggestions," he said and chuckled briefly. "She dressed you in it while I was getting the car out."

"It never occurred to you, Doctor Landau," I snarled at him, "that maybe your daughter wouldn't sleep through until you got back here? The thought that maybe she could wake up in the middle of the night and find herself inside a casket in a mortuary, didn't worry you at all? You figure your daughter's got nerves of sprung steel, or what?"

He chuckled again, and somehow managed to give that ancient wrinkled face a look of boyish embarrassment at having been caught out again.

"I see I have no choice but to confess, Lieutenant!" His shoulders lifted in an expressive shrug. "And now the second barrel of my practical joke misfires! There was no chance of Vicki waking up during the night, Lieutenant, because I'd sneaked a very adequate dose of sedative into that strange brandy and milk nightcap she always drinks before retiring. I confess, I cheated a little."

"That's my father," Vicki said, her shining eyes belying the sneering tone of her voice. "Got all the scruples of a tomcat when it comes to a practical joke!"

"Remind me never to call him when I'm sick," I grunted.

"Yeah," Polnik said hoarsely. "I bet you could walk into his office with a busted arm and come out wearing glasses!"

"Are you and your stooge quite finished, Lieutenant?" Landau asked bleakly.

"Not quite," I told him. "You made a real smooth transition there awhile back. How did it go? 'This was the first private mortuary we came to,' you said, 'and the casket in this room seemed ideal.' Just how did you get inside the mortuary, Doctor, to find this ideal casket?"

He rubbed one bony finger against the side of his nose for a little time while he thought about it, then quickly made a decision. His left hand slid inside his coat and came out holding his wallet. A moment later he extracted a large wad of bills and started counting through it slowly.

"Let me see now, Mr. Brenner." He glanced at the mortician with grave courtesy. "As I remember, we did agree on a figure of two hundred dollars as repayment for all the discomfort and inconvenience my stupidity has caused you?"

The avaricious gleam in Brenner's eyes burst into joyous flame. "Yes, sir, Doctor Landau, takes care of everything, you bet!" His plump white fingers almost tore the wad of money from Landau's hand.

"Forced entry, Doctor?" I growled. "It could be a felony."

"There must be some mistake here, Lieutenant." The little mortician smiled happily at the sudden opportunity to repay the law for its unkind comments. "My back door is always left unlocked in case of any emergency arising, like the one Doctor Landau had last night."

"Are you quite finished now?" Landau asked me. The smug, beatific smile on his face filled me with a strong desire to erase it with a blunt instrument.

"I guess there comes a time when even a cop has to quit trying," I admitted. "Let's go, Sergeant."

Polnik took one last look through the thin black veil at the vamp's delectable pink and white flesh tones, then sighed gently—it sounded like a shower of wet concrete emptying out of a mixer into a bucket, but then, nobody's perfect, I figured philosophically.

"I still figure I should explain daylight saving to her, Lieutenant," he muttered in bashful, gravel-like tones.

There was a kind of awesome fascination about the thought of the sergeant wrestling with that problem, and I was almost tempted to let him go ahead—but who wanted to stand around inside a private mortuary for a couple of days?

"I guess we'd better leave that chore to the doctor," I told him.

"Good day, Lieutenant," Brenner said smugly, and moved to one side to give me a clear run to the door.

"Do me a favor next time you have a problem?" I said thinly. "Insist the county sheriff himself handles it personally."

"I shall overlook your insolence this time, Lieutenant," he said primly. "Consider yourself fortunate!"

I walked past him toward the door because there was no

GIRL IN A SHROUD   131

percentage in trading insults with the little creep, then a warning light blinked in back of my mind and stopped to reconsider the whole situation. From an objective viewpoint, my life was all too short to risk tangling with the pint-sized mortician a second time. He'd cost me a couple of hours' sleep and probably advanced my incipient ulcer by at least six months, already. Had I then, I asked myself pedantically, taken all possible steps to prevent a second meeting?

"Mr. Brenner," I said, turning back toward him slowly, "you came in here, noticed the casket lid was out of line, looked inside, thought you saw a body that didn't belong in your mortuary—then what?"

He blinked a couple of times. "I called the county sheriff's office right away! How was I to know the girl was only sleeping?"

"There are many ways of checking," I told him, and gave a wistful glance in the direction of the black silk shroud. "A couple of them could have worked out real cute."

"A dumb detective is one thing," Vicki Landau said in an acid voice. "A dirty-minded one is something else again!"

"I mean," I went on, still concentrating on the mortician, "you didn't take time out to check if you had a couple more unsolicited corpses lying around the place?"

"Of course not! You don't think—" His eyes bulged suddenly at the thought.

"Before we go, I guess we could make sure," I said tiredly. "Just take a look inside the other caskets, Sergeant."

"Sure thing, Lieutenant."

Polnik lifted the lid of the casket nearest him and peered challengingly into the interior.

"It's empty, Lieutenant." He sounded disappointed.

"What a farce!" Landau sighed softly. "But I imagine you have to invent a few simple tasks for him, here and there, so you can justify his paycheck to the unsuspecting taxpayers?"

"Gosh!" I looked at him with a wistful expression. "I wish I worked for you, Doctor. I bet it's a barrel of fun and you keep your staff in fits like epileptic, mostly?"

"Lieutenant!" Polnik's shout re-echoed around the room.

I walked over to where he stood beside the last casket to be checked, the lid still held in his hands. There was a look of triumph on his sandblasted face.

"I got to hand it to you, Lieutenant," he said in an awestruck voice. "Second sight, that's what it is, and you don't wear glasses, even!"

The casket was occupied by a young, mousy-looking character who lay peacefully with his arms neatly folded across his chest. He would have been the classic man in a crowd except for one minor detail, the bullet hole in the center of his forehead.

"Good heavens!" a mildly astonished voice said in my ear. "What on earth is Marsh doing in there?"

Landau stood beside me staring down at the body inside the casket, his bushy eyebrows making two separate question marks. The doctor, I reflected bleakly, was the kind of guy who would ask what all the noise was about when the last trumpet sounded.

"Marsh?" I growled at him.

"Robert Marsh," Landau said, "one of my associates. What the hell is he doing in that casket?"

"Playing dead," I grunted. "That bullet through his head is a big help, of course."

Behind us, I heard a thin cry from the girl in the transparent black shroud, followed by a faint whimper from the pint-sized mortician as he staggered back and thudded against the wall again. It would have been a hell of a good morning to stay at home in bed.

Chapter Two

The Landau Research Foundation was housed in an old two-story house that rambled around the center of a five-acre plot which, by the look of it, had been running wild since Creation. I followed the doctor's beat-up sedan down the rutted driveway, then parked alongside it out front of the house. I had left Polnik back at the private mortuary to wait for Doc Murphy and the meat wagon, mainly because a lieutenant was entitled to some privileges, like not having to stand around sniffing formaldehyde and making small talk with that small creep, Brenner.

By the time I caught up with them, Landau and his daughter were already inside the front hall, waiting for me at the foot of the stairs. Bright sunlight streamed in through the open front door. It gave a whole lot more brilliance to the interior than the mortuary's stained-glass windows ever had, and the thin black silk shroud was suddenly completely transparent, exposing the ripe full curves and crests and Vicki's slender rounded body. Her breasts with their small but taut nipples jutted proudly, and the pale briefs that hung low over her pelvis only barely managed to cover her crotch. When she turned slightly, I could even make out the faint line of her reverse cleavage before it disappeared into the narrow clinging strip of her briefs.

"If you're finished looking, Lieutenant?" Vicki said from between clenched teeth, "I would like to go to my room and put on some clothes."

"How could I refuse such a charmingly put request?" I said in gallant, if baroque, syntax.

She turned around quickly and walked up the stairs. I watched the gentle, groin-grabbing motion of her elegantly shaped behind until she finally disappeared.

"You're like an open book, Lieutenant," Landau said. "The lechery in your eyes is a joy to behold."

I swung on him. "Okay, Doctor," I said drily, "you've made your point. Now back to business. Let's go someplace and talk about your late associate."

"My office is just across the hall." He gestured toward a closed door opposite. "We can talk in there."

Landau's office was frowzy in its furnishings. There was a desk that was littered like a trash dump; there was a clutch of straight-backed chairs; there was a bank of steel files streaked with rust; and there was a glass-fronted bookcase housing a jammed collection of technical and medical volumes behind cracked or splintered panes. It looked like a place where the owner worked like hell all the time and never quite made a living at it.

The chair creaked as the doctor sat down behind the desk. He pushed a stack of reports to one side so he could see me without standing up again, then lit a cigarette with a pyromaniac's fastidious attention to detail. I sat opposite him on one of the uncomfortable wooden chairs, which took the kinks out of my spine with unyielding brutality, and lit myself a cigarette to keep him company.

"Tell me about Robert Marsh," I suggested.

He shrugged. "There's not much to tell, Lieutenant. He'd been with the Foundation about six months—came straight to us after he'd finished a couple of years as an intern at one of the big Eastern hospitals. I advertised for a young M.D. interested in research and he was the best available." Landau smiled wryly. "I wasn't exactly deluged by applications—we offer a miserable salary and barely adequate working conditions! But Marsh was keen, almost dedicated, I think. We shall miss him."

"Do you know anybody who could have had a reason for killing him?"

He shook his head firmly. "None. I still can't believe it happened. Marsh was a very intense, very likable young doctor who was completely absorbed in his work. He was very shy and therefore naturally reticent, but his manner was pleasant. What appalls me at this moment, is just how little I know about his personal life. I don't even know if his parents are still living, or if he has any relatives back East, even. But

GIRL IN A SHROUD

I imagine you'll find out and inform them of what's happened?"

"Sure," I said. "When was the last time you saw him alive?"

"I wouldn't swear to the exact time," Landau said slowly. "Sometime last night after dinner. We all, including Marsh, had coffee in the living room, and I know that by ten-thirty only Vicki, Kaye Allen, and I were still there. It was then we started kidding Vicki about her being a heavy sleeper, and that was the start of a damned stupid practical joke—" He gave me a sudden piercing stare from beneath those heavy eyelids. "How in the name of sanity did Marsh's body wind up in the same private mortuary we left Vicki in, Lieutenant?"

"I was about to ask you the same question," I told him.

"It makes my blood run cold," he growled. "Thinking how we left her in that casket alone in the middle of the night, while all the time Marsh's body lay there in the same room!" His mouth tightened into a hard line. "One thing, this has cured me of practical joking for all time!"

"I'm so glad Robert Marsh didn't die in vain, Doctor," I murmured.

The darkly cynical eyes stared at me hotly for a few seconds. "You stinking son of a bitch!" Doctor Landau said elegantly. "I'd like to—"

A brisk knock on the door suddenly interrupted his wistful planning for my immediate future. Then the door opened and in came a girl wearing a neat white uniform and carrying a tray of coffee.

"I thought you could probably use some coffee, Doctor," she said in a crisp voice. "Vicki just told me about last night's tragedy. I'm very sorry about Doctor Marsh. He was a loyal and cooperative colleague. I shall miss him."

"Kaye," Landau said and nodded in my direction, "this is Lieutenant Wheeler from the county sheriff's office. Lieutenant, this is Kaye Allen, one of my associates."

The girl put the tray down on the desk, then turned and looked at me expressionlessly. "Good morning, Lieutenant."

Her whitish-blonde hair was pulled straight back across her head and held in a knot at the nape of her neck. The heavy black-framed glasses windowed a pair of china-blue eyes that were as warm as an arctic winter. Her face had a well-scrubbed aseptic look and was completely devoid of makeup. It was hard to say what lay beneath the neat white uniform, even though her breasts looked good enough, and her legs were of reasonable design.

"Ah," I said, looking at her closely, "so you're the girl with the rather strange sense of humor."

"I beg your pardon?" Her voice positively crackled.

"The girl who figured a transparent black silk shroud would be the chic fashion note for private mortuaries this year," I explained. " 'Be stylish when you wake up screaming'—was that your slogan, Miss Allen?"

"Oh, that!" she said distastefully, then deliberately turned her head away from me. "I brought an extra cup for the lieutenant, Doctor. Would you like me to serve the coffee?"

"Thank you." Landau nodded. "And don't mind the lieutenant's acidulous comments. Anything more complicated than a liquor store holdup by some teen-age delinquent armed with a toy gun confuses him. Naturally his limited intellect revolts against anything that remotely resembles a complex problem, and seeks refuge in childish insults and infantile repartee. The inevitable rationalization of a semimoronic mind!"

"Of course," she said tartly.

With her back toward me, the girl leaned forward across the desk, bringing her buttocks into slight prominence, and started to pour the coffee.

"No cream, thank you," I said politely. "If I may ask you a personal question, Miss Allen. What sort of underwear do you have on?"

Her hand shook slightly and a small steaming puddle of coffee suddenly glistened on the tray. She swung around and glared at me.

"What's that supposed to mean?" she demanded.

"Just curious," I said equably. "I wondered if there was anything to compensate for the frigid, sexless appearance women like you constantly present to the world. Something black and frothy, perhaps. Then maybe we can get together and you can tell me about your fantasies. I'm sure it would make interesting hearing."

She looked at me disbelievingly. "You mean you want to hear about my fantasies?"

I shrugged easily. "It would help pass the time."

GIRL IN A SHROUD

She looked at Landau. "You're the psychiatrist," she said steadily. "What do you think? He needs help?"

"You're the biologist, Kaye," he said happily. "Maybe it had something to do with his genes."

She brought the cup of coffee across to me, and stared coldly into my face for maybe five seconds after I'd taken it from her, before she shook her head slowly.

"Yes, I'd say there is a problem here, Doctor." She spoke to Landau although she still gazed at me impersonally. "A very definite problem, but I do think it comes more within your ambit. The strain is clear enough. Black hair, blue eyes, fair skin—predominantly Nordic, of course. All that dissipation is clearly self-imposed. Nothing wrong with the genes, so I'm afraid he belongs in your department." She turned and strolled casually back to the desk. "He has a thing about frothy black underwear, which tends to indicate a taste that is rather passé."

"Now, Kaye," Landau said with immense good humor. "You take care of the genes and I'll take care of the complexes."

"Okay," I said, looking the girl right in the eye. "If we're talking about complexes, tell me what sort of complex is it that makes a girl like you hide behind starch, glasses, and insults? As any headshrinker can tell you, that's the kind who is scared to death that someone might make a pass at them, break down the barriers, and maybe open up a whole Pandora's box of sexual pleasure that she can't control. Trouble is no one will make a pass, and it's all kind of sad, isn't it?"

Two red spots were flaming in the center of Kaye Allen's cheeks as she gave me a look of absolute loathing before she almost ran out of the office. The door shut behind her, and I looked at Landau happily.

"How did I make out as an amateur psychiatrist?" I asked.

He grunted. "You were unkind, Lieutenant," he said. "You upset her."

"A hell of a lot more than the news of Robert Marsh's murder did," I said thoughtfully. "Just how many people do you have here, Doctor?"

"Apart from a woman who comes in daily to do the cleaning," he said, "just the research team, and Vicki. She cooks our food and mothers us generally, you know? There are four of us, now poor Marsh has gone. Myself, a psychiatrist,

Kaye, as you know, a biologist; a chemist, Louis Gerard, and another psychiatrist, Theodore Altman."

"What kind of research are you working on?" I asked curiously.

"Psychopharmacology primarily."

"Drugs?"

"You could put it that way—yes."

I raised my eyebrows a fraction. "Drugs of addiction, like heroin maybe?"

"No, sir!" He smiled cynically. "This foundation is purely a private enterprise relying solely for its funds on a trust established by my late wife. We have no official, or even semi-official, support, monetarily or otherwise. Therefore, to research with any of the morphine derivatives would be asking for trouble. Especially—I'm sure you'll agree, Lieutenant?—for an ex-addict such as myself?"

"You—an ex-addict?" I gaped at him.

"An occupational hazard among doctors," he said easily. "I voluntarily admitted myself to the Federal Narcotics Hospital in Lexington in the summer of 1972 and was discharged as cured six months later. I didn't lose any of my professional privileges, but if I headed up a research team devoted to investigating the finer properties of morphine, I imagine the authorities might suddenly change their minds!"

"So what are you researching, exactly, Doctor?"

"Mescaline and LSD-25—lysergic acid—primarily. So little is really known or understood of their psychopharmaceutical value. We've been working hard here for five years and our significant discoveries—?" He shrugged wearily. "Ah, well, you have enough problems of your own, without listening to mine, Lieutenant!"

"Right," I said fervently. "I'd like to talk with the other two members of your research team I haven't met."

"Of course." He pressed a buzzer concealed beneath the desk top, and maybe ten seconds later his daughter walked into the office.

Vicki Landau had changed into a pair of tight faded jeans that were closely molded to her hips and thighs and came to a prominent V at the crotch. Beneath the pale green shirt, her unconfined breasts moved loosely.

"Ask Doctor Altman and Mr. Gerard to step in here for a moment, will you?" he said.

GIRL IN A SHROUD   139

"They're out," she stated with obvious satisfaction. "Louis has gone into town to pick up some stuff from the drug house and told Kaye he'd stay in for lunch and be back late this afternoon. Doctor Altman's over at the Baystone Sanitarium. It's his day for visiting with Doctor Schulmeyer, remember?"

"I had forgotten," her father admitted. "That means he won't be back much before five, either. I'm sorry, Lieutenant."

"I'll get around to them later," I said easily. "Meantime I'd like to take a look at Marsh's room."

"Of course. Vicki, will you show the lieutenant?"

"If you insist!" she said tersely.

I followed her out of the office, up the stairs, then along a winding hallway until she finally stopped and opened a door.

"This is it," she said flatly. "I just hope he left a couple of drawers booby-trapped in the dresser!"

"Somehow I get the feeling you don't like me," I said mildly. "Am I right?"

"You're so right," she snarled. "For Christ's sake, was it necessary to say those things to Kaye? You should be ashamed."

"Crap!" I retorted. "Kaye and your father were having fun taking my ego apart, so I figured it was a game, and any number could play."

I walked into Marsh's room and stood looking around it for a few seconds while I lit a cigarette. It wasn't exactly inspiring. The furnishings were along the same strictly utilitarian lines of Landau's office. There was a bed hard up against one wall, a motheaten three-by-four rug beside it. A battered dresser leaned against the opposite wall, and an ancient robe hung forlornly from the doorknob of the closet.

"What did he do? Camp here?" I grunted.

"What do you mean?" Vicki asked coldly.

"You wouldn't call it the lived-in look, would you?" I suggested. "The guy had been living here six months and the way it looks, you'd figure he was making an overnight stop in some cheesy hotel room."

"Doctor Marsh was a dedicated man," she said in a brittle voice. "Material things—physical comfort—meant nothing to him. But that's something you wouldn't understand, Lieutenant."

"I guess not," I grunted. "What did he do for

kicks?—besides taking naps in caskets where people could shoot at him, I mean."

"Kicks?" Her voice trembled slightly. "On Saturday nights he'd have a couple of beers before dinner. I suppose that makes him an alcoholic in your book?"

"Maybe. Maybe he was a Jekyll-Hyde drinker, even on two beers. Doctor Dedicated when sober and a corpse-hunting zombie when sozzled. This maybe accounts for him lying down so calmly in the casket, you think?"

"That's a horrible thing to say!"

I ignored that and walked over to the dresser. I pulled open the top drawer and started to search through an assortment of underwear, socks, and handkerchiefs. After a couple of moments I said casually over my shoulder, "And how come when I give you my version of Marsh lying down in that box, you take it lying down?"

"What do you mean by that?" she whispered after a pause. She had come to stand just behind me and I turned. She stood there motionless, and for once the air of calm superiority had disappeared.

"I mean I'd expect you to say to me how in hell do I know he lay down in the box before he was shot, and wasn't put there afterwards? That's what I'd expect you to say, unless you knew what really happened. Who ever heard of anyone obligingly lying down in a casket at a mortuary to get shot? *you* never did, did you? Or did you?"

A flash of the old arrogance showed in her eyes. "Well, what do you know? I've heard of cops getting mad when you don't *answer* their questions for them, but this is the first I knew that you're also expected to *ask* their questions for them. I should do your work for you? How should I know whether or not he was killed there or somewhere else—or doubt that he was killed there if you say he was? You're not by any chance implying that I killed him?"

"There's always a chance of that, honey," I assured her. "Why not—if he was killed on the premises? You had all the opportunity in the world, alone with him in that private mortuary."

"You're stupid! What earthly reason would I have for wanting to kill Bob?"

"I don't know," I admitted cheerfully, "but maybe I'll find out."

"If I had killed him, you think I could just climb back into that casket and go to sleep again?" Her voice choked at the monstrous thought. "What do you think I am?"

"Well, attractive for a start," I told her truthfully, "especially in a black shroud with the sun shining right through. Bad-tempered, too, which is a shame because it will put crow's feet under your eyes before you're thirty if you don't watch it."

"You!" She swung away from me in frustrated fury. "Screw you!"

I finished with the second drawer and started on the third.

"Who were his friends?" I asked.

"We were all his friends!" she said savagely, her back still turned toward me in rigid rejection. "Daddy, Kaye, Dr. Altman, Louis—"

"I mean outside the house," I said curtly. "Did he have a girl friend?"

"Bob?" She laughed incredulously. "He was married to medicine and infatuated with medical research. I don't think he ever looked at a girl in the six months he was here."

"Not even you?"

"Not even me," she grated. "I'll admit it didn't do much for my ego, either!"

"What about men friends?"

Her head swung slowly. "He hardly ever went out. He'd get his exercise walking around the garden. I doubt if he'd even been into Pine City twice during the six months he'd been here. Why don't you believe me? Bob Marsh was—"

"I know," I said wearily, "dedicated! Did he ever talk about his friends or his family back East?"

"He mentioned his parents a couple of times, and an uncle who'd helped him through medical school—that's all I can remember."

"And he got along just fine with everybody else in the house?"

"I told you—" She turned back toward me, her mouth set in a straight line. "Look, he's dead! Why are you so determined to destroy his memory before he's buried, even?"

"I'm trying to find a motive for his murder," I grated. "The way you tell it there just can't be one!"

"There isn't." She made it a factual statement. "If you

want to know what I think—he was murdered in mistake for somebody else."

"Like who?"

"How would I know?" She sniffed disdainfully. "You're supposed to be the detective around here. Find out for yourself!"

I finished the last drawer of the dresser and drew a blank with it, the same as I had with the rest of the drawers. Vicki Landau followed me across to the closet and stood with her arms folded under her breasts while she watched me go through the pockets of the clothes hanging inside.

"You think I'm about to steal something, maybe?" I growled over my shoulder.

"I'm just fascinated, watching a real live detective at work," she sneered. "You haven't used your magnifying glass once yet."

"I save it for examining the female suspects," I explained in a conversational voice. "It would save a lot of time if you took off your clothes now, Miss Landau, while I get my glass all polished up ready." I chuckled raucously. "The last time I forgot all about polishing it up first, I had a big, bouncing chorus girl quarantined for the measles!"

"Oh, you—" She spluttered helplessly for the right words. "You're obscene and I can't stand to be in the same room with you. I'm going to get some fresh air!"

She flounced out of the room and at long last I was left alone; I never did appreciate the help of any beady-eyed suspect, when searching the personal effects of a murder victim, anyway. A couple of minutes later I realized it wouldn't have made any difference if she'd stayed, because there was nothing in the closet of interest. The robe swung gently as I slammed the door shut; I slid my fingers into the pocket and heard a rustling sound.

It was a page torn from a cheap notebook that had been neatly folded a few times into a thin strip. I smoothed it out and read the name and address neatly typed on it: *Hal Kirby*, and underneath, *Pine City Bank and Trust*.

I tucked the folded page carefully into my wallet, walked out of the room, then retraced my steps toward the front door. As I reached the bottom of the stairs, I heard the faint rustling sound of starched linen as Kaye Allen stepped out of

GIRL IN A SHROUD

Landau's office in time to meet me face to face in the hallway.

Her china blue eyes looked at me—and through me—from behind the heavy black-framed glasses, then she made to walk past me like I didn't exist. I let her get two steps ahead, then said, "Miss Allen?"

She stopped, then turned back toward me with obvious reluctance. "Yes?" Her voice was crisp and completely devoid of expression.

"When was the last time you saw Robert Marsh alive?"

"Sometime after dinner last night. He said he was going to bed—somewhere around ten-thirty, I think."

"What time did Vicki go to bed?"

"About an hour later."

"And what time was it when you dressed her in that shroud and helped Doctor Landau carry her down to the car?"

"A little after one A.M."

"How long did it take to the mortuary?"

"Twenty minutes approximately."

"How long did it take Doctor Landau to break in the back door?"

"I thought it was already open," she said evenly. "We put Vicki into the casket, made sure she had plenty of air, then came straight here. I was in bed myself before two. Does that take care of the rest of your questions, Lieutenant?"

"I guess it does," I nodded. "Thank you, Miss Allen."

I walked past her to the front door and had almost reached it when she called my name. It was my turn to stop and turn around. "Yes?" I snapped.

"It's not my field, of course," she said in an impersonal voice, "but I was thinking about that problem of yours, and frankly, I guess it adds up to just one thing."

"Which is?"

"You're aggressiveness toward women is merely a cover. Beneath it is a basic insecurity. You're intimidated by them. They frighten you."

"Is that all?" I asked politely.

"I could even take it further and say that deep down, without you knowing it, you're possibly even a latent homosexual."

"That's quite some analysis," I told her sincerely.

She nodded. "It bears thinking about. But whatever, Lieutenant, I think you're a fraud. A bargain-basement eunuch, in fact."

"Is that all now?" I said patiently.

"Yes." Her voice crackled with contempt. "That's all, Lieutenant."

I opened the front door, stepped out onto the porch, then walked slowly across to the car. I shook my head slowly in wonderment. It was amazing the things people came out with sometimes. It was the first time ever that anyone had accused me of being a fag. But then, I thought, it mightn't be so bad at that. The way things were going, it was becoming a highly fashionable thing to be, and until now I had always just missed being in on the trends.

Chapter Three

Mr. Castle was the president of the Pine City Bank and Trust, and he managed to keep the warm friendly smile of your neighborhood banking buddy on his face, even after he discovered I was a cop and not a new account.

"Kirby?" He shook his head regretfully. "No Lieutenant, there's nobody by that name employed in the bank."

"Maybe he has an account here?" I suggested.

"There is a Henry Kirby who has an account with us," he acknowledged. His smile grew a little smug around the edges. "Although I doubt if our Mr. Kirby is the criminal you're looking for!"

"I'm not looking for any criminal," I said patiently. "I'm looking for a Hal Kirby who is a friend of someone who had a bad accident this morning."

"Oh?" He looked contrite. "I'm sorry I misunderstood you. Our Mr. Kirby has been with us for nearly three years now, and we're delighted with him."

"You mean he borrows money all the time?" I said.

"Our Mr. Kirby?" Castle looked shocked at the thought. "Hardly! He's a man of substance—investments, I understand. I only met him once—when he opened the account. An extremely pleasant chap, as I remember."

"Maybe you could get his address for me," I suggested.

"Of course."

Castle picked up the phone and spoke briskly. About thirty seconds later a harassed-looking pallid girl in her late twenties came into the room. From the mean look in her eyes she already knew she was doomed to die in single blessedness and considered it a fate worse than death itself. She presented Castle with Kirby's address neatly typed on bank stationery, gave me a sidelong glance from under short-fringed lashes, and asked would that be all.

"That will be all Miss Piper," Castle said curtly. "And next time I ask you to perform an equally simple task, I shall be grateful if it's performed with speed and dexterity, rather than sloth and tardiness!"

"Yes, sir." Her shoulders drooped under the added weight of one more injustice, then she walked listlessly out of the office again.

"Never let your staff take advantage of you, that's my slogan!" Castle said briskly. "Keep 'em on their toes the whole time, that's what I always say!"

He presented me with the address in a kind of swash-buckling Elizabethan gesture like he was Sir Francis Drake giving me the keys to the English Channel, or something. From the way he played the mannerisms of an English gentleman, I wondered if he'd ever seen one.

I thanked him politely and nearly had it made to the door when he cleared his throat loudly. "Lieutenant?"

I turned around and saw his warm smile had ripened to a point where it suggested the kind of intimate personal relationship I wouldn't want with my friendly neighborhood hooker, even.

"Have you ever considered opening an account with us?" He almost simpered. "Our services are unparalleled, you know?"

"What I've got left over at the end of the month will fit real neat into a parking meter," I confessed. "Maybe I'll come back when I quit being an honest cop."

"Well," he said heartily, "that would be just fine and we'll look forward to—" His mouth hung open for a moment while he blinked at me nervously. "How's that again, Lieutenant?"

"It's not unparalleled services I need from a bank," I explained carefully, "just money!"

He was still thinking about that when I closed the door gently and headed back toward the car parked outside at the curb.

Mr. Kirby lived in a luxurious new apartment house that looked so exclusive I wondered if the rugs were made out of imported chihuahua skins. His apartment was on the fifth

GIRL IN A SHROUD

floor, and it was a little after two in the afternoon when I rang his doorbell. After I'd left the bank I'd taken time out for a combined breakfast-lunch, which had happily given my stomach something else to think about besides garroting my throat.

The door opened and a statuesque blonde Amazon stood there watching me incuriously and shifting a wad of gum from one side of her mouth to the other. She was wearing a lightweight canary-colored sweater that was stretched tightly over the awesome thrust of her magnificent boobs, and white slacks that fit her so tightly that they looked as though they might have been painted onto her so that even the concavity of her pubis between her fleshy thighs was clearly delineated. She was built on a grand scale, her proportions were majestic. I could only stare at her.

"I'm a female," she said at last. "You never saw one before?"

"Not," I said humbly, "one like you."

She stopped chewing for a moment and her tongue absently pushed the wad of gum back to the other side of her mouth, while she tried to figure out if I'd just given her a compliment or an insult.

"You want to see Hal?" she said, getting back onto safer ground.

"Right."

"Maybe he don't want to see you."

Well, I thought, with an overgenerous body like that, one shouldn't expect much more. But it still seemed a hell of a shame to combine that body with a high-pitched strident voice and a plump face which gave her a cowlike look, enhanced by the big dumb brown eyes.

"Maybe he doesn't," I said helpfully and showed her my shield. "That's the trouble with being a cop, it gives you an inferiority complex."

"I'll go find out if he's in," she said quickly. "What's the name?"

"Wheeler."

"Sergeant?"

"Lieutenant."

"Yeah?" She pursed her lips critically. "You don't look smart enough for it, but then it's a small town, huh?"

"That's why we're so grateful when we're visited by strapping females like you."

A flicker of interest showed in her big brown eyes. "You like straps?" she asked. "Are you into bondage, that sort of thing?"

"I'm basically insecure," I told her. "Women intimidate me."

She snorted. "Maybe you're a fag."

Before I could say anything, the door closed in my face, and while I waited I conjured up an image of that great Amazon in a pair of black boots and nothing else, with a whip in her hand. She was just lifting it above her head and I was cringing at her feet waiting for the blow to fall, when the door opened again.

"Hal says he's in," she announced flatly.

I followed her inside the apartment, into the living room, which was large and ornately furnished.

"That's Hal over there." Like a professional tourist guide, she pointed out the guy sprawled on a low couch. She lowered her voice confidentially. "He's been thinking!"

"How about that?" I said admiringly.

On closer inspection, Kirby was a small thin guy with sharp features and greasy black hair. His undersized frame was wrapped in a gorgeous silk robe that had golden dragons spitting fire against a black background, and there was a white silk cravat daintily tucked around his throat. He looked like a high-class pimp on his day off, and maybe he was, with the king-sized female representing the best investment he'd made yet.

He selected a peanut from the bag on the couch beside him, tossed it into the air, and caught it neatly in his mouth. Then his narrow muddy eyes looked at me incuriously.

"You want to see me?" The voice was hoarse like maybe he'd spent too long a time barking in some carnival once.

"I'm afraid I've got bad news for you, Mr. Kirby," I said politely. "A friend of yours had a bad accident this morning."

"Friend?" he barked. "What friend?"

"Hal don't have any friends," the woman said proudly. "He figures people are just real lousy."

"Shut up, Sandra!" Kirby stared up at me with a malignant expression on his face. "What friend?"

"Robert Marsh."

He tossed another peanut into the air and caught it neatly in his mouth again. "I never heard of him!"

"That's strange," I said.

"What's strange? A cop makes a mistake and picks on the wrong Kirby—that's strange?" He laughed contemptuously. "It happens all the time, with cops!"

"He had your name written down and everything," I said, like I was only thinking out loud. "There's no mistake here, you're the right Kirby."

"What happened to him anyway?"

"He was murdered sometime last night," I said coldly.

"Nobody I know ever gets themselves murdered," he grunted. "Who was he? A hood or something?"

"He was a doctor, working with the Landau Research Foundation," I told him. "A real nice guy from what I can figure out."

"Nice guys don't get themselves knocked off!"

Most everything about the little creep was irritating, I figured, but maybe the worst thing was his infuriating habit of making statements instead of conversation.

"Hey!" He was so revitalized by a new idea that his head actually lifted a couple of inches off the couch. "You said this guy worked for some kind of research foundation, right?"

"Right."

"And he had my name written down and all, huh?"

"That's what I said."

"All these foundations are short on money, right?" he said contentedly. "Maybe they were looking for a couple of soft touches to give 'em a shot in the arm financially. Maybe he had me figured out to head up his sucker list. How about that?"

"You're already known for your generous donations to charities, research foundations, and so on, Mr. Kirby?" I asked dryly.

"Well"—he tried to look modest—"I guess there's always a first time." Sandra snorted and he closed his eyes wearily. "Shut up, Sandra."

"Maybe he was a friend of a friend?" I persisted. "You know anyone at all at the research foundation, Mr. Kirby?"

"No." He shook his head. "I got all the research I need

right here in this room, if she didn't keep opening that big mouth of hers the whole time!"

"He's strong for a little guy," Sandra said happily. "He's full of energy. Never stops. It's all those vitamins."

"Shut up!" Kirby grated.

"You've got a nice place here, Mr. Kirby," I said, looking around the room admiringly. "I guess you're in a pretty good kind of business?"

"I'm a consultant." He caught another peanut to prove it.

"Engineering?"

"Investments. I get rich making other guys rich, how about that?"

"A modern Robin Hood!" I said gravely.

"Damn fool," Kirby muttered. "Robbing the rich to give to the poor. Now where's the percentage in that, I ask you? History is full of well-meaning nut-cases."

"Come to think of it, there was a sheriff's office in his day, too," I murmured. "And they never did catch up with him, either."

"Well, it was nice meeting you, Lieutenant," Kirby said, without bothering to stifle a wide yawn. "Sandra, show the lieutenant out, huh? You want him to think we don't got any manners or something?"

"Good-bye, Mr. Kirby," I told him. "It was a real experience meeting you."

"Mostly it's only the broads say that." He smiled complacently.

"I told you," Sandra said with a chuckle. "It's the vitamins."

"Shut up, Sandra," Kirby said in a resigned voice. "So long, Lieutenant—and you can tell that research foundation to go find themselves another sucker. For Hal Kirby, charity starts at home."

"And with Sandra, you got a head start already," I respectfully agreed.

"I still think he's a fag," Sandra told no one in particular. "Beneath that rugged exterior there is a basic insecurity."

"You mustn't mind Sandra," Kirby said to me. "She gets it all from *Reader's Digest*."

When I stepped out of the apartment, big Sandra followed me and pulled the door almost shut behind her.

"That Hal!" She chuckled conspiratorially and her formidable boobs heaved alarmingly beneath the canary-yellow sweater. "He's always kidding."

"Hey," I said blankly.

"Acts so tough and all the whole time, but underneath he's just a great big kid, you know that?"

"No," I told her, "I didn't know that."

"Wouldn't give a dime to any charity—wouldn't let that research foundation make a sucker out of him!" She smiled fondly. "Don't you tell him I told you, Lieutenant, promise?"

"Cross my heart," I promised.

"It must have been a couple of nights back." She lowered her voice to a strident whisper, "I was just out of the shower and Hal didn't hear me come into the living room, I guess because I wasn't wearing anything to make a noise? He was talking on the phone and I heard him say, 'Don't worry, pal, I'll see that research foundation of yours gets taken care of.' How about that, Lieutenant?"

Sandra-baby's cowlike eyes were moist with pride in her big-hearted little man as she stared at me expectantly. "Hal is all heart, huh?"

"I guess that proves he does have an eighteen-carat gold-plated heart at that," I admitted. "He was talking to Max Landau then?"

"I wouldn't know," she said brightly. "He hung up right after that, then got mad when he saw me sitting on the couch. Hal's a real crazy man when he gets mad." There was an offbeat note of hero worship in her voice. "You should see my bruises, Lieutenant!" Modesty made her long eyelashes bat up and down a couple of times. "Or, on second thought, maybe you shouldn't?"

Chapter Four

I sat watching County Sheriff Laver's face slowly changing color from brick-red to illuminated purple, and thought almost fondly that his most endearing trait was his predictability. Right now he was about to bawl me out for having found a homicide at eight A.M. and not bothering to report back to him earlier than four P.M. I gave him a mental countdown and the opening bellow came precisely on "one!"

"Wheeler," he roared. "What the hell are you doing back in my office when you should be out questioning murder suspects!"

"Huh?" I said weakly.

"You mean you didn't hear me the first time?" he thundered.

"I just didn't believe my own ears, Sheriff," I mumbled.

"Well, you've lived with them long enough to know you can't trust them any more than the rest of you, I guess?"

"Oh, that's *funny*, Sheriff!" I snarled.

"Funny? It's hilarious!" He fell back into his chair and yelled with raucous laughter.

I watched him dubiously until he'd finally quieted down to the occasional ribald guffaw. "You've flipped?" I said accusingly.

"There are times when I suspect you take my reactions for granted," he said smugly. "That's when I start varying them a little, here and there."

"Did you get the autopsy report on Marsh yet?" I figured a change in the conversational line was needed fast right there.

"Not yet," Lavers grunted. "Doc Murphy said he'd be over with it inside the next twenty minutes and that was a half-hour back." He suddenly glared at me. "Don't ever send Sergeant Polnik back to report on a homicide again, Wheeler!

GIRL IN A SHROUD 153

Not if you want your temporary attachment to this office to remain on a permanent basis, anyway!"

"Yes, sir," I said carefully. "It was a real complicated-type homicide, at that."

"You don't have to tell me!" Lavers groaned and buried his face in his hands. "What with that vamp who just don't understand the time difference between West and East coasts, which is why she's sleeping nights in her coffin instead of days!"

"Polnik figured it out that far all by himself?" I asked wonderingly.

"Last seen wondering out loud how his old lady would look in a black silk shroud," the sheriff quavered. "Only he couldn't be sure she wouldn't get some of those vamp ideas along with it—and with a hot-blooded creature like his old lady, how could you tell for sure, when her white teeth fastened onto your jugular vein, if it was just passion, or she was helping herself to a vamp's idea of a martini!"

"That Polnik," I said, nearly choking. "He sure has his problems!"

"That county sheriff," he snarled back at me. "He sure has his problems, too. Like this homicide—so tell me about it."

I gave him a rundown on my day from the time the corpse Brenner had reported, sitting up in the casket with a bright smile on its face, up to the big broad's confidential report on how she'd overheard the proof of Hal Kirby's charitable benevolence toward the Landau Research Foundation.

Lavers just sat there and glowered at me for maybe ten long seconds after I'd finished. "You could have condensed that report down to one sentence, Lieutenant," he growled finally. "All you had to do was tell the truth—say you came up with a big fat zero!"

"At this juncture, sir—" and I smiled bleakly at him "—I'd like to go on record and say that it's only your faith and personal encouragement that makes my job really worthwhile!"

"Have you got one logical suspect yet?" He sniffed disparagingly. "You don't even have a motive! The way you tell it, this Doctor Marsh was a cross between a Galahad in shining armor and Tom Swift! And if there is a connection between this Kirby character and somebody in the foundation—and all you've got to prove it is hearsay!—what is its significance?"

"You're right!" I said, scrambling out of my chair. "I should be out questioning suspects, not just sitting here wasting my time listening to you, Sheriff."

"Sit down!" he thundered. "I—"

A thunderous tattoo on his door drowned out the rest of his words, as I sank back into my chair thankfully. Then the door burst open and Doc Murphy came in like a tornado straight out of Nebraska.

"I bring you greetings!" he boomed, then flung a neatly stapled folder onto the sheriff's desk, "and also one autopsy report as promised!"

"Any time anybody does what they're paid to do around here," Lavers said disgustedly, "they expect the Congressional Medal of Honor!"

"That's some routine you got there, Doc," I said admiringly. "Such flair, such style—panache if you like. With just a little polishing you sure could go places."

"It's therapeutic, if you must know," Murphy said from a great height. "Helps me limber up after all those stiffs. You've no idea how introspective a guy can become, working in the morgue all day."

The sheriff flicked over the pages of the report idly, then grunted. "Tell us about it, Doctor, it will save time."

"He was shot," Murphy said and looked at both of us expectantly. "That's a big surprise, huh?"

"I hate a doctor who's cute," Lavers confided to me in a thundering whisper. "It makes me start worrying that I could get sick sometime and he'd be the only help available!"

"How do you think I feel when I look at you, and start worrying my car could be stolen tomorrow?" Murphy asked in an indignant voice. "Very well, I shall break it down into a string of small one-syllable words renowned for their common usage, and hope, that way, you just may be able to get the gist of it, Sheriff!"

"Thank you, Doctor Murphy!" Lavers grated.

"He was shot," the doctor repeated happily. "A thirty-eight caliber slug—and I've taken enough of those out of people by now to recognize one when I see it without waiting for a ballistics report!—fired at close range, around five to six feet away, I'd guess. The bullet went straight into his brain so death would have been instantaneous."

"When?" I said.

GIRL IN A SHROUD

"Not earlier than midnight, say, and not later than one-thirty A.M. How does that sound?"

"Like another unrelated fact that doesn't get us anyplace at all," I groaned. "We found him in a casket—"

"I just love a murderer with a tidy mind!" Murphy enthused. "Don't you?"

"You figure he was already inside the casket when he was shot or put there later?" I finished my question with dogged determination.

"That's too big a question for me," he said cautiously, "but I can give you a part-answer. He was lying down when he was killed, because there was no blood spillage from the wound. But if his body had been left a few hours until the blood congealed, somebody could have moved him from wherever the murder took place, into that casket."

"Thanks," I said. "It doesn't help at all, but thanks anyway."

"He was a medico, wasn't he?" Murphy's voice hit a cold sober note. "I'm relying on you to catch his murderer, Wheeler, and uphold the honor of my profession! I wouldn't want anyone to get away with murdering an M.D.—the idea might catch on!"

"He was with the Landau Research Foundation," I said. "You know it?"

"So Landau told me this morning," I said. "You know anything about him personally?"

"Everybody knows about Max Landau," he said slowly. "A fantastic man—a fantastic doctor, too. Up until ten years back he was one of the four top psychiatrists in the whole country. Then he got bitten by the psycho-pharmaceutical bug—"

"How's that again?" Lavers queried.

"The use of mind-body drugs is therapy for the mentally sick," Murphy explained. "About the same time Landau married a very rich woman, so he didn't have to depend on his practice for income any more. He spent most of his time experimenting, and the rest of it as an honorary consultant to one of the state hospitals back East. He had to try everything himself first—some of his experimental dosages would have killed a half-dozen ordinary men! But he's got a fantastic metabolism."

"He told me he took a cure in Lexington for heroin addiction," I said.

"Did he tell you it was voluntary?"

"Sure."

"I bet he didn't tell you he insisted on a cold turkey cure, because he wanted to know just what the addict went through under those conditions?" Murphy grimaced. "In seventy-four, I think it was, he was experimenting with his own derivative from LSD-25 as therapy for a couple of paranoiacs who were regarded by the hospital medical staff as hopeless cases. Something went wrong—an overdose maybe, very possibly administered in error by a psychiatric aide—but both patients died and Landau took the rap.

"So that finished him with the hospital, and he retired from any kind of practice whatsoever. A few months later his wife died, leaving the bulk of her money to the children of her first marriage—but also leaving enough to set up a research foundation for Landau with just enough income to make it workable."

"You know if the girl—Vicki—is his daughter, or a child of his wife's first marriage?" I asked.

"She's his daughter and only child," Murphy said. "At the time Landau had his trouble at the state hospital, she was making headlines on her own, which didn't help her father any."

"Headlines about what?" Lavers asked.

"She'd gotten into an argument with her roommate at college and clinched it by sticking a knife into the other girl," Murphy said slowly. "Fortunately it went into the fleshy part of her shoulder and didn't do any real damage. The girl's parents refused to press charges so it was dropped a week later. There was a strong rumor that Landau's wife had paid off the girl's parents with a small fortune. It could have been—she didn't leave Vicki Landau a dime in her estate."

"Now maybe, Wheeler," Lavers said hopefully, "you've got yourself a suspect!"

"Maybe," I said. "Thanks, Doc, for the information."

"My pleasure." He inclined his head graciously. "I want you to find Marsh's murderer like I said, Al. I just hope it won't turn out to be Max Landau, is all." He looked at his watch and pantomimed a wild reaction. "I must fly, gentlemen! I promised my wife I'd be home early because Tuesday

GIRL IN A SHROUD 157

is our night for home-baked sweet-potato pie, and sex! If you find any more stiffs tonight don't embarrass me with any calls between eleven and twelve minutes after, will you?"

After he'd gone, Lavers looked at me with a brooding expression on his face for a while. "I can't make up my mind," he admitted grudgingly, "who is the biggest nut around here—him or Polnik."

"There's one easy way to find out," I said. "Call Murphy's wife—between eleven and twelve minutes after, tonight—and ask her if she wears a black silk shroud to bed."

"You know something, Wheeler?" he said in a wondering voice. "You have the fine devious mind of a natural-born assassin. Don't ever walk back of me in the unlikely situation that we should walk anyplace together." He made a production of shuffling the papers on his desk. "Well, I wouldn't know about you, but I've got work to do!"

"Yes, sir," I said dutifully and climbed onto my feet. "You know where I can find Sergeant Polnik?"

"Out buying his wife a shroud most likely!" he snarled. "After I'd listened to him for a solid hour this morning I sent him home before he drove me out of my mind, too. I told him to report back to the office tomorrow. You want him for something urgent, you can call him."

"It'll keep until morning," I said, "I'd be grateful if you'd check out Kirby with the FBI in Washington—and the L.A. boys. He looks to me like he should have a record. His voice didn't get that husky just by singing love songs to Sandra-baby!"

"All right," Lavers said. "You will close the door behind you when you leave?"

I went back into the outer office and stood watching in silent appreciation while a highly attractive chick with honey-blonde hair stood with one foot up on a chair, her dress hoicked up and calmly, almost abstractedly, scratching at a spot on her upper thigh, just beneath a pair of pale yellow briefs. Good manners bring their own reward, I reflected smugly, remembering how I had closed the door of Lavers' office so gently that it hadn't made a sound.

Then she stopped scratching, and lowering her foot from the chair, smoothed down her dress and turned to see me watching her. She froze and glared at me fiercely.

"Just what do you think you're doing?" she muttered savagely. "I should have known. Why couldn't you cough or something?"

"Annabelle Jackson," I said, gazing at her in gentle reproach, "am I the kind of man who'd come between a girl and her itch?"

"Given half a chance you'd come between a girl and her—oh, never mind." She retreated to her desk and sat down. "Don't you have someplace to go and do some work for a change?" she snapped. "Instead of just standing there playing the voyeur."

"Oh, but haven't you heard?" I said cheerfully. "Deep down, I'm really a fag, so you don't have anything to worry about."

"A fag?" She looked at me suspiciously, then gave a harsh laugh. "Oh boy, that's a new line. What do you want me to do? Mother you?"

"I'm basically insecure."

"You're basically a prick."

"You don't like fags," I said accusingly. "You've been listening to Anita Bryant. You're the one who's insecure, the crumbling pedestal of womanhood, the sexual challenge."

She was looking at me shrewdly. "Maybe it's not such a bad idea at that," she said quietly. "I mean about you being a fag."

"Oh? Why?"

"It means you've finally lost interest in sex."

Chapter Five

Vicki Landau opened the front door of the Landau Research Foundation headquarters, and looked at me with no enthusiasm at all showing in her dark eyes.

"I told you this morning that I'd be back," I said defensively.

"I know." She shook her head regretfully. "I just hoped you might have had a fatal accident through the day. Father's very busy in the lab right now. Do you have to disturb him?"

"No, I wanted to see Doctor Altman and Mr. Gerard," I said.

"They're both here." She opened the door a little wider and stepped back so I could walk into the front hall.

"Maybe I can use your father's office?" I suggested.

"I guess so," she said indifferently. "Maybe you could talk to Louis Gerard first. Doctor Altman's with Father at the moment but I know he'll be free inside the next quarter-hour."

"I am an obliging lieutenant," I said, my voice almost choking at the thought of my own generosity. "Gerard first, and you might ask Doctor Altman to come to the office once he's free?"

"Sure," she said, nodding. "How's your investigation coming along? Did you get to use your magnifying glass on another chorus girl yet?"

"I'm saving it for you, honey," I said soberly. "Maybe you'd like to step into the office now and get it over with before I talk to the others. It shouldn't take more than a couple of hours."

Her face suddenly flamed crimson a moment before she spun on her heel and marched down the hallway, her rigid back eloquent with suppressed fury. I walked into Landau's office and sat down behind his desk, shifted some junk to one side so I could see across the desk top, then lit a cigarette.

A couple of minutes later there was a polite tap on the door and a serious-looking guy around thirty came into the room.

"Lieutenant Wheeler?" His voice had a pleasantly deep intonation. "I'm Louis Gerard."

I told him to take a chair and he sat down on one of the straight-backed variety, facing me with a look of polite attention on his face. His sandy-colored hair was receding fast across his head and had already added a couple of inches to the high-domed forehead, giving him an impressive intellectual look that was enhanced by the deep-set, brooding gray eyes.

"How long have you been with the foundation, Mr. Gerard?" I said for openers.

"A little over two years, Lieutenant. I'm an analytical chemist. After I graduated, I did some work with a research team in immunology, and—"

"What the hell is immunology?" I pleaded.

"Oh, sorry!" He grinned faintly. "Well, basically, I guess it's the study of why some people are immune to a certain disease, and others aren't. Anyway, our research inevitably expanded into the psychiatric aspects, and then into psychotherapy. For me, the chemist on the team, the link was in the usage of drugs, the hallucinogenics such as LSD. When I heard of the work Doctor Landau was doing here in that field, I knew this was what I wanted, and contacted him. Six months later he had a slot for a chemist and I got the job."

"What kind of a man was Doctor Marsh?" I asked.

"Dedicated."

There was that damned word again, I thought sourly. Why would anybody want to kill a man simply because he was dedicated?

"How did you get along with him?"

"Just fine," Gerard said easily. "Everyone did. He was a nice guy, very shy and introverted, but that maybe made him even more likable. Everybody tried to be friendly with him, break down the barriers his own shyness created."

"Were they successful?"

He smiled wryly. "Not very! But they tried. I can't think

of any one reason—sane or insane—why someone should murder him, Lieutenant."

"When was the last time you saw him?"

"Last night after dinner, we all had coffee in the living room. I went to bed early—before ten, anyway—he was still there then. I'd just gotten into bed about ten minutes later when I heard him walk past my room on the way to his own. But the last time I *saw* him was in the living room."

"Marsh wasn't involved in any kind of dispute or agrument with any of the others?" I queried. "Something about the work you're doing, or any emotional relationship with Miss Allen or Vicki Landau?"

Gerard grinned broadly. "No, sir! I think he looked on Doctor Landau as a genius who was close to being a saint. Whatever Doctor Landau said was gospel! As for the two girls—" he shook his head slowly "—poor old Bob got along just fine while he was working with them, but any kind of personal relationship was out of the question. If one of them admired his tie even, he'd blush and get so embarrassed he couldn't even speak!"

"Well, thanks for your time, Mr. Gerard," I told him.

"No trouble, Lieutenant." He hauled his compact, muscular body out of the chair. "If there's anything at all I can do to help catch Bob Marsh's murderer, you just let me know!"

He reached the door, then stood to one side to let another guy come into the room, who had to be Doctor Altman. I watched him walk toward the desk, as Gerard closed the door gently and I listened to his footsteps fade down the hallway.

The newcomer was a big man—tall, and fat without being gross. He was completely bald, and the contrast between the pink shining skin of his head and the dark-jowled face was most ludicrous. His mouth was firm and sensual; his bright blue eyes looked unwinkingly from their cavities sunk in creased rolls of fatty tissue, and gave the impression of an alert intelligence coupled with ruthless purpose. I was impressed.

He stopped a couple of steps away from the desk, almost clicked his heels together, then jerked his head forward in a stiff movement. "Altman!" he said harshly.

"Why don't you sit down, Doctor?" I suggested. "I'm Lieutenant Wheeler."

He sat down facing me, his arms folded across his chest,

like I was his superior officer and not to be trusted—like a sergeant with a long memory who knows goddamn well whatever the chicken colonel says to the contrary, he's still a stiff-necked bastard from way back.

I worked my weary way through the same bunch of questions I'd asked Gerard, and got about the same unhelpful answers. Altman had left Marsh in the living room after dinner with the others, and that was the last time he'd seen him alive. He had no idea why anyone would want to kill him, and there certainly hadn't been any friction in the research team between Marsh and anyone else.

"What kind of a man was Marsh, Doctor?" I asked finally.

He smiled slowly. "A very earnest young man! You have just talked with Louis Gerard? Compared with Marsh, Louis is a frivolous butterfly, Lieutenant!"

"Everybody else uses the same word about him—dedicated," I said gloomily.

"After five years of it I am a little tired of the word." He smiled with an ironic twist to his mouth. "Even Max—Doctor Landau—is dedicated, in spite of his vitality and humor. The biologist, who is so brilliant, is so dedicated she hasn't yet discovered she is also a female! Sometimes I get a little tired of it all."

"How long have you been with Doctor Landau?" I asked.

"We worked together in a state hospital on the Eastern seaboard for about two years," Altman said. "When the foundation was established he asked me to work with him here, and I willingly accepted—and that was more than five years ago, Lieutenant."

"That was the hospital where he killed two patients with an overdose of drugs?"

"You know about that?" His eyebrows lifted for a moment, then he smiled. "But of course you do—I almost forgot you are a police officer! It was not Max's fault, someone else administered the overdose against his explicit instructions, but he had to accept the blame! Max Landau is a very great man, but unfortunately ahead of his time."

"How do you mean that exactly?"

Altman shrugged. "It is not important, and the answer would be so complex and immaterial, I would not presume to waste your time with it, Lieutenant," he said easily. "Let me just say that Max has an intuitive flair for the research we

GIRL IN A SHROUD

are doing that is close to genius. And genius, without lecturing you, Lieutenant, is something that is always deeply distrusted by ordinary men!"

"What is the line of research you're doing right now, Doctor?" I queried, without any real hope it could open up a new angle. "Is it very important? Something to be kept secret, maybe?"

His smile had all the slightly contemptuous tolerance of the scientist for the lay mind. "I hope it will be important, we all do, but it's hardly secret! Putting it in nonscientific terms, Lieutenant, we are exploring the possibilities of combining a hallucinogenic drug, such as LSD-25, with a hypnotic sedative, such as hyoscine, for use in psychotherapy."

"Hyoscine?" I thought for a moment. "That's another name for scopolamine, isn't it?"

"Of course."

"The truth drug?"

"Truth drug?" The bright blue eyes scanned my face for a moment, then he chuckled. "Ah, yes! The law enforcement officer's dream!—I had almost forgotten. Yes, Lieutenant, it's been called that many times but unfortunately it just isn't true. The hypnotic effect will certainly in many cases inhibit the subject's strength of will and leave his mind unguarded. In that case the chances are the subject will answer any question, however personal or dangerous to himself, with the absolute truth. But with another personality, the unguarded mind will indulge in fantasy, so of course the answers will then also be pure fantasy. Hyoscine is like a beautiful woman, Lieutenant, fascinating, but not to be trusted!"

He took a thin black cheroot from his top pocket, unwrapped the cellophane with great care, then lit it with obvious pleasure.

"A cigar, a beautiful woman, a great wine—these are the things I have come to appreciate through my life. I saw too much dedication in Nazi Germany, Lieutenant. I say this to you by way of explanation, I wouldn't want you to think I sneered at the young doctor while he was alive. It is a built-in reaction for me that I can't help. Marsh was a very sincere young man, and my only wish for him was that just once he would have gotten the young female biologist drunk and seduced her. I tried to prescribe it as therapy for him, and he nearly lapsed into a state of catatonic shock at the thought! It would have done them both a lot of good!"

"I must say, Doctor Altman, if you're not the most informative suspect I've talked with, you're certainly the most entertaining!" I grinned at him. "You were a practicing psychiatrist in Nazi Germany? They must have kept you busy?"

'Busy?" There was a bitter undertone to the irony in his voice. "What a useful word that is in the English language! Yes, they kept me busy." He watched the smoke drifting from the cheroot held between his fingers for a few seconds. "In 1938 I was practicing psychoanalysis in Vienna, Lieutenant. After I had gotten my degree in medicine I studied psychiatry for four years under the great Professor Edelstein. I was fortunate enough to become his favorite pupil, so later when I was in practice, he would recommend me to anyone who inquired about analysis. With his recommendation, how could I go wrong?"

He sighed gently. "I was a young man—in my early twenties—with a successful and growing practice and, thanks to Professor Edelstein, my professional reputation was established on firm ground and also growing. That was 1938, that was Theodore Altman—then the Nazis moved into Vienna.

"Edelstein was Jewish—everyone knew that Freud was a Jew and therefore the whole theory of psychiatry and allied subjects was suspect and anti-Aryan. Teaching was the professor's whole life, so when they tried to limit him, he spoke out against them—and vanished. I kept up my practice, tried to ignore the pressure brought against me, and watched it steadily dwindle away to nothing. A year later the Gestapo discovered my grandmother on the maternal side had been Jewish and that, coupled with the former association with Edelstein, was enough for them to take action."

"You were imprisoned?" I asked him.

"Sent to a forced labor battalion," Altman said harshly. "That was the year in which World War Two started, you may recall, Lieutenant. After three weeks in the labor battalion they put me to work cleaning the latrines of S.S. barracks, which I did for five years—first in Austria, then in Germany, and finally in Poland. Then in 1944 we were being moved again in Poland. We were herded like cattle into railroad cars, and because of the bombing the train moved slowly. Some died en route. A young S.S. major was in charge of the train and Jewish corpses didn't worry him unduly. But on the fifth day, one of his own men died and he was interested enough to look at the corpse. The train was stopped while the guards shouted for anyone with any medical experience to come outside. I went, and when I told them I was a doctor, they hustled me in front of a badly frightened S.S. major who didn't want to report an outbreak of smallpox to the authorities for fear of what might happen to himself."

Altman sucked on his cheroot, blew a stream of smoke from the side of his mouth, and continued: "I did the best I could, which wasn't much under the circumstances. Another thirty died before we reached our destination. When we arrived we were told we were going to work the land and would be first bathed and deloused in decontamination sheds at the camp. I was pulled out of my squad just before the time came for me to strip and enter the shed, and I was taken before the camp's commandant, who had learned from the S.S. major that I was a doctor and had practiced psychiatry. It seemed he wanted me to discover why there was such a high incidence of nervous disorders among the Auschwitz guards." He paused, looked at me unblinkingly for a moment, and added, "That's where we were—Auschwitz." He flicked his cheroot and studied its glowing end. "For almost a year after that, I watched the trains arrive, heard the speech about working the land, and saw the naked march, squad by squad, to the 'decontamination' sheds, from which, as you know, they never returned.

"I soon discovered the commandant wasn't interested in nervous disorders as such. He wanted me to find out which of his men had any distaste for their work so he could weed them out fast. It was his contention that these men would naturally be inefficient, and he had a mania for efficiency. That commandant was the most dedicated man I ever met in my whole life, Lieutenant, which is why I can never wholly like or trust any man who is dedicated, regardless of his high purpose!"

"What happened when the war finished?" It was a hell of a detour he'd taken in explaining why he had no use for dedicated types, and I didn't see why he wanted to talk about all this, but I figured if he wanted to tell it I might as well listen to it—and besides, I was kind of curious.

"I managed to escape one night, just before the Russians came. I worked for them for a while, and then I had a year in a refugee camp, and then I managed to get to America as an immigrant. It took time to learn a new language, to requalify as a doctor, to catch up with the tremendous advances made during the war years in psychiatry. After that, I worked in hospitals. The third hospital was where I first met Max Landau—and you know the rest."

Chapter Six

By the time I got home to my apartment it was eight-thirty that night. I made myself a large Scotch on the rocks, added a little soda, then slipped a Bette Midler cassette into the player.

About the same time I went in search of a second drink, I remembered there was a steak in the refrigerator and I was hungry. Using an old and well-tried recipe, I grilled it for as long as it took to turn it almost to charcoal, smothered it with fried onions, dunked it in French mustard a couple of times, then set it to do battle with my digestive juices.

By nine-thirty I was sprawled happily in an armchair, contentedly digesting my meal, a glass in my hand, listening to the velvet voice of Mel Torme. I was in an extremely good mood and pondered on the advantages of living alone when one could do one's own thing without the fear of treading on someone else's toes.

Nothing, I reflected happily, to break your mood—then jumped a foot in the air when the one exception made itself felt. I moved toward the front door reluctantly, wondering who the hell would blast my door buzzer at this time of night.

I opened the door and was suddenly face to face with an apparition in a raincoat, a pale face devoid of makeup, and blonde hair pulled tight back across her head and tied in a knot at the back. A pair of china-blue eyes regarded me expressionlessly from behind glasses with thick black frames. The gender was definitely female, and I could even pin it down more exactly as one called Kaye Allen, who had been trained as a biologist but preferred libelous psychiatry, as I remembered.

"What the hell do you want?" I growled. It's all that innate breeding that makes us Wheelers that way—we just can't help being gracious, no matter what!

"We have some unfinished business, Lieutenant," she said calmly, then walked straight past me into the apartment.

"Hey! Who asked—" But it was too late then. I slammed the door shut and managed to catch up with her in the living room.

"What's that you're drinking?" She pointed toward the glass balanced on the arm of my chair.

"Scotch on the rocks, a little soda," I said automatically. "Listen! What the—"

"I'll have one!" She started to unbutton her raincoat unhurriedly.

"Are you out of your tiny biological mind?" I yelped. "You come busting into my apartment like this and—"

"I'll leave," she said easily, "the moment after you admit I was right."

"About what?" I growled suspiciously.

"About your aggressive complexes adding up to the one thing."

"You mean that crap about my being a latent fag?"

"A theory—just a theory."

"You're out of your mind," I snapped.

"Okay then." She shrugged. "Maybe I should try and prove it to you. Show you once and for all, so that you might come to terms with it. Once you've come to accept it, then we're well on the road to recovery."

I stared at her blankly for a few seconds, while I slowly realized she meant every word of it. What the hell? Maybe it could turn out to be more interesting than a game of gin at that.

"Okay." I grinned at her. "The floor is yours, Miss Allen, so prove it!"

"I think you'd better call me Kaye before we start," she said briskly. "Otherwise the situation might suddenly strike you as being comic—and I wouldn't want that. I presume even police lieutenants have a first name?"

"Al."

"Al?" Her nose wrinkled faintly. "I guess I shouldn't be surprised. It suits you very well—Al!"

"So now we've established a buddy-buddy basis, what comes next?" I demanded impatiently.

GIRL IN A SHROUD 169

"My drink," she said casually. "Remember? That Scotch on the rocks and whatever—the same as you're having."

She pulled off her raincoat and threw it carelessly onto the couch. Underneath, she still had on that white coat-dress she wore around the Research Foundation. I'd known plenty of people in white coats who took care of nuts, I thought bitterly, but this surely had to be the first time a white-coated nut took care of people. But I'd told her to go right ahead and prove her theory, and that meant I had no choice now but to do as I was told, so I went out into the kitchen and made her a Scotch on the rocks, with a little soda.

When I got back into the living room, she was sitting in my armchair, her legs crossed neatly, the hem of her white coat riding slightly back over one well-fleshed thigh.

"Here is your drink, as ordered—" I thrust the glass under her nose "—Kaye!"

"Thank you." She picked up my glass from the arm of the chair and thrust it under my nose. "And here is yours—Al!"

We exchanged glasses and glared at each other for a while, until those china blue eyes started bugging me again—didn't they ever show some sign of life?

"It's your party—Kaye," I reminded her. "What happens next?"

"Let's drink," she said gravely. "Bottoms up!"

"Why bottoms up?"

"To tell you the truth, I'm a little nervous," she said. "I mean, as an experiment, this is going to take some nerve. That's why it has to be bottoms up."

"Okay," I said easily. "If it makes you feel better."

I drained my glass in one long gulp; Kaye Allen took two, but then I reluctantly remembered she'd started with a fresh drink and I hadn't.

"Now what?" I asked.

"Don't be so impatient!" She cleared her throat tentatively. "That was good Scotch! Now we talk for a little while, so sit down on the couch and behave yourself, Al!"

She was still calling the game, so I did like I was told and sat down on the couch facing her. After a couple of minutes had tippy-toed by, I got restive with the great big silence.

"You really need those glasses?" I asked her. "Or are they just another part of your defense mechanism?—you know—men never make passes at girls who wear glasses."

"Dorothy Parker's always misquoted on that one," she said evenly. "It's 'seldom make passes,' not 'never.' I do really need them, I'm myopic. Compared to me a bat has twenty-twenty vision. Without my glasses I can't see more than a couple of feet in any direction."

"Why don't you use any makeup?" I persisted.

She glanced at the neat no-nonsense wristwatch on her arm. "I'm not here to discuss myself," she said sharply. "The object of this experiment is to prove something about you, not me."

"You have another appointment?" I said coldly.

"In a sense, but not the way you mean." Her eyes stared straight into mine and seemed to grow steadily bigger and bigger. It had to be some trick of the light, I figured nervously, something to do with the lenses in front of them. Whatever it was, it didn't stop. Now her eyes were enormous, blotting everything else from my sight.

"Al?" Her voice was so faint I hardly heard it at all.

"What the hell are you whispering for?" I asked hoarsely.

"I'm not whispering," she whispered. "What are you staring at me like that for?"

"I'm not staring," I croaked. "You're staring!"

The huge china blue eyes reacted indignantly, rippling in and out of focus in time to a steady drumbeat I couldn't hear. The silent frenzy built, and the china blue world gyrated in a whirling mass of vivid color that made my head spin with it giddily.

"Al?" A million miles away she spoke my name softly and expected me to hear!

"I spin like a top," I confided out loud to myself. "I *am* a top! A spinning top, how's that for a topper? Topping, don't you think, old top?"

"Al?" She had come closer, but why did she bother to whisper my name to the ocean, and expect me to hear? "*Al!*"

What the hell was the matter with her? I wondered savagely. She figured I was deaf or something, she had to lean over and shout in my ear?

"Yeah!" I shouted right back at her.

"Are you all right?"

Everything snapped back into sharp focus, and I saw Kaye Allen was leaning forward in her chair looking at me anxiously.

GIRL IN A SHROUD 171

"Sure, I'm okay," I told her. "Why?"

"You looked—I don't know—odd, for a little while back there," she said awkwardly, "and you were talking away to yourself like crazy! I thought it was a pity to waste all that good conversation on yourself, and if you'd only speak up a little I could join in."

"I guess it was something I ate." I gave her an embarrassed smile. "I guess that teaches me to never eat my own cooking again!"

"You're sure you feel all right now?"

"Sure," I said confidently. "What were we talking about?"

"It's time to take the experiment a stage further, Al." She stood up and started across the room. "I need a couple of props—it won't take a minute to organize them. You don't mind waiting?"

"I'm fascinated!" I said truthfully. "It's one of those classic cliff-hangers! What will happen next? I almost can't wait to find out."

She closed the door into the kitchen and switched off lights so the living room was in deep shadow except for one warm pool of light that splashed onto the rug from the one remaining lamp still alight. She turned her back on me deliberately, then reached up and fumbled with the tight knot of hair at the nape of her neck. Suddenly a riot of molten white-gold cascaded down her back to within a few inches of her waist. She shook her head gently and the silken strands of white-gold rippled sensuously, like the pagan dance of a wheatfield in the summer breeze at harvest time.

She turned back toward me slowly, her right hand placing the heavy, black-framed glasses down on the coffee table. Freed from the savage pull of the knot at the nape of her neck, her hair now made a soft frame of spun-silk for her face. Without the glasses, the china blue eyes had come alive with a glowing warmth.

"Now here comes the worst part," she said huskily. "I'm going to hate it, but it has to be done."

"What has to be done?" There was a cracking sound to my own voice, too, I realized.

"I'm doing this only for you. One has to make sacrifices if the therapy is to be complete, no matter how distasteful."

Her fingers were suddenly busy unbuttoning the uniform all the way down the front, then she shrugged her shoulders free and stepped out of it. Her lower lip pouted at me for a moment. "Here!" She tossed it carelessly in my direction and it landed on the couch on top of the raincoat.

The last remaining vestiges of the sexless biologist vanished along with the white uniform, and in her place stood a wanton and intensely desirable woman wearing only a small black bra from which her full, creamy breasts swelled up and out of the cups that just barely contained them, and an abbreviated pair of black briefs that were molded to the gentle concavity of her crotch, above which showed a very faint line of pale curling hair. She stood in front of me, her pelvis thrust forward a fraction, her hands running up and down her flanks which gleamed in the soft warmth of the lamplight.

"You were right, Al." There was a gentle mocking note in her voice. "Black underwear, you see. No froth, that would have been carrying it too far—but black. I hope you approve."

"I approve," I said thickly. "I approve."

"Does it stimulate erotic images?"

"You're my kind of woman," I croaked.

"Then there's the question of arousal," she said softly.

Her legs were really elegant, her thighs firm and rounded with just a hint of steel beneath the vibrant flesh. Then, as I watched her, my throat suddenly dry, a quick stirring in my loins as the messages from my eyes were transmitted through the central exchange of my brain down to my genitals, she reached up behind her and unclipped the bra, and bringing it away from her superb milky breasts, threw it to one side. Her breasts thrust proudly forward, the pink tips pushing rigidly from their surrounding areoles. Still smiling at me in a smoky sort of way, she slipped her fingers beneath the waistband of her briefs, and slowly rolled them down her thighs, then stepped out of them, one shapely leg after the other. She stood in front of me, her pose relaxed and inviting, completely naked.

My yard throbbed wildly at the sight of her. She was some woman, and she was offering herself to me, just like that, with nothing asked for in return. Her hands were running slowly down her smooth, marblelike flanks again. Between them, her delta was whitish-blonde, like her hair, the slit clearly discernible beneath the wispy, curling growth.

"Well?" she said huskily. "What are you waiting for? Don't

GIRL IN A SHROUD 173

you want to make hard, passionate love to me? Or was I right the first time around and this is going to be more challenging than I thought?" She glanced down at my packed groin, and nodded to herself in some sort of satisfaction. "Well, at least the arousal is there. It's a start. Come here, Al ... Come here and make love to me."

"I'm coming," I croaked happily. "I'm coming." I came from the couch like an arrow straight from Cupid's bow and hurtled across the intervening space toward her. Then, just two steps away from her, my hands reaching out for her, ready to crush that alluring body hard against me, the fantasies of what I would do to her, and how, swirling through my desire-clouded brain, I came to a sudden stop. That is, my legs did—the rest of me kept pounding right on toward her, but it was a kind of futile effort unless the legs cooperated.

Kaye still stood motionless, her magnificent body arched in a provocative, inviting pose, her legs parted, her pink labia distended a little. I felt the sweat trickling down my forehead as I made a valiant, titanic effort of will to get my legs moving again. Nothing happened—I was frozen to the spot, unmoving and apparently immovable. It was a nightmare, I figured hopelessly, a living nightmare, and I was trapped right in the middle.

"What's the matter, Al? Why have you stopped?"

"Something's happened to my legs," I muttered. "I can't move."

"Just try and relax a little. You're too tense. You have to fight it, Al, this awful inhibiting curse of yours."

I tried to relax—by Jesus I tried, but it didn't make any difference. I was doomed to spend all eternity as a monument to man's ultimate frustration.

"Okay, Al." Kaye took a deep breath. "So you just can't relax right now, which I guess leave it up to me. Don't worry about it. I know just what to do." The china-blue eyes shone brightly with exotic promise. "You'll be surprised how quickly I can make you relax."

She took a step toward me, and at the same moment my legs twitched violently and I took a step back. A faintly puzzled look showed in her eyes for a moment, then she shrugged gently and took another step toward me. There was another violent twitch, and I was still two steps away from her.

"Is this some sort of game?" she asked coldly.

I looked down at my legs, struck dumb by their treachery—and with that body just in front of me, tempting and flowing like pale honey, that was the only way I could describe it.

"Relax, Al," she said. "You're fighting your inner self. But you must relax. Try. Don't be frightened. I'm here to help you. You must realize that. I'm your friend."

She walked toward me determinedly, her breasts moving with a gentle rhythm, the nipples still erect—and I backed away from her with equal determination. She walked faster, and my lousy legs backpedaled faster. We circled the room this way until at last the backs of my knees slammed into the couch so all at once I was sitting down.

"Now!" she cried triumphantly, hurling herself into my lap and grabbing my still rampant, demanding stalk, as pulling my head forward with her other hand, she began to push her tongue between my lips.

A feeling of stark terror suddenly engulfed me, and I vaguely felt a blind muscular reflex in both arms. Suddenly I knew beyond all doubt that it *was* a living nightmare, because Kaye had vanished completely.

"You bastard!" someone cried passionately. "You fucking miserable bastard!"

I looked down and saw that Kaye was sprawled on the floor, her legs up in the air with the pale flanges of her vulva meshing as she brought them down onto the rug. One long silken strand of her hair hung down straight over one eye, then curled demurely in the valley between her snow-white breasts.

"I think that's enough." Kaye's voice was suddenly tired. "I give up. I was right about you in the first place, and I don't know if it's worth the effort to continue. Look at you now. Terrified at the very thought of making physical contact with a woman." Her beautiful breasts expanded majestically as she took a deep breath. "You're almost crying."

And who wouldn't? I thought bitterly. "The experiment's over," she snapped. "You've shown I was right, and I'll leave you alone."

"I was bewitched, tormented by demons, so please get out

GIRL IN A SHROUD

of here right now," I muttered feverishly. "I'd like a little privacy so I can kill myself."

There was one exquisite refinement left to add to the torture I had already suffered—I had no choice but to sit helplessly on the couch, my prick limp and forlorn again, and watch while Kaye put her clothes back on. Finally she was fully dressed again, the raincoat buttoned over her uniform, and on her way out of the apartment.

She stopped when she reached the entrance hall, turned around, and looked back at me with an expressionless face.

"You know what a trigger is, Lieutenant?" she asked.

"Part of a gun," I said thickly.

"What happens when you pull it?"

"The gun fires," I said.

Maybe there was a faint malicious gleam in the china blue eyes, but now they were hidden in back of the black-framed glasses again, it was hard to be sure.

"I'll let you in on a secret, Lieutenant," she said softly. "You have a kind of gun in your mind right now and it's fully loaded."

"Huh?" I grunted.

"I guess I should pull the trigger before I go," she said, almost to herself. "It'll take about five minutes before it fires, Al, so don't get impatient."

"Huh?" I repeated.

"Sucker!" she said in a loud clear voice.

"What?"

"I just pulled the trigger for you, Lieutenant." She gurgled with laughter. I'd love to be here five minutes from now, but I'm not brave enough to take the risk. Good night, Lieutenant, pleasant dreams! And remember, nobody fools around with a female biologist and gets away with it—not even a cop!"

Chapter Seven

Sucker!

The word suddenly exploded inside my brain in a white-hot flash of pain. I pressed both hands hard down on top of my head to stop my skull flying apart and closed my eyes. The throbbing pain subsided slowly while my mind examined its brand-new memory with a masochistic attention to the smallest detail.

I was on the couch facing Kaye, who was sitting in an armchair, I remembered, and we had been talking when her china blue eyes suddenly had grown bigger—and had kept on getting bigger until they'd blotted out everything else from my sight. Then I'd had a kind of dizzy spell which was real weird—kept hearing her voice calling my name from a long way off—but a couple of seconds later everything had snapped back into focus and I had been just fine again.

Now I had this brand-new memory of what really happened during that dizzy spell, which had lasted a lot longer than the few seconds I'd thought it had—ten minutes was a far more accurate guess. There was that whirling mass of vivid color, my mind remembered objectively. Now let's superimpose this nice new memory and see what really happened.

I closed my eyes obediently.

"Al?" The new memory ticked over, bringing me Kaye's voice as if from a great distance.

"Yes?"

"You hear me?" The voice was suddenly much stronger, and real close.

"I hear you fine," I said.

"Then listen closely. Everything I said about you is the absolute truth. You're really terrified of women. You're in-

GIRL IN A SHROUD 177

timidated by them. Aroused, yes—I could see you were aroused. But after that—" she had paused for a moment, then said, "Tell me the truth about yourself and your feeling's toward the opposite sex."

"You're right," I replied without even hesitating. "I'm a latent fag."

"Perhaps that's only because you're frightened of being rejected by a woman—found wanting. It happens a lot with men, to a varying degree of course."

Her voice had continued at length, telling me how she would attempt to seduce me—that at first I would be eager and filled with desire, but when I got close to her, just two steps away, my true feelings would overwhelm me. My legs would remain rooted to the spot. She gave me a detailed layout of my physical reactions from start to finish, then made me repeat it word for word.

"In a few moments now," she had said finally, "you will wake up, but your conscious mind will remember nothing of this conversation, even though your subconscious will ensure you carry out my instructions. Only when I say the word *Sucker!* will your conscious mind be permitted to remember this conversation—but not until five minutes after I have said the word. You understand, Al?"

Oh brother, my mind sneered, did you ever!

I dragged myself off the couch and walked into the kitchen—legs functioning perfectly, no latent muscular twitch—but the hungry ache of unfulfilled desire still remained as strong as ever. The first drink I didn't even taste, but the reaction hit about five seconds later, so I decided to take the second back into the living room with me and take more time over demolishing it.

Sucker! The word was etched in fire across my mind as I dropped into an armchair, and stared morosely at the innocent ice cubes floating around busy about their business of chilling the Scotch. Somehow Kaye had put me into a hypnotic trance; it didn't seem possible those big china blue eyes could have done the whole bit by themselves. But what else?

I raised the glass to my lips, then held it stationary a couple of inches away from them and stared blankly at the busy ice cubes. That was how she did it, of course! Slipped something into my drink—some kind of hypnotic drug. That was why she'd checked her watch just before the dizzy spell hit me. She'd handled it real cool, I admitted grudgingly to myself. Demanding a drink—the same as whatever I was drinking!—so she had plenty of time to slip the drug into my glass while I was outside in the kitchen making her drink. Then the bottoms-up toast to make sure I got the full prescribed dose!

A sudden vivid recollection of how she had looked—her hands clasped behind her head and her whole body arched in a pagan hymn of invitation—made me close my eyes and groan in torment. Then—for no good reason at all—I got an equally vivid picture of how we both must have looked when I was backpedaling fast around the room, and she was running after me.

Five minutes later I was still laughing helplessly, the tears streaming down my face, when the buzzer gave a faint apologetic-sounding squawk. Somehow, I managed to get out of the chair and totter toward the front door.

I was confronted by a white-faced apparition with long white-blonde hair tumbling around her shoulders. She stood there giving me a distinctly nervous look.

"You wouldn't hit a girl while she's wearing her glasses?" Kaye Allen asked in a small voice.

She came into the front hall and I closed the front door firmly in back of her; the sound made her jump like a startled gazelle. Her shoulders hunched under the drab raincoat as she walked stiff-legged into the living room, then turned around slowly to face me again.

"I got down to the street and into my car," she said sadly. "That was going to be my greatest moment of triumph—to sit there and wait until the five minutes was up—and gloat over just how you were reacting to the sudden revelation of the whole truth up here in your apartment." She bit her lower lip painfully. "You know something, Al? I didn't enjoy it one little bit! I kept on thinking about how you must be feeling right now. Not only the humiliation you'd feel when you knew how I'd taken you for a ride, but the physical frustration—the way I'd thrown my body at you, knowing damn well the whole time you had no chance of even getting close!"

She stared moodily at the floor for a while, then slowly lifted her head again. "All in all, I came to the conclusion that it had been a pretty stinking kind of trick to play on anyone—and it needed a pretty stinking kind of personality to do it. So I finally figured out the only honorable course left for me was to come back up here and take my lumps!"

Her hand shook a little as she suddenly whipped the heavy-framed glasses from her face.

"You want to slug me, Al Wheeler?" The china blue eyes screwed tight shut. "Go right ahead!"

"I don't want to slug you, Kaye Allen," I said, fighting desperately against the bubbling laughter inside me.

She opened her eyes again quickly and stared into my face for a long moment. "Oh, Al!" Her eyelids blinked rapidly. "You've been crying!"

"I couldn't help it," I said in a muffled voice. "I kept on thinking after you'd gone—"

"I'll make it up to you, Al." Her voice throbbed with the ecstasy of absolute guilt, and once again there was the beginning of a reaction in my groin. "I promise." Her eyes sparkled at the chance of nobly sacrificing herself to the wild passionate frenzy that beat within my chest, not to mention my awakening loins.

"Tell me," she whispered eagerly. "What were those bittersweet thoughts that brought tears to your eyes?"

"The way we were moving around the room—remember? You were running after me. It was wild, crazy. Christ Almighty, what a sight we must have made." The humor of it struck me forcibly, and I began to laugh while she watched me, a faint doubt clouding the sparkle in her eyes.

I bent double, my hands clasped to my sides, then staggered across to the couch and fell onto it gratefully. Laughter racked my body unmercifully, and more tears streamed down my face, until I was sure my lungs would burst. Then, gradually, it died away in an uneven procession of occasional guffaws and sudden giggles. It took one hell of an effort to drag myself up into a sitting position again, but I made it, and looked vaguely across to where Kaye stood, one foot slowly tapping the floor.

The naked fury in her eyes sobered me completely in one terrifying glance.

"Oh?" she said in a soft, menacing voice. "So you think it's funny? The thought of making love to me is simply hilarious, is it?"

"Kay," I said cautiously, "I—"

"Shut up!" The vicious rasp in her voice had a blood-curdling quality. "After all, I did come back up here to try and make up for what I—how mistaken can I get!—thought was a cruel trick I'd played on you. Now I know the whole thing amused you so much, I think it's only fair I provide you with a few more laughs!"

"Listen, Kaye," I said nervously. "I—"

"Shut up!" Her fingers worked with incredible speed. "Can't you see I'm busy?"

I relapsed into an uneasy silence, and right after that she started throwing things at me, beginning with the raincoat and ending with the tiny black briefs.

A remembrance of things past slowly took shape in the center of a warm pool of lamplight. She was naked again, and my prick was throbbing again. We had come full circle, and as she waited for me with a misty look in her china-blue eyes, I was halfway across the room toward her before I was conscious of having even moved.

"Your clothes," she said softly. "It will be easier without your clothes."

An oversight which was remedied in about five seconds flat. In a state of full rampant awareness, I faced her and saw the look of admiration in her eyes as she glanced down at my straining member.

"That's better, Al," she whispered. "Now I think we're getting somewhere. All it needs is the right amount of encouragement.

I put both hands on her bare hips and pulled her hard against me, the length of my yard pressing against the softness of her pelvis. Her hand dropped and closed gently around it. I held her even tighter and kissed her with a bruising intensity for some moments before leading her across to the couch, and laying her down on it, brought myself over her, easing her legs apart to receive me, then guiding the tip of my penis to the opening of her vagina, eased myself into her.

We made love quickly and intently, our bodies rippling against each other in pleasing harmony. She made soft moaning sounds and her hands fluttered across my back. My own hands pressed down on her shoulders, pinning her down as I lunged powerfully against her. Latent fag indeed! She writhed beneath me, and started calling me dirty names which seemed to turn her on even more. And then, slowly, inevitably, we brought each other to a shattering climax, and even as my juice was still pumping into her, and her body was bucking violently beneath me with the force of her own sweeping orgasm, she cried out in sheer triumph.

"My God, you're cured! We've done it, Al! You and I! We've come through!"

She lay on her back, her china blue eyes idly gazing at the ceiling, her long wheat-colored hair spread like a silken fan around her head.

"What time is it?" she murmured.

I made a herculean effort and lifted my watch from the bedside table. "Five after two."

"Shit! How time goes when you're enjoying yourself."

"Never mind," I murmured wearily. "We've got all night."

We had spent ourselves in an absolute welter of lust, experimenting, trying out a fair number of the positions so artfully drawn in Xaviera's handbook—or those that I remembered, and limited by the fact that there was no horse or stepladder, or even a sheep dog. We had made love every which way, with Kaye Allen on top of me, straddling me, facing me, her back to me—and each time it lasted that much longer.

"Do you feel better now?" she asked, during a quiet spell.

"Why don't you ask if it was nice for me too?" I said.

"Was it?"

"Uh-huh."

"I was wrong about you," she said. "I couldn't have been more wrong."

"Does that mean I'm no longer a latent fag?" I asked.

"You should be pleased you're not."

"Oh, and I had such great ideas about becoming trendy at long last."

She laughed. "You're quite impossible, Al."

"Sure I am," I said, and gently nuzzled her nearest dimple which happened to be tucked away in the hollow of her shoulder.

I lifted my head a moment later and stared down at the white puckered scar my lips had discovered a moment before.

"You beast!" Kaye said in a tragic voice. "You've discovered my dread secret! Now you've discovered the one flaw in my beauty, I'll probably kill myself!"

"What is it?" I asked curiously.

"A permanent keepsake from my college days," she said lightly. "Ah, what innocent girlish fun we had then! The saber duels! The night we burned a sophomore, the—"

"It looks like a knife wound," I said.

"Does it?" Her voice was carefully noncommittal. "Now it's your turn to reveal your scars—that's only fair."

"Is that where Vicki Landau stuck a knife into you?"

"Yes, damn you!" She turned her head away suddenly. "Don't you ever stop being a detective for a while? First you make love to me, then while I'm still purring, you start giving me the third degree! Just what kind of a monster are you, anyway?"

"You want to tell me about it?" I asked gently.

"No, but I guess I don't have any choice!"

She sat up suddenly and swung her legs onto the floor. She stood up and I lay there admiring her buttocks as she looked around the room.

"I want a robe," she said.

"In the wardrobe," I told her.

With a gentle grinding motion of her buttocks, she moved across to the wardrobe, pulled out a robe, and wrapped it around herself.

Five minutes later, also berobed, I sat respectably in the kitchen and watched Kaye make a pot of coffee. After she had served it, she sat down opposite me across the midget-sized table, with one lozenge-shaped boob protruding from the opening of the robe.

"Well?" I prompted. "Aren't you going to tell me the story of your life?"

"You know what?" She winced slightly. "All that screwing. Now I'm bruised and sore."

"So you have something to remember me by," I said. "A token, a momento."

"Maybe it was because you were overcompensating," she said thoughtfully. "Proving something to yourself."

"Does that mean I could still be a fag," I groaned.

She sipped her coffee and pulled the robe tighter around her, covering the wayward boob. "One minute we're making it together like crazy; the next minute you're the interrogating cop again."

"That dedicated doctor," I said coldly. "The young, shy

doctor everybody liked so much. I haven't gotten any closer to finding his murderer yet. Or have you forgotten?"

"All right!" Kaye said savagely. "Only I just don't see what my life story has to do with Bob Marsh's death."

"Neither do I, until I've heard it."

"Promise you won't tell anyone else about it, unless it somehow ties in with catching your murderer?" she murmured.

"Of course."

"I was an only child," Kaye said in a colorless voice. "My mother was forty when I was born—that didn't make me a love child exactly, did it? Neither of my parents wanted me—I was an embarrassment they tolerated but never loved." She smiled uncertainly. "I'm sorry about the hearts and flowers, but it's important because of what came after."

"Sure," I said. "All true life stories are corny—ask any cop."

"Vicki Landau was my roommate in college," she continued, "and right from the start we got along together just fine. She was crazy about her father—worshiped him! All the time she never stopped talking about him—how wise and kind he was, what a brilliant psychiatrist he was—and how much he loved her. I guess that was the bit that got me—the one thing I'd never had from either of my parents was love, and it was the one thing I wanted more than anything else in the world."

She drank some more coffee, settled the heavy blackframed glasses more firmly on the bridge of her nose, then ran out of excuses so had to start talking again.

"All that first year in college I listened to Vicki's neverending stories about her brilliant, wise, handsome father, who cherished her more than anything else in the world—and I loved every minute of it! I used to listen to Vicki talk, and pretend in my mind that it was really *my* father she was talking about, and *she* belonged to that dull, aging, petulant little man who lived in our house!

"Then Vicki suddenly asked me if I'd like to stay with her for a few days during the summer vacation. I said yes, great, and I went. I was quite excited about it. Until then, I guess you could say I had had a fairly sheltered sort of life.

"Anyway, I went to stay with her at their home on Long Island, which was much bigger and far more impressive than ours. But the wonderful thing was that Doctor Landau in real life was everything Vicki had said. He was such a striking man, I thought when I first saw him, with his beautiful gray hair and that clever satanic face which sent shivers up and down my spine every time I looked at him.

"His wife was very sick then, and almost a permanent invalid. I was introduced to her when I arrived, then never saw her again so she seemed completely unreal. Vicki naturally assumed the three of us would do everything together, and her father didn't seem to mind me always tagging along. We went swimming and walking—barbecued on the beach—we had a ball! After the first week, Vicki said why didn't I stay for a couple more and I was almost delirious with joy!

"It was sometime during the last week I was there . . ." Kaye's voice faltered for a moment. "Vicki had to go to her dentist, which meant a trip to Manhattan, and she insisted I stay home and enjoy the beach because it was such a terribly hot day. Her father drove her to the station, and I went down to the beach for a swim. I came back about an hour later and met him in the front hall. There was a funny look in his eyes and he told me how great I looked in a swimsuit. He kept looking at me—you know—up and down, very obvious. Anyway, I went up to my room and took a shower."

She took a cigarette from the pack on the table, and lit it. "He was waiting for me," she went on in a flat voice. "Sitting on my bed, the door already locked from the inside. He was in a robe, and it was hanging open, and he had nothing on beneath it. He was aroused, hard, and he looked sort of pleased when he saw the look in my eyes. And there I was, just out of the shower, without even a bath towel wrapped around me. He said something about my body, and the next thing I knew he had grabbed me and thrown me down on the bed."

She studied the burning tip of her cigarette with sudden absorbing interest. "The first thing he did was give me head, which wasn't so bad, although his stubble did tickle a bit— and then he wanted me to go down on him, forced me to go down on him, and I kept gagging all the time. It was the first time I had gone down on a man and I didn't know there was such a thing as technique. I bit him and he didn't like that. Then he screwed me, hard, and tore a few membranes into the bargain. It didn't last long, but Jesus, it was painful. Just before he left the room he said he knew I was smart and wouldn't tell anyone about our little secret, because who would believe me anyway? The next morning I made some excuse to Vicki and went home.

"I had nightmares until I found I wasn't pregnant, then the summer vacation was over and I went back to college. What I hadn't realized was the reaction I'd get every time Vicki told another story about her wonderful father. After a few weeks my nerves were raw. One night she trotted out a particularly revolting story, about how he had cried like a baby when he had had to have an old dog destroyed.

"That did it. I had had enough. A fucking hypocrite he was, and I told her so. She demanded to know what I meant by that, so I gave her the whole story, chapter and verse, not leaving out a single gruesome detail. When I'd finished she went berserk—grabbed a letter opener and lunged at me with it. I screamed my head off, and by the time someone rushed into the room, I was covered with blood and convinced I was dying. But it was only a flesh wound."

"You didn't bring any charges against Vicki?" I said casually.

"I intended to," Kaye said. "I'd had more than my share of the Landau family by then, but her mother got up from the sick bed and came to see me in the hospital. She asked me to drop them for Vicki's sake and I told her the hell with Vicki. Think of my husband's reputation, he's a doctor, she said. I told her about the original treatment he'd given me that summer, and she didn't even look surprised. But when I told her how I planned to tell the same story in court, she just looked at me for a couple of seconds, then pulled out her checkbook!"

"You want some more coffee?" I asked her.

"No," she said flatly. "Now I want you to hear the rest of it quickly, so it's finished with! I graduated at another college, still carrying all the traumas the Landau family had given me inside my head. I hated all men from that day when I walked out of the shower and saw Max Landau waiting for me with the lust shining in his eyes! I worked at developing a kind of dual personality—the sexless dedicated scientist you saw at the foundation, and, when it was to my advantage, the kind of girl you saw in your living room tonight!

"But it didn't really work for me. I figured Max Landau had destroyed for all times my chances of a normal relationship with any man, based on trust and affection. I thought a hell of a lot about that. I was the innocent victim who'd done all the suffering and was still suffering—while the Landaus, father and daughter, hadn't suffered at all!"

Kaye bit her lip savagely. "I guess you'll think I'm crazy—but I made up my mind that I had to have revenge. If they had destroyed me, then I'd make it my business to destroy them! A year back I saw the Landau Research Foundation were looking for a biologist. I wrote Vicki a masterpiece of hearts and flowers—she was the best friend I'd ever had, how could I have invented those dreadful lies about her father?—the whole bit. She swallowed it. A week later I had a cozy interview with Max—he patted my knee a couple of times and I had the job."

"You haven't succeeded in destroying either of them yet?" I asked.

"Not for the want of trying!" she said coldly. "Doctor Altman is Max's oldest friend, you know? I confided in him right from the start! Blushed when I said what could I do because Vicki was my dearest friend, and her father tried to take advantage of the fact? Most always I've kept Max at a distance, but here and there I'd curl up against his manly chest, and plead with him to keep that beast, Altman, away from me. After the first three months they weren't speaking outside the lab.

"Dear little Vicki was hot for Louis Gerard, and making progress, too! One night I let my hair down and sneaked into his room. If Vicki Landau could spend five out of seven nights a week in Bob Marsh's room, I told him, I didn't see why I couldn't visit with him occasionally!"

The smile suddenly faded from her face, and the china blue eyes blanked out. "Things like that," she said listlessly. "I know they're only small things, but you give somebody enough of the small frustrations and one day they suddenly build into something big! Anyway—you've heard enough for one night!"

She got up from the table and walked into the living room. I sat where I was and smoked a cigarette. Then I followed, and found her fully dressed, buttoning up her raincoat.

"You're going?" I said obviously.

"You turned detective on me, lover," she said easily, "and sometime the night got itself disenchanted!"

"You sure you don't want to stay the rest of the night—even on a strictly platonic basis, which means I take the couch?"

She shook her head firmly. "No thanks, Al. It was a lot of fun and now it's back to biology!"

I walked with her to the door and she gave me a placid, old maid aunt's peck on the cheek as a farewell.

"Did my story help you toward catching your murderer?" she asked suddenly as she stepped out into the corridor.

"I don't think so," I said.

She smiled complacently. "I told you it wouldn't."

"Who do you think killed Marsh?" I asked lightly.

"Either Max or Vicki Landau," she answered promptly. "Who else?"

"You're prejudiced!"

"Right!" she said, nodding. "How about you, Lieutenant?—unofficially, of course?"

"I think maybe you did," I told her.

"Thank you!"

"Or it could have been a friend of yours," I added.

"You just heard the story of my life," she said in a hurt voice. "You know I don't have any friends!"

"Hal Kirby is everybody's friend, honey." I grinned knowingly at her. "Right?"

"Hal Kirby?" she repeated slowly. "I don't think I've heard the name before—I know I've never met him. What does he do?"

"He sits around his apartment all the time, figuring out the charities and research institutes he'll reward with a generous donation," I said, "only he never does."

"You're joking?" Kaye said politely.

"I'm deadly serious," I assured her. "I was sure you knew him. I know he's got a good friend in the foundation."

She nibbled her lower lip for a moment. "Would you like me to ask around when I get back?"

"What are you trying to do?" I grinned again. "Deprive an honest cop of his livelihood?"

"I'm depriving him of his sleep already," she said. "Goodbye, Al, I shall always cherish the memory!"

I watched her walk down the hallway, wait a few seconds, then step into the elevator. Then I went back inside the apartment, and wondered.

Chapter Eight

Annabelle gave a keen, discerning look when I came into the office a little after nine the next morning.

"Beautiful morning!" she said brightly.

"Where?" I grunted.

"You know"— she cupped her chin in her hands and leaned her elbows on the desk top while she took time out for a detailed study of my face—"maybe you weren't kidding about being a fag. I've been thinking about it, and maybe you are compensating for something. If you hadn't told me that, I would have been sure you were up to your old tricks again."

"How can you even think such a thing!" I groaned.

"The sunken, bloodshot, apathetic eyes," she said enthusiastically. "The faint tremor in the hands. The dry lips, and the ghastly colored tongue that keeps trying to moisten them! All the old sure signs are there this morning, Lieutenant. Isn't it nice that I don't have a suspicious mind?"

"Be grateful for what you were given from the neck down, honey!" I grated. "Hoping for a brain would be pushing it a little too far, don't you think?"

"Wheeler!" I shuddered involuntarily at the frantic bellow which suddenly blasted out of the sheriff's office.

"Somebody wants you, Al," Annabelle said sweetly. "I think that's hysterical!"

I tottered past her desk and fumbled my way into Laver's office, then sank quickly into the nearest chair.

"My God!" he said in a shaken voice. "I never dare ask what you do with your nights, Wheeler, in case you tell me, but whatever it is, you'll have to stop! The county can't afford the expense of keeping blood donors permanently on call just for you!"

188

GIRL IN A SHROUD   189

"Everyone is so bright this morning," I said from between tightly clenched teeth, "so witty! It makes for such a stimulating prelude to the day's work. I find myself chuckling merrily on my way to another unsolved homicide—whistling homely little songs while I'm standing in the morgue—"

"There must have been some good reason why I insisted you drag that death mask you're using for a face in here," Lavers grunted. "I remember! Kirby!"

"Hal Kirby?" I felt a small stab of interest pierce my throbbing skull.

"You were right about him—amazingly enough," he said sourly. "I had a call from Captain Songar in L.A. From what he said, this Kirby is a real sweet character."

"What did he say?" I snarled.

"He's one half of a time," the sheriff continued in an unperturbed voice. "The other half is a man named Johnny King. 'Kirby and King'—sounds like an old-time vaudeville act, doesn't it?"

"Save the sparkling asides for your memoirs, Sheriff," I pleaded. "I may not have long to live, and I'd like to hear it all before I go."

"Blackmail—extortion," he growled. "The dirtiest kind is their specialty. I understand from Songar. Kirby is the ferret who sniffs around anything that looks promising—you know the thing, who's sleeping with whom, who likes to screw young boys, orgies among the well-placed, drugs and financial double-dealing—it's a rich, productive field in this free society of ours. Once he's had a lead he's worse than a bloodhound, Songar says, and his files of clippings and cross-references would be a fortune to anyone."

"I've met Kirby," I said. "I can imagine! How about the other guy—King?"

"The strong arm," Lavers grunted. "When they've got a victim already lined up, it's King who makes the first approach. It makes for a double threat—if the victim doesn't pay up he's not only scared of being exposed, he's also scared of the physical violence King's promised him, too. So, if you want my advice, Wheeler, you'll—"

His phone rang sharply and he glared, like it had just delivered a personal insult. "You'll take Polnik and—" The phone rang a second time. "Useless damned thing!" he snarled. "Why the hell would anybody bother investing it in the first place?" He grabbed it off the hook and grunted "Lavers" into the mouthpiece. "Put him on!" He pinched his fourth chin reflectively while he waited. "Yes, this is the county sheriff! Now, hold it! . . . Calm down and start over, I didn't understand a goddamn word! . . . That's better, much better! . . . You . . . *what?*"

I got a certain vicarious pleasure out of watching his face slowly change color from its normal flushed pink to a bilious green. "Of course," he croaked. "Right away!" He hung up and stared at me blindly for a few seconds.

"Good news, sir?" I said gleefully.

"The Pine City Bank and Trust opened their vault this morning as usual," he said hoarsely. "The timing mechanism was set for nine-thirty, as usual. Only after it was open, they found something this morning that's most unusual!"

"You have me breathless," I assured him.

"They are missing a little money from inside their vault," he said thickly. "On first count it's around two hundred and forty thousand dollars, but they think it could be more, the second count should be more accurate!"

"Sheriff," I gulped hard. "I'm impressed!"

"Well—" the normal color slowly seeped back into his face "—just don't sit there, Wheeler! Get on over to the bank!"

"And what do I do with my homicide investigation? File it?" I snarled. "Why don't you get the FBI for this? The Pine City bank is insured by Federal Deposit Insurance, isn't it? That makes it FBI business."

"Thank you so much, Lieutenant Wheeler, for reminding me that this involves a violation of a Federal statute! It so happens I was already aware of the fact—and was already about to call the local FBI office. Now—a few facts for you, Lieutenant!" His voice rose to a sudden thundering crescendo. "That bank is in Pine City County—and it's stacked full of employees who all vote in the same county! So that's why you're about to rush right over there and make a big impression—I do mean a favorable one!—of the sheriff's office, and its speedy, efficient response to a call for help!" His bulging index finger sliced the air in my direction. "You strut around that bank and ask a million questions and look wise at every answer, Wheeler! You keep on doing just that until the FBI agents get there, you understand? I need those votes come next election!"

GIRL IN A SHROUD

"Yes, sir!" I said respectfully. "I'm gone already."

Sergeant Polnik was talking happily to Annabelle Jackson as I came back to the outer office. It was easier to grab his arm and pull him along after me than to stop first and explain. I bundled him into the passenger's seat, got in the other side, then drove out from the curb at a rapid rate of acceleration.

"We're on our way to the Pine City Bank and Trust," I told the sergeant briefly.

"What's up?" Polnik demanded. "I hadn't finished talking to Annabelle. Actually, she was even beginning to show some interest."

"What could be more interesting," I snarled, "than a bank being knocked over for close to a quarter-million?"

"How's that?" Polnik shook his head violently a couple of times, then stared disbelievingly out the windshield.

"A bank," I said deliberately. "Robbed."

"So what's new?" he demanded gruffly. "Banks are getting robbed all the time. This is the age of the bank robber. It's a growth industry."

Ten minutes later, we had pulled up outside the bank in question. "Take the car," I told Polnik, "and nose around the immediate neighborhood of that funeral home where we found the corpse yesterday morning."

"What's up?" he asked.

"I got a line on the mortician," I told him. "I want you to check and find out what kind of a guy he is—how much work he does, what time does he usually start in the mornings, when does he finish—stuff like that."

"Yes, sir, Lieutenant." Polnik stuffed himself into the seat I had just vacated. "I'm on my way."

There was an agonized scream of tortured brakes just as I reached the curb. I looked back reluctantly and the sergeant waved happily before heading the car out into the traffic, charging into it like a wounded buffalo and blithely ignoring the outraged horn blasts and screeching brakes.

I could see right off when I walked into his office that there was something missing from Mr. Castle himself. Where had the warm friendly smile of my neighborhood banking buddy gone?

"Lieutenant Wheeler, thank heaven you're here!" He gave

me a haggard look. "That this should happen to us! A quarter of a million dollars stolen from within our very vault!"

"Maybe we could take a look at the vault first?" I suggested politely.

"It's impregnable," Castle muttered, "impregnable!"

And so it was still, when I looked at it a few minutes later. I carried out the sheriff's instructions to the letter, spending the next hour asking questions and looking wise at all the answers, until the two Federal agents arrived.

I took them into Castle's office and tactfully suggested he take a coffee break. The tall, fat, tough-looking FBI agent, who said almost nothing, was called Peters, I discovered. While the tall, thin, tough-looking one, who also said almost nothing, was called Kardos.

"The vault hasn't been touched," I told them. "The timing mechanism was set yesterday afternoon as usual, for nine-thirty this morning. When they opened it up at nine-thirty this morning, they found almost a quarter of a million dollars missing."

"No outside locks or windows tampered with?" Kardos asked mildly.

"Nothing," I said.

"Makes it easier, I always figure, when it's an inside job," Peters said comfortably.

"Well," I said carefully. "Only two people know the combination and how to set the timing mechanism. Castle, the president; and the vice-president, McPhail. Castle claims he was at a school reunion dinner until after midnight, then he, his wife, and three old school buddies who were staying the night, drove back to his place. His wife went straight to bed. The old school buddies got to talking about old times and would up playing stud poker through until seven this morning."

"McPhail?" Kardos rasped.

"Is in Seattle until the day after tomorrow, attending a bankers' conference," I said woodenly.

"Don't let's get nervous until we check out Castle's alibi," Peters grunted, but the tone of his voice left no doubt that he was nervous already.

"I hate to do this to you boys," I said apologetically. "There is just one more thing."

"I don't want to hear it," Kardos grated, "but I guess I don't have the choice?"

"The night guard has to punch a time clock on the hour, every hour, through the night," I said. "He did just that last night, and also swears he didn't see or hear anything unusual the whole night through."

The two agents looked at each other for maybe ten seconds, then they both started talking at once.

"I hate muscling in, anyway," Kardos said with a big affable grin plastered across his face. "After all, it is county territory and—"

"You've done all the hard work already, Lieutenant," Peters said, with a look of frank admiration on his face. "It's not right we should cut in now and steal your glory—"

"Good day, gentlemen," I said quickly, "and may I wish you the best of luck?"

Chapter Nine

"Sure was lucky me coming back when I did, and seeing you standing on the sidewalk outside the bank, huh, Lieutenant?" Polnik said cheerfully.

"Yes," I said thoughtfully, "and I'd only been there a half hour, too!"

"Sure was lucky," he repeated happily. He stared through the windshield at the road ahead for a few seconds, then shrugged massively. "When you think about all the traffic there is around nowadays."

"Not to mention the hazards," I said with a shudder, remembering the outraged horn blasts and screeching brakes.

"I guess," he said absently. "Like I told you, Lieutenant, there's this gas station on the other side of the street, almost opposite the mortuary. And does the guy who owns it hate the mortician's guts! He says Brenner never starts work before nine at best, and he quits any time after three in the afternoon."

"You did a good job, Sergeant," I told him. "Let's go see if he's found any more unknown stiffs lately."

The pint-sized mortician didn't look delighted to see us exactly, when we walked into his office ten minutes later.

"It's Lieutenant—uh—Wheeler." He made a big effort and almost achieved a smile of welcome. "And Sergeant—uh—"

"How are you, Mr. Brenner?" I said cheerfully. "Haven't found any more strange stiffs lately?"

"Dear me, no!" He dabbed his forehead with a fine linen handkerchief. "I hope I never shall! One experience like that is quite enough to last a lifetime, don't you agree, Lieutenant?"

"I don't know," I said doubtfully. "At a couple of hundred

bucks a time, I'd figure one a week would be just fine. What do you think, Sergeant?"

Polnik fixed the little mortician with a fish-eyed stare he'd obviously stolen from some medieval torturer. "I think he's a creep!" he said stolidly.

"Well, really!" Brenner said, dabbing faster. "I won't be insulted like that again!"

"Next time I'll do better!" Polnik said, his voice sounding like a cement-mixer in low gear.

"We don't mind you making a fast two hundred, Mr. Brenner," I said easily. "We just don't like the way you involved us in the deal. It cost us sleep."

"I really have no idea what you're talking about!" he quavered.

"Mr. Brenner!" I gave him the real cold cop stare, the one that takes a couple of years' regular practice before anybody can get it right. "I'll do this just once, and you tell me where I'm wrong!"

"I still don't understand?" Brenner whimpered.

"It would be a wonderful practical joke on his daughter," I said. "There was no chance of her waking up inside your mortuary because he'd be sure she was under sedation. All you had to do was leave the back door unlocked, get here early in the morning to make sure everything was okay, and he'd come by at eight and pick her up. There was a—hundred?—in it for you."

"Fifty!" The little guy said, without thinking.

"Fifty?" I looked at him curiously.

"That was the first time we talked it over." He shook his head piteously. "If I'd known it would cause all this trouble!"

"Tell me about the second time?" I suggested.

"He called me quite late the evening before," Brenner said nervously. "Said it would make the joke even better if I reported an unknown body in one of my caskets. I argued, but he said he'd double the original payment if I'd go along with it."

"So you did, of course," I grunted. "The first time, he came here in person?"

"Yes, yes, indeed!" Brenner nodded vigorously. "I wouldn't have considered it, only him being a doctor and all, I thought—"

"This place stinks, Lieutenant!" Polnik rasped suddenly. "Can we get out of here?"

"Sure," I said, "we're all through now."

"What about me?" the plump little man whimpered. "What's going to happen to me, Lieutenant, sir?"

"I don't know yet," I said truthfully, then gave him an encouraging smile. "But don't worry—we'll think of something!"

We left him gnawing a bunch of fingernails and I hoped he'd gotten down to his wrists before he realized nothing was going to happen to him, anyway.

Polnik grunted suddenly as we got back into the car.

"Hey, Lieutenant? How did you figure out it was a phony—a put-up job—huh?"

"A string of coincidences," I said. "I should've seen it right away if I'd been smart. A mortician who happens to start work at seven A.M. and right off finds an unknown corpse in one of his caskets?—Doctor Landau so wonderfully casual about the whole bit—it was the first mortuary we came to, he said! The back door coincidence being left unlocked? Remember when the corpse sat up and smiled at us?"

"I've been trying to forget it, Lieutenant!" There was a plaintive note in his voice.

"It was a hell of a shock," I admitted. "But we survived it. Only Brenner reacted violently. He hammed it up a little too much. He overdid it. For the sweet love of Jesus, the man's a mortician after all, dealing with dead bodies all the time, which means he has to have some sort of nerve."

When we arrived at the apartment, I rang the doorbell, and a moment later the door opened. The blonde Amazon was standing there looking blankly out at us. Polnik gave a small yelp, and I could tell he was impressed. If he had had a tail, he would have been wagging it.

Sandra had traded the canary-colored sweater for a dusty-pink silk shirt which might as well not have been there at all, if it was worn for the sake of modesty. Through it, I could make out the heavy hang of her breasts in almost every loving detail. She was wearing the same tight slacks which were every bit as revealing as they stretched snugly over the sweeping grandeur of her hips and traced the dominant rise of her venus mound.

GIRL IN A SHROUD

"So I'll let myself in," I told her, "while you stay here and keep the sergeant company." I made a dramatic flourish. "Meet Sergeant Polnik, the bravest guy on the force. He thinks you're magnificent, and he does like his women big and strapping."

"Yeah?" She looked him over critically then nodded as if satisfied with what she saw. "Strapping eh? Are you into bondage, too?"

"Huh?" Polnik looked at me helplessly.

"Just her little joke," I told him.

"I must say, with his size, he might look a little bit stupid," Sandra observed. "Still, it might make an interesting change. Who needs sensitivity all the time? I mean, some of the guys—the ones I've met—get so broken up and emotional."

It was time to leave them. "Just look after Sandra here, will you?" I said quickly to the sergeant. "I'm sure she'll keep you entertained."

"Yeah," Polnik said, almost licking his thick lips. "I bet she will."

I walked inside the apartment and there was Kirby still horizontal on the couch, still catching peanuts in his mouth. Behind the couch stood a massively built guy who looked like he carried around 250 pounds on his six-foot-four frame, at minimum. Someone had taken a sledgehammer and roughly pounded out a few primitive features where his face should have been—a spreading nose that had been busted in a couple of places—a horizontal slit for a mouth—a couple of small agate pebbles rammed each side of the nose for eyes. A loose sprinkling of coarse brown hair on top of his skull completed the make-shift job.

Kirby looked up and scowled at me. "It's you," he barked hoarsely, "back again?"

"Hi, Robin Hood," I said brightly, then glanced at the man-mountain standing in back of the couch. "Who's that? Little John?"

"Who's the creep?" the mountain growled in a voice so deep it sounded like it never touched his lungs, but kept right on going down to his boots

"C-O-P!" Kirby made a production of whispering the word from the protection of one hand held in front of his mouth. "I also figure he's some kind of nut, but he's carrying a badge."

"The celebrated duo—Kirby and King—masters of extortion!" I made like an emcee for a moment. "How many of the Landau Research Foundation team have you got tucked away in your cross-indexed files, hey, Kirby?"

He tossed a peanut into the air and caught it neatly, then shook his head slowly. "Where do you get this stuff from?" he asked plaintively. "I never heard of the joint until you came barging in here yesterday, yelling your head off about it!"

"Where were you last night?" I asked. "Both of you?"

"What's it to you?" King growled.

"I know it's not an original thought," I said coldly. "But we can do this the easy way, or we can go downtown!"

"Tell him, Johnny!" King croaked. "What's the big secret we got? We was here all night, right?"

"Sure," King said.

"The three of us," Kirby added. "Sandra, too. You ask her! We had a wild night watching television and drinking beer! What's so important about last night, anyway?"

"Somebody knocked off the Pine City Bank and Trust for a quarter million," I said.

"Yeah?" King looked real impressed.

"Hey, Lieutenant?" Kirby's voice was derisive. "Do we look like a couple of guys who'd knock off a bank?"

"No," I admitted. "You look like a couple of guys who'd let somebody else knock off a bank for you—then double-cross them out of their cut!"

The peanut hit the tip of his nose, then bounced onto his chest, and he didn't even notice. "Just what's with that crack?" he asked carefully.

"All that money must be burning a hole someplace," I said idly. "You mind if I take a look around the apartment?"

"Help yourself," Kirby said with a shrug.

"In that case I won't bother," I told him. "The FBI's handling the bank job so maybe you'll get more visitors through the day."

"Feds—cops—what's the difference?" King growled disgustedly. "They all got nothing better to do than get in your hair the whole time!"

"There's not too much room in yours either, is there?" I looked critically at the bald patches showing through the sparse brown crop on top of his head.

GIRL IN A SHROUD

"I'd offer you a drink only I guess you have to go now, Lieutenant?" Kirby barked hurriedly at me.

King's face slowly turned a mottled red. "I hate a wise guy!" he said thickly. "Some bum who comes around making personal remarks!" He lumbered around the couch toward me, and Kirby was so alarmed, he actually sat up.

"Johnny!" he yelped. "Take it easy."

"Let him come," I snarled. "I'll put a slug in him for resisting arrest!"

The lumbering mountain came to a sudden halt. "What did you say?" he mumbled wildly.

"You heard me!" I snapped. "Me and the county sheriff have got this town sewn up! By the time the boys finish working you over in the tank, you'll be convinced it was your own fault and plead guilty—either that, or you never will get into court!" I always figure the best lies are the real wild ones, because most people figure nobody would try and get away with an outrageous lie, so it has to be true.

"Don't stay in Pine City much longer, boys," I said gently. "Or I'll have to organize something for the both of you, so you get to stay a real long time!"

I went back out of the apartment, detached Polnik from the warm approving gaze of Sandra, and dragged him toward the elevators. By the time we reached the sidewalk, his eyeballs were only partially glazed.

"I want you to keep a stake-out on the apartment house," I told him. "Go call the office first and let them know, so they can organize your relief, right? Tell them I'm going out to the research foundation, and if either Kirby or King leave the building I want them followed, and I want to know where they go."

"Sure thing, Lieutenant," Polnik said blissfully. "Jeez, that woman, she sure is something. And every bit of her real."

"Just make sure somebody tells me if either of those hoods make a move," I reminded him.

"Don't worry about a thing, Lieutenant," he said confidently. "Christ, those boobs—"

I walked across to the car, leaving him standing in the center of the sidewalk blissfully confiding his secrets to an incurious dog and—by the time I pulled away from the curb—to a little old lady who wore a hearing aid and was doing her best to tell him the quickest way to the downtown shopping mart.

Chapter Ten

The girl in the neat white uniform coat had white-blonde hair pulled straight back across her head and held in a knot in back. Her face had a well-scrubbed aseptic look, and the heavy black-framed glasses windowed a pair of china blue eyes that were arctic-bleak.

"Doctor Landau is busy in his office right now," she said crisply, "so if you wish to talk to me in private, Lieutenant, we can go up to my room."

"That will be fine, Miss Allen," I murmured.

I followed the crackling starched uniform up the stairs, then along the hallway until we reached the room. It had that aseptic, scrubbed look too, and the furnishings were strictly functional in keeping with the rest of the house. Miss Allen closed the door behind her carefully, then looked at me with a discerning expression on her face.

"Oh, brother!" she said. "You're pooped!"

"Big day!" I told her, and sat down gratefully on the side of the bed.

She leaned against the door and lit a cigarette. "And I thought you came all the way out here just to see if you could talk me out of my black underwear during working hours!" She pouted. "I'm hurt!"

"A quarter of a million dollars taken from the bank," I said slowly, "Marsh's murderer still running loose. Time is also running out fast, honey. We got to talk about a lot of things but they all have to be true—like no more direct lies, half-lies, evasions, omissions, okay?"

"Go on," she said crisply.

"A fantasy!" I said in a wondering voice "Right out of a comic book, even. Who would believe it if you told them?

GIRL IN A SHROUD   201

Only me, Kaye, honey, I guess—because you gave me a practical demonstration last night?"

"I won't say I don't know what you're talking about"—she smiled briefly—"but I'm not commenting, either!"

"Altman told me you were working on the possibilities of combining a—hallucinogenic?—and a hypnotic sedative. That's it, I guess, the Mickey Finn you slipped me last night?"

"That's it, Al," she said soberly.

"The final test was Vicki Landau—have her sleep in a casket, in somebody's private mortuary, and make sure she remembered nothing about it when she woke at eight, as ordered. Did they give her a trigger word the same as you gave me, so afterwards she would remember?"

"They gave her a trigger word," Kaye said, nodding.

"But they didn't give one to the president of the Pine City Bank and Trust, I guess? Or the night guard inside the bank?"

The china blue eyes were carefully blank as they stared at the wall above my head.

"I was thinking about it while I was driving out here," I went on. "Once you'd given Castle—the bank president—the drug, you gave him his instructions and told him when he'd carried them out he'd never remember a thing about it, of course. Tell him to reset the time lock so the vault could be opened at the time you wanted—say, midnight? Learn how to reset it from him, so it will open again at the usual time in the morning; and don't forget the name and address of the night guard, either, because he has to get a shot, too. So you can tell him to open up the back door of the bank for you just before midnight, and lock it after you leave with your quarter million—and he's told he'll never remember what happened, either."

"I love to hear you talk, Al," she said softly, "even when it doesn't make any sense."

"I kept asking myself why a bunch of dedicated research scientists would plan a bank robbery," I continued slowly, "and the funny thing is, it's because they *are* dedicated—and led by a man who's part-genius, and has no morality at all. This drug of yours could be about the biggest thing yet in its field, I guess?"

"The biggest!"

"But before you publicized it in the medical field—before

you could expect anybody to take it seriously—you'd have to come up with a track record for the drug. Maybe thousands of test cases where it had been used successfully in psychotherapy and so on? Having discovered the drug, I guess the team, especially Landau, would want to handle all that themselves and it would take more money than the Landau Foundation would get in a hundred years! Max Landau's answer to that would be typical of his own peculiar genius—why don't we use the drug to help us get the money we need to establish the drug so we can help the mentally sick?" I took a deep breath. "A beautifully simple equation—drug equals money equals drug established!"

"Is that the end of the story?" she asked politely.

"Only the beginning," I grated. "Let's take a closer look at Landau's research team for a moment, huh? Landau himself—we've about established what he is. Then there was Marsh and Gerard—both young, intensely loyal, and *dedicated!* They would be no problem. Vicki—his own daughter—would be no problem, either Altman, I figure, is not a dedicated guy, but he's Landau's oldest friend and owes him a lot, so he'll go along. That leaves just you, honey?"

"Did you save me for last because I'm something special, or merely the least important, Al?"

"You were dedicated to the destruction of the Landaus, father and daughter," I said. "But you'd go along with this kind of deal happily, because you'd see a greater chance for their destruction in this kind of wild project. So why was one of the most passionately loyal members of the team murdered the night before the robbery was planned? The same night the final test with Vicki as the subject took place?"

"You're asking me?" Kaye raised her eyebrows.

"Telling you, what else?" I grinned briefly at her. "Once you know of the team being involved in a conspiracy, it has to be one of two reasons why Marsh was murdered. He was a traitor to the conspiracy and was found out—or he discovered a traitor who killed him before Marsh had a chance to expose him to the others."

"Which side are you on?" she asked casually.

"Marsh was no traitor," I said confidently. "When I searched his clothing I found a typed note with a name and address—Hal Kirby, and the name of the bank that was knocked over last night. It was a deliberate lead to the reason for a traitor. Kirby and his partner Johnny King are a notorious partnership specializing in blackmail and extortion. The traitor was being blackmailed by Kirby, and saw his chance to get free if he cut him in on the robbery. Somehow Marsh discovered his plans and was about to tell Landau—so he had to be killed."

"This is starting to get real complicated," Kaye said easily. "I'm not sure if I can keep up with these convoluted twists and turns."

"If Marsh had any idea his life was in danger he'd have left a note naming his suspected murderer and giving all the details he knew about the traitor," I said. "That neatly typed lead to Kirby was put into the pocket of Marsh's suit after he'd been murdered."

"By whom?"

"The same person who's been so busy helping me all along in the investigation, I guess," I told her. "The one who gave me a practical demonstration of the drug so I would know it could work on the bank personnel because it had worked on me—the same person who gave me such a detailed rundown on the lives of the Landau family last night—you, honey."

"You think I'm the traitor who killed Marsh?" she whispered.

"I think there's more than one traitor who could have killed Marsh," I grunted. "I think there's more than one person in the research team being blackmailed by Kirby. I want Marsh's murderer real bad, and I want Kirby, too. But there isn't much time—"

"What do you mean by that?" she asked quickly.

"When Landau and his fellow conspirators took that money out of the bank last night, they had to hide it someplace," I said. "I figure the deal the traitor's already made with Kirby is to tell him where he can find the money, and later they'll split it between them."

"Oh?" Kaye said faintly.

"You want to tell me what Kirby's got on you, for a start, honey?" I said gently.

She shook her head mutely, the china blue eyes staring at the wall above my head again, with a look of sudden fear in them.

"Okay," I shrugged, and got onto my feet. "Then I'll go

downstairs and start going through the same routine with the others."

"I don't think that will be necessary, Al." Her voice shook slightly, while she still stared at the wall. "I have a strong feeling that right after Bob Marsh was found murdered, Landau bugged every room in the house!"

"Can you see the microphone from where you are?" I asked.

"Maybe, I'm not sure—but it doesn't matter now, does it?" she said listlessly. "If he has got the house bugged, he's heard every word we said!"

"Why don't we go down and find out?" I suggested.

They were waiting for us at the bottom of the stairs in a tight group. Max Landau, that cruel clever caricature of a face saturnine and watchful; Vickie, with her mouth twisted petulantly, her natural arrogance now cold and calculating as her dark eyes looked at Kaye Allen with a smouldering hate. Theodore Altman's fleshy face had a carefully neutral expression, the bright blue eyes sunken in fatty tissues more bland than ever. Louis Gerard had a deeply troubled look in his brooding gray eyes, and a nervous tic jumped spasmodically in his forehead a couple of inches above his left eye.

Landau smiled jovially and the fine mesh of wrinkled skin that covered his face suddenly tautened, aging him another fifty years. "A welcoming party, Lieutenant!" He chuckled boyishly, while his dark eyes made an openly obscene mockery of me and everything I represented. "You will stay for lunch? Vicki has it all ready and waiting. Beef hash—her speciality!"

"Thank you," I said gravely. "You're sure that quarter of a million dollars will keep until after lunch, Doctor? You don't think Kirby and King might get to it during that time? If they did, it would make that beef hash about the most expensive there's been yet, huh?"

"I can't think of the right word to describe your sense of humor, Lieutenant!" His rich baritone flooded the whole ground floor of the house. "Let me see now? *Delightful* is not exactly the word I'd want. *Roguish*—there's an implication of cuteness which isn't strictly true, is it?"

He took my elbow and walked with me into the dining room, with Kaye directly in back of us, and the others behind her. "Do sit down, Lieutenant. The head of the table if you please—after all, you're the guest of honor here today!"

I sat down at the head of the table. Landau took a chair next to me on one side and gestured for Kaye to do the same on the other side. Vicki looked at him inquiringly and he nodded. "By all means, my dear, serve it right away. And a bottle of the good claret, I think? This is an occasion, admittedly unexpected, but still an occasion!"

Altman left space for Vickie next to her father, and then sat down. Gerard took a chair next to Kaye's—and then it was set for a real cozy family-type meal, I guessed.

"Kaye was absolutely right," Landau said in a conversational voice. "I've had every room in this house wired for sound since poor Bob's death. We were quite fascinated by your incredibly imaginative theories, Lieutenant." He laughed. "They were really quite wild. You have a fertile mind, which I suppose in some fields would stand you in very good stead. But for a police officer?" He shook his head. "A police officer has to deal only in facts."

Vicki served the hash, poured the claret, then sat down next to her father. She glanced at me coldly. "You must have had a wild time at your place last night," she said. "Kaye looked positively exhausted this morning. I'm sure you must have opened up a whole new world for her. Or was it she who was teaching you how?"

"Vicki, darling," Landau said good humoredly, "you mustn't insult our guest of honor."

"I don't mind," I assured him. "The hash is just great. Reminds me of what my uncle used to say—if you've got to marry a bitch, then marry a bitch who can cook!" I smiled innocently around the table, and collected an assortment of stony glares.

"It's the coarseness that repels you more than anything else, I think," Vicki said in a detached voice to nobody in particular. "You can never really ignore breeding, can you?"

"Right," I agreed. "Look what happens to the lemmings."

Landau threw back his head and guffawed. "Touché! I think both of you should concede a draw. Lieutenant, just for the hell of it, why don't you continue your little game of fantasy you were playing in Kaye's room? We'd all be fascinated to play, we really would!"

"To find the traitor?" I said. "Why not?" I looked at Kaye

and saw the panic shuttered in back of the heavy-framed glasses. "I have to know," I said softly. "What has Kirby got that he can blackmail you with?"

"Photographs," she said, and stared down at the plate in front of her.

"Photographs of what?"

"Some charmingly intimate scenes played in a hotel room without knowledge of the camera in the background," she said in a flat monotonous voice that was close to the edge of hysteria. "There are only two people featured in them. Myself—and Max Landau!"

There was a sharp hissing sound as Vicki drew in a deep breath. "You're lying again," she said shrilly, "you dirty little—"

"Vicki!" Landau snapped, and she stopped saying the words out loud, but her eyes kept saying them over and over again.

"Why are they worth paying blackmail for?" I asked Kaye. "The only person it could hurt would be Vickie—and you wouldn't have cared about that?"

"At the hospital, when I told Mrs. Landau I'd testify that her husband had raped me while I was a guest at their house, she finally bought me off with a check for twenty-five thousand dollars." She closed her eyes for a long moment. "Those photographs were taken later the same year—it's very obvious that I'm no older than eighteen or nineteen. The picture of the lily-white flower despoiled can't possibly hold up, can it," she stated bitterly. "I'm afraid that maybe her estate can claim back the money she paid me. Kirby as much as said so. And of course I haven't even got it now."

"Har, har, har," Vicki sneered with real venom. "You were taken, in more ways than one!"

"Let's return to the lieutenant's game," Landau said easily. "Lieutenant?"

"The traitor has to be someone being blackmailed by Kirby," I said. "We now know Kaye is—so she's the first candidate as traitor. Is there anybody else at this table being blackmailed, too?"

"I doubt if anyone will come right out and admit it, Lieutenant," Landau said after a few seconds' silence. "I think you'll have to detect it out of them, you know?"

"Why don't we start eliminating the unlikely ones?" I suggested. "Marsh was killed to prevent him telling you who the traitor was—that alone is obviously enough to take your name off the list."

"I'm flattered!" Landau smiled. "Anyone else?"

"Louis Gerard." I nodded down the table toward the chemist. "He's one of the original dedicated boys, along with Marsh: thinks you are God's gift to science and humanity and therefore can do no wrong! I imagine this will be about the last of the childish fantasies he'll allow himself to indulge in. I hope so, for his sake!"

Gerard's face flushed slightly and he carefully concentrated on the blank wall opposite.

"That narrows down the field to two," I said easily. "Your daughter, and your oldest friend, Doctor Landau, by some unhappy coincidence."

"Go on!" he grated.

"Vicki doesn't seem a very likely candidate—from what I've heard she's always worshiped the ground you wiped your shoes on, so I figure if she'd ever been in any real trouble, the first thing she would have done would be to come crying to you for help. If she was being blackmailed, you would have known about that long before now."

"Don't do me any favors, Lieutenant!" Vickie said petulantly.

"Then that leaves only my oldest friend, and trusted colleague, Doctor Altman?" Landau said softly. "How do you rate him, Lieutenant?"

"I can only generalize, and you'll have to bear with it for a little while," I said. "What a cop learns about people, that sort of thing. If somebody tells you a long story you haven't even asked for: or carries it a hell of a lot further than you asked for—as Kaye did with me last night, for example. You wonder why they took all the trouble and almost invariably you come up with the same answer—because they're hoping to pass off a pack of lies as the truth—or some truth mingled with some lies as the whole truth.

"Kaye gave me a long sad story of how her life was ruined by what happened that day you were waiting in her room when she came out of the shower." I looked at Landau. "A stack of tear-jerking lies to cover up the fact she obviously enjoyed your company or those photographs could never have been taken, could they?"

"May lightning strike you dead, Al Wheeler!" Kaye said bitterly.

"Getting back to Doctor Altman," I said. "He gave me an immensely detailed story of his life from 1938 on. Why? I know Kirby has a fantastic collection of clippings that must go back at least as far as the end of the war. It's just possible he tied in Doctor Altman as being someone else—maybe a Nazi doctor at Auschwitz who was wanted to stand trial for the war crimes he'd committed. I don't say it's likely, even, only that it's possible."

Landau stared across the table at Altman, and for the first time the innate savagery showed on the fine-wrinkled face, so it was no longer distinguished, only ugly and ruthless.

"Well, Theodore?" he snarled.

Altman slowly mopped the sweat from his shining head with an outsize handkerchief. "It is not true, Max! I swear it, by our friendship, by everything you have ever done for me since that first day we met! I could not betray you, old friend."

Landau nodded slowly, then looked at me again. "I know Theodore," he said softly, "and I believe him. Doesn't that bring us back to where we started, Lieutenant?"

"With Kaye Allen," I said easily. "Yes, it does! Whose idea was it, Kaye, that you should get a job here with the Landau Foundation?"

"Al?" Her eyes pleaded with me fearfully. "It's not me, I swear it!"

"Whose idea?" I repeated coldly.

Her shoulder slumped; the china blue eyes gave up fighting, and gave up hope at the same time. "Hal Kirby," she said tonelessly.

"Now we're getting close to the real truth at last," Landau said with savage satisfaction. "Why did Kirby send you to spy on us a year back?"

"I don't know," Kaye said helplessly. "He told me to do something, I did it. While he's got those photographs I don't have any free choice!"

"How about that?" I said loudly, without looking at anyone in particular. "From the time Kirby had those pictures, he could control her whole life! But for my money, the real smart operator is the one who *took* the pictures. Whoever it was that figured out how they could conceal themselves and

GIRL IN A SHROUD   209

their camera close enough to get a whole series of action shots—"

"All right!" Landau winced. "That's enough, Lieutenant. We'll never know now who did take the goddamn things, anyway!"

"I don't know." I shrugged easily. "What were you doing at the time, Vicki?"

She straightened her back, arching her neck proudly, while the malignant laughter danced and whirled in her eyes.

"You know something about sex when you're not a participant, only an observer?" She giggled abruptly. "It's the most hilariously funny thing to watch you've ever seen! Half the time I had trouble holding the camera, even!"

"Vicki!" Landau stared blankly at his daughter's face like he was seeing it for the first time. "You!"

"Yes, me!" She turned toward him with the swiftness of a striking snake. "I worshiped you from the time I could crawl!" she said in a soft, venomous voice. "Kaye was my best friend! And the first time I left you alone together, you both jumped into bed—under the same roof where my mother—your wife—lay dying! I swore then that both of you would pay for it, and keep paying as long as you lived."

"How did you know Kirby, that you could give him the photographs?" Kaye asked bewilderedly.

"There was an—accident—at the new college where I went after you caused me all that trouble!" Vickie said sullenly. "It was kind of hushed up, but Kirby saw a garbled report in the local newspaper and tied it in with the first one. So I'd do as I was told or he'd match both accounts and give them to the new college. He's a real bright man, that Hal Kirby!" She giggled again. "He even had a kind of points system. If I could bring him a better piece of blackmail to use against somebody else than the one he had against me, he promised to make a deal. Those candid pictures of dear old Daddy rolling in the hay with my best girl friend took me off the hook just fine!"

She smiled weirdly at Kaye. "And it was my idea to have Kirby make you get a job here. I wanted you close so I could see you squirm, honey! But the wildest thing of all, of course, was dear old Daddy and his nut-house gang setting out to rob a bank!"

Vicki swung back toward Landau, and laughed in his face. "What a pompous intellectual idiot you are!"

I grabbed his arm warningly. "Vicki," I said urgently, "how about Marsh?"

"That creep?" She shrugged distastefully. "If he *would* wear sneakers around the house all the time, it was his own fault what happened! He overheard me talking to Hal Kirby on the phone when I was sure everybody else was in the lab. I didn't know anything about it until that night when he walked into my room—then got into bed beside me and said we'd have to think of the best way to tell my father—later!

"I stalled him the next day, and that night was the big experiment when little Vicki took the dope and performed. So I used my little-girl manner and pleaded with him to wait until the next day, so I didn't have to tell my father until I'd helped him a little, anyway! The drug went down the sink, of course! I listened while dear Daddy gave me all that involved crap about driving myself out to the private mortuary and sleeping in the casket until eight the next morning. I suffered while darling Kaye wrapped me in that cute winding-sheet, then off I went. I parked a couple of blocks away and waited an hour, then came straight back to the house."

She giggled again. "I slipped into Bob Marsh's room, woke him up with passionate kisses, and told him I was lonely and scared so would he spend the night with me? Would he just! We sneaked out of the house again and drove to the mortuary, and that casket display room made him a little nervous. I told him it was a hilarious place to make love, but if he was chicken he could get lost. He said he *wasn't* chicken, so I told him to prove it by getting into one of the caskets and lying down. I'd brought my purse in with me from the car, and dear old Daddy's trusty thirty-eight was inside the purse."

The sound of her sudden laughter made my scalp crawl gently. "You should have seen his stupid face—lying there in the casket!—when I pointed the gun at him and pulled the trigger!"

"Where's the gun now, Vicki?" I asked softly.

"Back in dear old Daddy's drawer," she sad. "I wiped it clean, of course, the same night, and left it in my purse in the car outside. I had a couple of sedatives with me—special for the occasion! so I took 'em, hopped into the casket next door to Bob's, and went to sleep!"

"It's—macabre!" Landau said hoarsely. "She shot him in cold blood while he lay in a casket in a private mortuary, then casually took a couple of sedatives, lay down in the next casket and went to sleep!" He stared at her wildly. "What kind of a monster are you?"

"The one that you reared, Landau!" I snapped. "She learned her morality from your example."

"Anyway," Vicki said, leaning back in her chair contentedly, "Hal will have the money by now, he knows exactly where to find it, dear old Daddy!"

"I don't think so," Landau muttered.

"Don't kid yourself!" Vicki laughed harshly. "I told Hal the exact place where you put the money last night when you all came back from the bank—under that old cedar tree right out in the—"

"While none of us knew who had killed Marsh, or why," he interrupted her, "I thought that nobody but myself could be trusted. I got up early this morning and moved it to another place a long way from the cedar!"

"Why, you stupid—" the color drained from her face as she stared at him with wide eyes. "Hal must be going crazy out there looking—" Her eyes glazed, as if she'd been suddenly placed in a trance, then her right hand swooped on a table knife, grabbed it, and in one continuous movement, plunged it down toward her father's chest. Landau managed to deflect it with his arm, and the knife clattered on the floor.

At the same moment the door crashed open and the mountainous Johnny King thudded into the room, followed by Hal Kirby. It was the first time I'd seen Kirby on his feet, and I figured he looked more like a carrion bird than a ferret. Both of them had guns in their hands, and from the look on their faces they were just hoping for an excuse to shoot somebody.

"Nobody moves!" King rumbled. "You—cop!" He scowled at me. "Just give me one reason, huh?"

Kirby stared at Vicki, his thin mouth twisted into a fixed sneer, while the tight-controlled fury in his eyes looked dangerously close to breaking point.

"Okay, Vicki," he barked at her. "What sort of joke is this? We've been out there digging in all that dirt, and there's no money—nothing. So what's the game you're playing?"

"No, Hal!" she said quickly. "I only just found out myself this moment, and when I did, I tried to kill him!" She nodded toward Landau. "The stinking louse got up early this morning and moved it again!"

"Real cute!" Kirby moved slowly down the table toward Landau, his mouth working all the time. "You want to tell us where it is now, huh?" he asked.

"You are Hal Kirby?" Landau looked up at him with an expression of arrogant contempt on his face. "The blackmailer, extortionist, and panderer too, I imagine? I think I would have recognized you anywhere. You look just about as dirty and sordid as you should—the way you make a living!"

"Don't push it, little man!" Kirby whispered. "I had a hard day already! Where do we find the money?"

"You'll never find it if you're waiting for me to tell you!" Landau sneered. "If you think I'm frightened of a—"

There was a faintly sickening sound as the gun barrel slammed against the side of Landau's face.

"I told you already," Kirby said in a thin voice, "I had a hard day!"

Landau took his hand away from his face, and his eyes widened as he saw the blood dripping down his fingers.

"You made me bleed!" His voice was thick with shocked indignation. "You dare to use physical violence on me? Why, I'll kill you for—"

"Doctor Landau!" I snarled frantically. "Just shut up, and tell them where you hid the money!"

He glanced at me with searing contempt in his eyes. "I am not a physical coward, Lieutenant! If your nerves won't stand it, mine will!"

"Hit him again, Hal!" Vicki said thinly. "Beat it out of him, why don't you?"

"One last time," Kirby said wearily. "Where do we find the money?"

"Try and beat it out of me!" Landau sat back in his chair, his arms folded across his chest, with a look of stupid pride on his face like he'd just won a victory, or something.

I concentrated on Hal Kirby, because every time I looked in Johnny King's direction I was looking straight down the barrel of a thirty-eight, which is one hell of an aid to the digestion right after lunch.

"I guess not," Kirby said.

GIRL IN A SHROUD

"Ha!" Landau boomed triumphantly. "You see? Stand up to them and—"

There was that faintly sickening sound again, punctuated by a thin, high-pitched scream of pain. Vickie Landau slumped back in her chair, her eyes wide with naked fear, while the crimson welt down one side of her face visibly grew bigger.

"I'll beat it out of her," Kirby whispered. "She's your daughter—right? Well, maybe if I get to work on her, mark her so she'll never look the same again, you can make up your own mind, and if you're wise, decide it would be better to cooperate with us and tell us where to find that money."

"All right," Landau said slowly. "The garage roof—stacked on top of the timbers, you can't—"

Vicki spun around in her chair with startling speed, and raked her nails viciously down the side of Kirby's face. He yelped, pulled back his head instinctively, and Landau lunged out of his chair toward him. I saw the gun barrel waver for a moment as King's attention was distracted, and I went sideways out of my own chair onto the floor, grabbing my thirty-eight from its belt holster.

A slug exploded into the tabletop six inches above my head, as I was halfway up onto my knees. I heard another shot real close, and a scream, followed by a sharp scuffling noise. I lifted my head above the top of the table and ducked back again in one continuous movement; then two more slugs plowed into the solid wood. With a fast-ebbing faith in the luck of the Wheelers, I jerked my head up for a second time, and the gun with it.

Fon a split second I stared at the mountainous bulk of Johnny King, as my gun moved in a small arc toward its target, then I suddenly realized the giant had his back toward me—facing the doorway into the front hall—and was taking a fast powder. I looked around to see what was happening to Kirby just as his gun pointed directly at me. At the same moment, a wild harpie with blood-stained face, wild staring eyes, and a black void where her mouth should have been, dragged herself up from the floor and threw herself onto him.

Kirby's gun exploded, and as her body went limp and slid back toward the floor, Vicki Landau's head suddenly rolled to one side. For a fragment of time, her dying eyes looked at me with stark disbelief in their own mortality, then her head vanished beneath the tabletop level.

For a moment there, I figured Kirby was confused by the unexpected attack from Vicki, and by his accidentally killing her. His confusion wasn't going to last any time at all, I was sure, and the barrel of his gun only needed a two-inch deflection at most to put a slug straight into my stomach. So I took advantage of his momentary confusion and put three slugs into his chest which punched him back against the wall. He was dead before he had time to be surprised, even. The three shots were no self-indulgent luxury, only an insurance. One sure way to get yourself killed while you're still comparatively young is to take a shot at a guy facing you with a gun in his hand, and neglect to make real sure he's dead.

Max Landau sat slumped in his chair like he was tired and the hell with everything. The last time I'd seen him he was coming out of the chair toward Kirby. The second shot I'd heard must have been the one that put a slug through Landau's left eye—and punched him back into the chair again.

A tall thin guy and a tall fat guy came charging into the room from the hallway, and suddenly relaxed when they saw it was all over. I walked around the table to meet them, seeing the various expressions on the faces of the three living people still sitting on the far side.

Kaye Allen's face had a greenish tinge, and the china blue eyes a wobbly kind of look. Theodore Altman's face had a deep sadness as he stared silently across at the body of the man he had regarded as his one true friend. Gerard, the chemist, just sat there looking plain bewildered like he wanted to ask what time was the next hurricane, but he wasn't real sure who to ask.

Kardos, the thin one of the two FBI agents, gave me a brief grin that was almost friendly, as I came up.

"It was busy for a while there, Lieutenant?"

"I assume you took care of Johnny King," I said.

"All that much man," Peters, the fat one, said with an academic interest, "took hardly any killing at all."

"Just how did you manage to arrive at the exactly right moment?" I asked curiously.

"The night guard at the bank," Kardos said with a grin. "He kept on having this nightmare, so his wife said if we'd go hear him tell it, then maybe he could get some sleep. We

GIRL IN A SHROUD 215

figured him for a nut when we heard it the first time around. The way it went, he dreamed he was on his way to the bank in the early evening, when one of the bank's clients stopped and offered him a lift. This client was a Doctor Landau, and his daughter was in the car with him—Vicki. The girl told him it was her birthday, and he just had to drink to her health. So, a small one, he said.

"Then, a few minutes after he's had the drink, his eyes went funny on him and all he could see was a blur. The doctor told him he was to open the back door of the bank at precisely eleven-thirty that night and let the doctor and his daughter in. Once inside, the guard would ignore them and keep about his business until they told him to let them out again. He was to lock up after they'd gone, then forget they'd ever been there, and never remember it for as long as he lived!"

"So they gave him a Mickey Finn in the drink?" Peters said. "But what kind of Mickey Finn will make a guy forget, then remember, then forget again for the rest of his life?"

"Funny thing was," Kardos said slowly, "it worried the guard that he remembered! Somehow he felt he'd done the wrong thing by the doctor. When we checked and found this Landau was bossman of a research institute experimenting with drugs, we figured we'd better come out and take a look!"

I gave them a capsuled rundown. Landau had discovered the new drug and used it on the bank president as well as the guard. The daughter was being blackmailed by Kirby and King, had tipped them off where her father had hidden the money, but he'd moved it again in the morning without her knowing—that's why the blackmail team had come into the house.

"These three people here," I raised the level of my voice a fraction to make damn sure they heard me, "are the other members of the research team. You can see from the stunned looks still on their faces that they had no idea what was really going on."

"Sure." Kardos wasn't interested. "We still got to find that quarter million!"

"The garage roof, on top of the timbers," I said. "I think the garage is—" But they had gone already.

"That was very generous of you, Lieutenant!" Altman said quietly. "I don't think any of us really deserve it!"

"A man like Max Landau doesn't happen very often," I said. "Maybe it's a good thing, huh?"

"You were dead right about one thing, Lieutenant," Gerard said in a slightly shaking voice. "This was my last indulgence in childish fantasies!"

"How come the drug worked perfectly on me and the bank president, but not the night guard?" I asked.

"The IQ factor," Altman said. "We thought it would be a problem. The drug has a different reaction at different levels of intelligence, Lieutenant."

"You mean the night guard's intelligence level was lower than mine or the bank president's?" I said modestly. "That's why he remembered?"

Altman looked faintly embarrassed. "Actually—uh—the reverse is true, unfortunately, Lieutenant!"

"Oh, really?" I snarled, and walked down to the end of the table.

Kaye's face had regained its normal color, more or less, but the china blue eyes were real forlorn.

"I have a few short, sharp things to say," I said bleakly. "All those stories Vicki told you about her wonderful father helped you build up a nice fat, completely false, image of the guy. You couldn't help it he was waiting when you came out of the shower!"

"I know," she whispered. "But I thought I was in love with him—after his wife died I—well, those photographs!"

"So you screwed your best friend's father," I snarled. "Such a big deal. You want to make a Federal case out of it? It was Vicki who was real sick—kinky, she probably got her kicks out of you both. If she hadn't taken the pictures and given them to Kirby, that session with Landau could have been strictly therapeutic, gotten him right out of your system. You could have worked him around and made a laughingstock out of him, had your revenge, anything you wanted. Now, having established that, what you need to do is stop feeling sorry for yourself, get a new pair of glasses, buy some clothes, work on your appearance so you don't look so dowdy all the time, find yourself a lover—for Christ's sake, why do *I* have to tell you what you need? I'm just a police lieutenant who's not even a latent fag any more."

GIRL IN A SHROUD 217

"You're the best psychoanalyst I met yet!" She smiled softly.

"I'll see you around, honey," I said. "I have to go call some law to clean this up, then I have to go back to town and retrieve a sergeant who, I'll bet, is still studiously watching the front door of an apartment building waiting for King and Kirby to come out. I guess it's my fault, I never told him those buildings have back doors, too!"

I got back to my apartment around seven-thirty, made a drink, slipped a Carole Bayer Sager cassette into the player, and sank thankfully into a chair. The FBI agents had found the money in the garage roof. Castle was deliriously happy when they returned it, and wanted them both to resign so they could run for county sheriff in the next election, only I forgot to mention that to Lavers.

Polnik was still drooling over the massive blonde Amazon in the dusty-pink see-through shirt, and I had no difficulty wondering what direction his thoughts had taken while he had staked out the front of the building. It was a depressing prospect, so I dismissed it from my mind.

Even the sheriff seemed pleased, which doesn't happen too often even when a homicide case is finished. He told me I looked pooped and it couldn't all be due to my dubious personal life, so why didn't I take a couple of days out from the office right now? He could have been coming down with something, of course, but I didn't stop to find out.

So life was but a breeze. I put my feet up comfortably and let my mind drift in all directions, careful to avoid the short-lived memory of what it had been like to be a latent fag. Then the buzzer sounded and I wasn't thinking about anything at all.

I opened the door and a complete stranger was standing there—a stranger who brushed straight past me and deposited herself in the living room.

"Hey." I said nervously.

She spun toward me with a dazzling smile, her china-blue eyes twinkling behind a pair of lightly tinted glasses with lightweight frames, and then I knew who she was. She had done something rather cool with her hair.

"You approve, Al?" she asked cautiously.

"Do I approve? Kaye, honey, you look just great," I said truthfully.

"You see? I took your advice."

"I'm glad you did."

"I feel like a new woman."

"Yeah." I studied her admiringly. She was wearing pale jeans and a checked shirt, which emphasized all the curves she had kept hidden until now beneath a starched white uniform.

"I called your office and they said you were taking a couple of days' vacation. Is that right?"

I nodded. "It sure is."

"That's fine," she said. "Just you and I. We could make it a very special vacation. Tell me, have you eaten yet?"

"Not yet," I told her.

"Neither have I. Are you hungry?"

"Not really."

She sighed. "Neither am I."

"I'll go make you a drink," I told her. "I'll be right back."

It took a little longer in the kitchen than I had figured, because this was an occasion I celebrated by making up a brace of old-fashioned Old Fashioneds. The living room had changed while I had been away, I realized that the moment I came back into it. It had gotten a hell of a lot darker than it was when I left, so I had to grope my way cautiously toward the one oasis of light by the couch.

She was standing in the middle of the room, completely naked, the lamplight caressing her breasts with their erect tips, the shadows bunching between her rounded thighs. I put the two Old Fashioneds down carefully onto the coffee table, then walked toward her with a slow, determined stride, and as I grabbed her around the waist, lifted her from the floor, and carried her across to the couch where I laid her down and began to take off my clothes, I thought I wasn't doing too badly for someone who had once been a latent fag and who was about to embark on a fresh round of therapy, just in case.